Seasons of
Bliss

Also by Ruth Glover
A Place Called Bliss
With Love from Bliss
Journey to Bliss

The Saskatchewan Saga

Seasons of *Bliss*

A NOVEL

RUTH GLOVER

Fleming H. Revell
A Division of Baker Book House Co
Grand Rapids, Michigan 49516

© 2002 by Ruth Glover

Published by Fleming H. Revell
a division of Baker Book House Company
P.O. Box 6287, Grand Rapids, MI 49516-6287

Printed in the United States of America

ISBN 0-8007-5792-0

Library of Congress Cataloging-in-Publication Data is on file at the Library of Congress, Washington, D.C.

For current information about all releases from Baker Book House, visit our web site:
http://www.bakerbooks.com

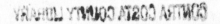

To Hal
Best of husbands
Best of friends

The arms of Robbie Dunbar! Was there another place to compare with them in the whole wide world? How many times had Tierney dreamed of them being around her, tight and warm, as they were now? How many times had she cried herself to sleep for lack of them? Never having felt them, still she knew how they would feel—hungry, loving, sheltering. A haven.

Having dared the dangers of wild and tossing seas, Tierney knew about the need for a haven. But hadn't she declared that she would follow Robbie Dunbar to the ends of the earth? Even to Timbuktu, if necessary? And hadn't Robbie gone off two years ago, as to the ends of the earth, and left her in Scotland, hopeless of ever seeing him again and helpless to do anything about it?

Saskatchewan was a far cry from Timbuktu, but it was no less inaccessible. Yet here she was, and—wonder of all wonders—here he was!

Standing in the circle of Robbie Dunbar's arms—feet planted in the freshly turned furrow of a raw homestead, far, far from Scotland and all things familiar—Tierney felt herself to be in a dream. One moment, it seemed, she had been amid familiar mud-dabbed, straw-thatched crofts, the next, in the wilds of northern Saskatchewan.

Of course, it hadn't been that simple. Or that quick.

But already fading from memory were the miseries of the long ocean voyage. Even the face of Ishbel Mountjoy, that intrepid advocate and employee of the British Women's Emigration Society responsible for her move from Scotland to Canada, seemed dim and distant, in memory as in fact. All, all was forgotten in the feeling of unreality that gripped Tierney now.

But a horse, a very real horse, stomped a foot nearby, somewhere a bird sang, and the arms—the very real arms of Robbie Dunbar—tightened.

"Robbie . . . Robbie Dunbar . . . is it ye, Robbie? Is it yoursel'?"

Leaning her head back and raising her eyes to the suntanned face so close to her own, so close and so familiar, Tierney asked the question wonderingly.

Robbie's arms—those arms denied her heretofore—seemed unwilling to let her go. His lips, the lips that had never kissed hers, pressed themselves into the abandon of her hair—her hat having fallen off as she ran—as he pulled her close again.

As clearly as though it were yesterday rather than more than two years ago, Tierney recalled their farewell moments high on the hillside above the small Scottish seaside town of Binkiebrae, he to leave forever for Canada, she to remain behind. Remain forever in Binkiebrae, and with few if any memories to cherish, just a dream of what might have been, of what she had always supposed would be, had taken for granted would be.

With all of life ahead, in which their love could ripen and come to fruition and fulfillment, Tierney and Robbie had never felt any urgency about it. Rather, they had accepted and nourished it with joy and satisfaction, allowing it to grow and deepen naturally, confident they had a lifetime to savor it. They, as their parents and grandparents before them and *their* parents and grandparents before them, and back and back, would settle into a croft of their own, becoming a small, insignificant but solid part of the history that was Binkiebrae's. Robbie Dunbar and Tierney Caulder were meant for each other.

Then had come the shattering edict of Robbie's father: Robbie and his brother Allan were to leave for the new homesteads opening in Canada and offered free to all comers. Eventually, if everything went well, the rest of the family would follow; certainly Robbie and Allan would never return.

With her mother dead and her own father dying, with no money and no hope of following, Tierney had seen her dreams crumple and die, that morning on the hillside, like a bud that had been cut down before it blossomed. And indeed, the possibility of her going with him, or even following at some later date, had not been mentioned or considered, so remote was the idea. Robbie Dunbar knew as surely as did Tierney that it was impossible. The parting was forever. He was going off to the ends of the earth; she was remaining in Binkiebrae. She was remaining, with no choice but to become a dried-up, lonely old maid. For with Robbie gone, love and marriage and children were gone; there would never be anyone for Tierney but Robbie Dunbar.

Even then, in their final moments together, with the wind skirmishing sadly about them and the distant sea sparkling like tears, Robbie had not kissed her. But he had touched her. Taking her chin in his hand, his eyes burning with unexpressed emotions, he had turned her face toward him. Tenderly he had placed a hand on each side of her face, her tear-streaked face, and looked deeply into her eyes. As though she were experienced in the tender art of kissing, simply and naturally Tierney had lifted her face. Her eyes closed, her heart breaking, she had lifted her lips to Robbie Dunbar.

But Robbie had not kissed her. With a low sound that from a less fine man would have been something between a curse and a groan, Robbie had dropped his hands and stepped back from her, clenching his jaws. "I canna, lass, *I canna!*" he had groaned. "I canna kiss ye, else I'd ne'er leave ye!"

And Robbie, resigned to his fate as she was to hers, had stumbled backwards, turned, and was off, leaping and bounding down the steep hillside, away from her. It was her last sight of Robbie Dunbar; it was her lasting nightmare.

⸻

After her father's death, and Robbie long gone, Tierney had met up with Ishbel Mountjoy and her incredible offer: Sign up with the British Women's Emigration Society, go to Canada, and experience a new life in a new land.

It had taken but a short moment's consideration for Tierney to fling caution to the winds and join the throng of girls and women agreeing to become "domestics" on the prairies of distant Canada. Amazingly, it was at no cost to them, except that a part of their pay would be returned, for a while, to the government so urgently desiring their services. And though no one could see at the time that it would be so, these same domestics—eventually tens of thousands of them—would change history as they married, had children, and raised up a new generation of Canadians.

Most of them, however, had no intention of setting out to change the world; they were simply following the only opening there was; single women, particularly, had few if any options. Thus it was that Ishbel Mountjoy's proposal had sounded a note of hope that Tierney and others like her had been unable to resist.

For many of them it meant flight, flight from meaningless lives with no future. For Tierney it meant escaping a pointless existence in the home of her brother and his wife. That the flight took her halfway around the world, to end up in the expanse of prairie or the wilds of the bush, no matter!

Tierney, after a few months on Will and Lavinia Ketchum's chicken ranch, accepted an opportunity to go northward, and had, earlier in the day, alighted from the train in the heart of the bush, or parkland, immediately falling in love with the flourishing growth, so different from the barren prairies to the south. She was met by Herbert Bloom, father of Lavinia, prepared to take up her duties as a domestic in the home of Herbert and his wife, Lydia.

The buggy ride from Prince Albert to Bliss had been a time of getting acquainted. Tierney told Mr. Bloom about Will and the chicken ranch. She told him the sad details of Lavinia's death in childbirth. Herbert wanted to hear about his grandson, Buster, and how he was settling down happily with his new mother. Will, like others in the same situation, had found it expedient to marry quickly. Herbert, in turn, described the Bloom homestead, assuring her that he and Lydia were eager to have Tierney join their household, needing her badly. Lydia, he explained, was cruelly incapacitated with rheumatism and no longer able to keep up the many tasks required in the running of a farm.

They stopped at the small hamlet of Bliss to pick up the mail and, at various homes along the way, dropped it off, which was the custom and a friendly, helpful thing to do.

One final stop was the homestead of a young man who had recently taken up residence in the community of Bliss. They found him plowing, turning over the soil of his homestead for the first time. Tierney, cramped from the train and buggy rides, had offered to take the letter across the small field to him. Hopping from the buggy she sprinted, long-limbed and free as a feather, across the furrows, holding the letter aloft and calling for attention.

Herbert Bloom, waiting in the buggy, soon had cause to be astonished. The plowman, eventually hearing Tierney's call over the sound of the team's clopping feet and the roots tearing loose as the soil came free and rolled back, turned, froze in place, dropped the reins and ran, fleet as any colt, to meet the girl. The lassie, pausing momentarily, had taken flight into the arms of the man, a young man who was known only sketchily to Herbert Bloom, but who was, apparently, well-known to the girl Tierney Caulder, incredible as it seemed. Why else would a proper young woman fling herself into a man's arms? And linger there, rocked there, weeping there? Herbert Bloom, unaccustomed to imagi-nations and flights-of-fancy, may be excused for gaping blankly.

<hr />

For Tierney, it was enough, at the moment, to rest in the arms of Robbie Dunbar, to hear the broken words he was whispering into her hair. Her face was pressed to his chest, broad and strong, as she had known it would be, had known all her growing up years but had never experienced before. To think that here—in the rampant bush of the parkland strip of Saskatchewan, far from croft and brae and bracken, far from sea and shore, far from home and hearth—she would have come, as straight as a bird to its nest, to the arms of Robbie Dunbar.

"Aye, lassie, it's me," Robbie was saying huskily, adding, "an' is it ye, Tierney Caulder, yersel' so far from Binkiebrae and home? How can it be? Is't a dream?"

Her renewed clutch, his tightened embrace, were answer enough.

It was the threatened straying of Robbie's team that broke the spell.

"Whoa!" Robbie turned swiftly and reached for the fallen reins.

Loosed from his embrace, Tierney half-staggered for a moment, her head awhirl as the world slowly came back into focus. Pressing greenery—bushes and trees unknown to her—took the place of her barren Scotland hillside, and there was no wide and sweeping view of the sea; indeed, sight ended where the bush began. Tierney's feet did not press Scottish soil but trampled the rich black dirt of a homestead in Canada's west. Her nostrils were assailed by scents she had never known before—soil turned over for the first time, sweaty horses, growth so verdant and lush as to be almost overwhelming, flowers of unknown variety nodding heads in the ground at the edge of the small plowed plot. It all added up to perfume of a rare vintage, a fragrance she would always equate with this lovely, unexpected moment.

As Robbie got his team under control—they had been head-ing toward the small log buildings and the well with its hand-hewn water trough—and as Tierney's bemused gaze focused again, she remembered the driver who had brought her here, still sitting in his buggy.

Herbert Bloom's face was a study. His fading eyes blinked, his mouth had fallen slackly open, and his lips were puckered as if in a soundless whistle.

And no wonder! What a sight! This young woman, Tierney Caulder by name—recently employed on a chicken farm on the prairie, just off the train and committed to helping him and Lydia on their homestead in the bush—was *sparking* with a strange young man. One didn't expect, when merely stopping by to drop off the mail, that the person delivering it would be swept up into the arms of the one to whom the mail was addressed—Robert Dunbar, in this instance.

Herbert Bloom knew his neighbor slightly as a newcomer to the area of Bliss and recalled now that he had a decided Scots accent. Could they—the girl and the man—be old acquaintances? It was the only explanation that made sense. Herbert Bloom scratched his head, dumbfounded.

Tierney—her amber eyes and head of abundant auburn hair being her distinguishing features and chief claim to beauty—had seemed, to her prospective employer, a self-controlled, well-man-nered, perfectly normal young woman when she had alighted from the train in Prince Albert, eminently suited to meet the needs of the Bloom household.

Now, here she was—having started out sedately enough across the fresh-turned sod to give a letter to a stranger—dazedly pick-ing up the hat that had flown from her head when that man had turned toward her and she had run to meet him. No wonder Her-bert Bloom was transfixed by the strangeness of it all.

While she scrabbled in the earth for her hat, the man was get-ting his team under control. He turned, took the girl Tierney's hand in his own, and together they made their way over the fur-rows toward the buggy waiting at the edge of the field.

It was all too much for a staid Englishman like Mr. Bloom. He sat in his rig holding the reins numbly, his aging face sagging with the perplexity of his thoughts. If this didn't beat all! What a story to tell Lydia! The very idea brought him up short— Lydia! That proper lady would be shocked at the *im*proper goings-on he had just observed.

Ahem! Herbert Bloom straightened himself, cleared his throat, swallowed, and attempted to look stern. But his kindly heart melted at the joy he saw pouring from the countenances of the young people approaching the buggy. Rather than an expression of disapproval, it was a face full of curiosity that Herbert raised toward Tierney Caulder and Robbie Dunbar as they stepped from the last furrow and walked—*floated*—to the side of the buggy.

"Mr. Bloom." Robbie Dunbar held out an earth-stained hand, grasping one that was equally work-worn, if cleaner at the moment, and shook it heartily.

"Good day to you, Mr. Dunbar," Herbert Bloom answered automatically.

For a second or two, under the midday sun, a silence fell. The young people were starry-eyed but tongue-tied, and Herbert was merely at a loss for words. The birds of the bush filled the moment with outpourings of song, the horse's harness creaked as he shifted his feet, the buggy jiggled as the older man shifted his weight.

"Ah," Herbert began, "it would seem . . ."

Robbie and Tierney were looking at each other again, and though there was now no physical touch, there was an intimacy apparent in their very absorption with one another.

"Ahem." Herbert cleared his throat again and, with a start, the young man and woman turned back toward him.

"Mr. Bloom?" Robbie asked quickly.

"It seems to me," Herbert Bloom said to their lifted faces, "that you two may know each other. Either that or you've gotten acquainted very quickly! You must be old . . . friends, or," he added, and who could blame him if he spoke dryly, "perhaps . . . more."

Merry laughter from Tierney, along with a pretty flush to her cheeks. As for the young man, Mr. Bloom's words seemed to bring a startled look to his face.

"Miss Caulder and I," Robbie Dunbar said slowly, "are from the same place in Sco'lan'—"

"Binkiebrae," the girl interjected rather breathlessly, as though the place were heaven's gate.

"Aye, Binkiebrae," Robbie Dunbar affirmed. "We thought niver to see each other again. I can hardly believe—"

The eyes of the young man turned again, this time in sheer disbelief, on the handsome girl at his side, made even more vivid because of the color suffusing her face and the light of happiness setting her eyes aglow. Ah yes, it was a happy meeting, even an amazing one, all things considered. What were the odds, Herbert wondered fleetingly, of coming half a world from all things familiar only to run straight into the arms of someone you knew? And knew very well, if appearances meant anything. The odds were against it, for sure. Unless, that is, one were a praying person. Herbert Bloom was a praying person himself and could see the possibilities, could even see the *im*possibilities that could be surmounted if one indeed prayed.

"Ah . . . Binkiebrae," Herbert repeated for lack of anything better to say and still much in the dark about the whole thing. "Both from, er, Binkiebrae . . ."

It was as if all three of them were mesmerized by something, perhaps the rare combination of sounds that made up the name Binkiebrae, and silence fell again. The man Robbie Dunbar cleared his throat.

"This land . . . this homestead," he began, speaking primarily to the girl, explaining to the girl, "is mine. This is what I came over to find; this is what me da had in mind for me. I filed on it all legal in Prince Albert, at the Lands Office. Allan, me brother," he said, turning to Mr. Bloom momentarily, "filed on the quarter section next to this. Maybe y' know him. Together," he said, with an exultant note to his voice, "we hae half a section. And wi' any kind o' luck," his glance wavered, "we'll be able to get the other quarters of the section."

"Oh, Robbie," the girl rejoiced, "tha's wonderful. An' is this your hoosie?" She nodded toward the small cabin at the edge of the field, not far from where they were standing.

"Thass it, Tierney," he said, with some pride, some humility. "An' sma' though it is, it's not any smaller than some o' the crofts in Binkiebrae. Aye, an' Allan has his hoose, too. We've made a good start, Tierney."

"I'll tell you what, Mr. Dunbar," Herbert was bold enough to interject into what could well be a continuing conversation, "why don't you come over to our house for supper tonight? I know Lydia will be preparing something special for this first night when Miss Caulder is with us, and you're welcome. Then you and Miss Caulder can continue your talk and get acquainted again. I'm sure there is much you have to say to each other."

"Aye, Robbie! Please coom. I've sae much to tell ye . . . all aboot how I came to make the trip—"

"Aye! And I have sae many things to ask," Robbie said in reply.

"She'll tell you all about it this evening," Mr. Bloom said hastily, remembering that his wife was probably wondering where he was and why he was delayed, and supposing the conversation was about to take off again into lengthy explanations and reminiscences.

"Oh, aye," Tierney said happily. "That's verra nice o' ye, Mr. Bloom. Do coom, Robbie."

"Let's set it for about seven o'clock," Herbert Bloom said, pulling out his pocket watch, shaking it, checking the sky, and speaking judiciously. "That'll give us time to do the chores first. I suppose you'd be free after that, wouldn't you, Mr. Dunbar?"

Robbie Dunbar, brought back to earth and something so routine as farm chores, seemed to collect himself with a start. Strangely—or so it seemed to the watching Herbert Bloom—the glow had faded from the dark eyes, the eagerness slipped from the square, good-looking face, and (it couldn't possibly be true, could it?), the suntan was actually replaced by a definite paling of the complexion. The picture Robbie Dunbar presented, Herbert Bloom concluded, was very like that of a gunnysack that had been punctured and out of which the grain was dribbling away.

"Ah," Robbie stammered. "Ah . . . I dinna think I can come tonight after all."

Disappointment changed the girl's bright face to shadow.

"Aye," Robbie Dunbar continued, sounding more certain of his decision, "I'm quite sure of it, now that I think aboot it."

"Robbie . . ." the girl objected, half pleading.

"Tomorrow, tomorrow for sure," Robbie said quickly.

"Weel, then," Tierney said uncertainly and stepped toward the buggy. Robbie took her elbow and helped her up into the rig, which rocked and righted itself and engaged her attention momentarily.

"For supper tomorrow night, then?" Mr. Bloom asked, with some relief, aware that his wife would not thank him if he surprised her with an unexpected guest. Besides, he and Lydia needed the evening to get acquainted with the girl.

"Aye. Seven o'clock."

Robbie Dunbar stood at the side of the buggy, looking up, his face—if Herbert Bloom was any judge—suddenly haggard, his eyes almost desperate. Herbert Bloom clucked to the horse, made a wide turn, and headed the buggy toward the road. The girl Tierney kept turning her eyes, whichever way they were headed, so that she could see the face of the man standing alone beside his plowed field and watching them until they were out of sight.

As the horse and buggy reached the road, Tierney turned apprehensive eyes on her new acquaintance, her employer, and said, through stiff lips, "Somethin's not reet . . . right, Mr. Bloom. I know Robbie Dunbar well, and somethin' . . . something's not right."

2

As though in a dream, Robbie Dunbar turned back to his plowing. The letter, a communication from Prince Albert concerning the sale of a seeder, delivered by—was it indeed a dream?—Tierney Caulder herself, was stuffed into a pocket and forgotten for the time being. Who was there to write him anything personal? Certainly no one here in this new land in which he found himself, a stranger among strangers. Except for Allan, his brother, Robbie was as alone as though he had gone to the end of the earth and found it uninhabited. And mostly uninhabited it was, this isolated corner of the world.

Hard as it had been to leave Binkiebrae, home, and all things known and dear, still something in him had thrilled at the challenge opening before him—to tread on land never before stepped on by human foot, to slide a plow into soil that had never felt a blade's bite, to build a "hoosie" of his own on land of his own. Yes, it had been the chance of a lifetime, and, to a young, healthy man with little to look forward to, tremendously challenging.

Robbie's gaze drifted to the cabin. Just down the road stood its duplicate—Allan's. Crude they both were, and rough, the one rougher than the other, for they learned together as they erected Allan's cabin, then turned their attention to Robbie's, to proceed with a little more finesse. They had been warned that the logs, being green and unweathered, would undoubtedly shrink, allowing for drafts, even snow, to blow in. But just now they were snug and sturdy dwellings, and Robbie felt king of all he possessed when, at night, he shut the door behind him, sat up to the side of his small stove, and took his rest from a hard day's labor.

Simple and rustic as things were, they had not been easy to come by. Though only $10.00 was needed for the filing fee, there was much to buy before the two men could live on the land and make it productive. Houses, of course, were made from the trees on their own property, but the motley assemblage of items to put in them—a stove, a few dishes, a bed, a couple of chairs—all basic and necessary, had to be purchased. Besides the small supply of household goods, there were windows to buy, doors, nails, axes and countless other tools. As for horses to work the land, a cow for milk, and a few hens for eggs, these items were being shared between the brothers, one set doing both places for now. Certainly there were no frills on the Dunbar homesteads. Even as Robbie used the team for plowing today, he could hear Allan's axe as he worked doggedly and persistently at the task of clearing land so that, in three years, he might have the proper number of acres cleared and so fulfill that requirement to prove up his land; it took constant and persistent work.

Allan and Robbie had chosen to build separate cabins rather than live together. Each wanted the satisfaction of stepping out of his house in the morning and looking over land he could call his own. But their cabins were not far apart, each built almost on the line dividing the properties. The thick, unrelenting bush between the cabins remained intact, dividing house from house as surely as though it were a curtain. At times the brothers could hear the ring of an axe or the bawling of a cow or smell the smoke of a chimney, but they could not see one another for the thick and rampant bush between them; they rather liked it that way. A narrow path threaded the bush and made quick contact possible; what it would be like in the dead of winter was yet to be seen.

Robbie and Allan had come too late to be among those fortunate Scots who had settled a dozen years and more ago near Wapella. The philanthropic Lady Gordon Cathcart had proposed a plan to the Department of the Interior whereby she, and her funds, would assist Scottish families to settle in the Northwest Territories; she had advanced up to 100 pounds each, a tremendous encouragement to anyone considering such a move. The first ten families were followed by forty more, and though they suffered much hardship and deprivation in the early years, the settlement had taken root and eventually prospered.

Such knowledge encouraged the Dunbar brothers—it could be done!—but was no real or practical help. They had to make their own way, every step of the way, every cent of the expense. However, Robbie and Allan, attending the Bliss church one Sunday, had been happy to make the acquaintance of at least one Scottish family who lived nearby—the Morrisons. The Morrisons' story was still largely unknown to them, but it seemed their daughter Molly was keeping company with the pastor.

Church services, held in the schoolhouse, were a good deal different from those in the kirk back home, but they offered the best chance of meeting other members of the community. The dear and friendly people of Bliss had gathered Robbie and Allan to their collective bosom and had showed their welcome and friendship by turning up for a "building bee" when the young men had erected their cabins.

Before that, however, having arrived in Canada with no resources whatsoever, Robbie and Allan had spent their first months in the territories working for the railroad. The money earned had been used for the filing fee and the basic necessities to begin homesteading. With the land near the Wapella settlement taken up, they had turned farther north, ending up in Bliss.

Whether or not it would live up to its name they would have to see.

With the astonishing appearance of Tierney Caulder, it certainly had every opportunity to be blissful for Robbie Dunbar.

Robbie's sturdy Scottish heart had nearly failed him when he had told Tierney of his father's decision regarding his and Allan's future. The awful blankness, followed by anguish, that he had seen reflected in Tierney's amber-colored eyes that day, had almost been his undoing. Yet with heartbreaking reticence she had said little or nothing, realizing, as he did, the uselessness of it. Therefore, the words he had never said, planned someday to say, dreamed of saying, were never spoken. He had left her, lonely as the passing cloud, and leaped away, never to see her again. Until today.

"Think on't," he muttered now, still half dazed, shaking his head.

Making a few more rounds he concluded the day's plowing, then turned the team homeward, to unhitch, water the horses, and turn them loose in the small pound he had built at the side of his barn, working and walking through it all with a feeling of unreality.

Dreams, it seemed, did come true. But was it too late?

3

Herbert Bloom, though intent on his driving, could sense the troubled spirit of the young woman sitting next to him in the buggy.

"Ahem!" he said, being given to clearing his throat at auspicious moments. Tierney jumped a bit, startled into giving attention to something other than Robbie Dunbar's peculiar reaction to an invitation to supper during their final moments together.

"This place we're passing," Herbert said, nodding to his left, "is the homestead of Robert Dunbar's brother, Allan. As he said, the two places are much alike."

Tierney studied with interest the small cabin in the clearing in the bush and the collection of additional buildings, which she supposed were barn, chicken house, and perhaps shed or granary. It was rough, it was raw, it was rudimentary—just the basic things needed to get started. And yet there was a charm about it that caught and held a breath in Tierney's throat.

Perhaps it was the trees, in their crisp new spring green. Perhaps it was the blossoms that graced some of those trees and promised a harvest of fruit, wild though it might be and of a sort unknown to her. Whatever it was, the buildings *cuddled* in the arms of the bush, Tierney thought fancifully, rather than *huddled*. Both places—Robbie's and Allan's—looked so homey.

Far from home, still it seemed to Tierney that she had found home.

It was a strange sensation. And confusing; it was a feeling she would have to explore as time and experience allowed. Perhaps it would pass as the people of the community became known as humans with joys and problems the same as any other spot in the world, their homes just places of abode like everywhere else.

"Ahem," Herbert said, getting Tierney's attention. "Your comment back there—about something being wrong where Robert Dunbar is concerned—"

"Aye?"

"Maybe," Herbert Bloom said, "you are imagining it. You haven't seen Robert for a while, have you? How can you be certain you are reading the signs correctly? I'd give him the benefit of the doubt, if I were you. This country changes people, you know. Why, I myself—"

"I know Robbie Dunbar, Mr. Bloom," Tierney said quietly, though positively.

Herbert Bloom took a moment to reflect on the fact that indeed even he, a stranger in most ways to Robbie Dunbar, had noticed the definite paling of the ruddy face and the almost stricken look that had touched the gray eyes.

"Well," he said placatingly, "it'll all straighten out tomorrow when you see him. He had to be very surprised, isn't that so?"

"Verra surprised indeed," Tierney confirmed. "As I was to see him. I had no idea he was within a thousand miles o' here. You see, I left Binkiebrae before his family had heard from him and his brother. I mean, they didn't know where he was, so they couldn't write and tell him I'd coom over too. And even if they had, letters take a long time, goin' overseas and all."

"Yes, I suppose it seems very far indeed. Lydia and I were born in Canada, in the east, actually, so we never had that long ocean voyage to endure, though our parents did, and have told us about it many times. They always talked of taking a trip back—to England, that is—back home. But we never made it, of course. Once here it's very unusual to be able to afford to go back just for a pleasure trip. No, it's good-bye for all time."

"Aye, and that's what Robbie and I thought when we parted, he to coom to Canada, me to stay in Binkiebrae. Heaven knows we niver thought to meet up like this. I hoped that in time I'd hear from me brother, and maybe he'd have some idea where Robbie was, and I could write to him. Even then—well, it's a big land, reet?"

"Right, a big, big land. It was no picnic for us, either, coming this far west, I can tell you." Herbert Bloom clucked, as though recalling very difficult days indeed. "Maybe Lydia and I left it too late in life; one needs to be young to make such changes. But our daughter was coming—Lavinia, and her husband, Will. And they moved. And she had our first grandchild.

"And here we are, Lydia and I," he continued, "permanently situated, I suppose. It's too much to think of picking up and moving again. And of course our parents are long gone and we don't have any reason to go back east anymore."

Herbert Bloom fell silent, thinking, Tierney supposed, of his move, his so permanent move west, his only child gone. "So I guess," he finished eventually, "Bliss is our home. Sink or swim, survive or perish, it'll be in Bliss."

"It's beautiful, at least this time of year." Even while talking to her companion, Tierney had been engaged in absorbing her surroundings. And indeed, she found them beautiful past expressing.

"Oh, it's beautiful any time of year, though in different ways. Trouble is, one is so isolated, especially in the winter, though the land is quickly filling up, and neighbors are not as unusual as they once were. Do you," Herbert Bloom said, changing the subject abruptly, "attend church, Miss Caulder?"

Tierney brightened, weary though she was and distracted by her meeting with Robbie Dunbar.

"Oh, aye! Do ye?" In her enthusiasm Tierney forgot—as she was apt to do in moments of excess feeling, whether joy or sorrow—to mute the Scots accent that she had been told, by Ishbel Mountjoy and others, made it difficult to understand her.

But now she tended to forget all else except her satisfaction in her recent conversion. Church, Christians, the Bible, to Tierney Caulder, were subjects of supreme interest. Having known the Lord Jesus a short time, still He was a dear friend to this lonely misplant from home and family and all things known and loved.

So "Oh, aye!" she said enthusiastically. "That is, I attended kirk, back home in Binkiebrae. Here, I've had nae chance. Still, I would love to. Do ye and yer guid lady go, by any chance? Tell me aboot it!"

Thus invited, Herbert, first, breathed a sigh of relief. It would make things so much more pleasant if the newcomer to their home knew and loved their Savior as they did.

"We passed the local church—kirk to you, I suppose—when we passed the schoolhouse in Bliss. We make good use of that building. It's the center of much that goes on. Not far from it, by the way, is the small log house that the congregation erected on land donated for that purpose, and we call it a parsonage, though it's just like many another homesteader's first home in the area."

"And do you," Tierney interrupted, mending her speech in order to be better understood, "also live in a cabin?"

"No. We sold out back east before we came, and so we arrived with sufficient funds to build a frame house and barn and so on, though I don't suppose we're any more comfortable than many folks are in their cabins. But it's larger, having an upstairs, for one thing. I guess that's one of the reasons why we need help to keep it up—it's too big for just the two of us. Our daughter and her husband wanted a place of their own. They preferred the prairie, and it meant a move away from us. So we ended up rattling around in a big house. I guess," he finished with a sigh, "we thought our children and grandchildren would share it with us from time to time." Herbert's tone was melancholy.

He sat up alertly—a rig was approaching—and began sawing on the reins, pulling the horse from a trot to a walk and urging it toward the side of the road, not an easy thing to do because of the wild tangle of pea vine and other growth.

Her attention taken from him, Tierney turned her head to see the rig and to note that it was coming fast. The driver, finally becoming aware of them, pulled to the side also, and both buggies stopped, almost wheel to wheel.

"Well, Miss Molly," Herbert Bloom said cordially, doffing his hat with one hand while restraining his horse with the other. "Where are you off to so frisky-like?"

"Now where would I be going, Mr. Bloom, except to Bliss—"

"And the parsonage," the man supplied good-humoredly.

"The dear parson would starve, I do believe," the young woman Molly said, tapping a box at her elbow, "if we didn't take pity on him from time to time." Her gaze shifted to Herbert's passenger.

Before the cool beauty of this Molly, Tierney felt sorely bedraggled and travel-worn. It had been a long day.

"Molly, this is the young lady come to help Lydia and me. I think you may have known we were expecting her. The good preacher prayed about it in church a time or two, you may remember. Her name is Tierney Caulder. Miss Caulder, meet Molly Morrison."

Tierney nodded, at a loss for words before this vision of grace and energy. Molly Morrison was a natural beauty. Simple, lovely lines of body, and a lively expression on a piquant face under a mane of wild black hair, made up the wholesome person who smiled at Tierney now. Her voice, when she spoke, was kind and friendly. Here was a rare gem indeed, Tierney decided on the spot—one who had everything going for her and either knew it not or cared not.

"Welcome to Bliss, Miss Caulder."

"Ta . . . that is, thank you," Tierney responded.

"And guess what?" Herbert was continuing. "Miss Caulder is an old friend of that newcomer down the road, Robert Dunbar by name."

"Is that so? How wonderful to come so far and meet someone you know. But it won't take you long to feel at home, Miss Caulder. Homesteads are filling in, and there are many like you, new to the area, looking for friends. We need each other here. There are not many strangers in the territories."

The young woman's horse was fractious and not inclined to stand. Molly was distracted as she hauled on the reins, her small feet braced against the buggy's dash, her slender form curved in her effort to keep control.

"Well, Molly, Kip isn't going to give you any time for visiting today," Herbert Bloom said, obviously acquainted with the horse. "And Lydia is waiting and wondering where in heaven we are. So—"

Herbert loosed his grip on the reins, and his buggy inched forward; Miss Morrison did the same.

"I'll look forward to getting to know you better, Miss Caulder—"

"An' I hope to get better acquainted with you, Miss Morrison."

The last Tierney saw of the sparkling eyes and vivacious face of her new acquaintance was when Molly turned long enough to call over her shoulder, her horse once again commanding her attention, "Molly! Call me Molly!"

"Do you suppose," Herbert Bloom asked as soon as horse and buggy were back in the center of the road, "she'll ever settle down to making a minister's wife?"

"I'm verra sure she will," Tierney answered wholeheartedly, fully won over by the charm and graciousness of Bliss's Molly Morrison. "Is a weddin' day set?"

"Gracious no. As far as I know they're not even promised to each other. But the preacher is definitely looking her way, and our Molly, without any doubt, has her cap set for him. Half the community thinks she'll never tame down enough to fill the bill, if you know what I mean—"

"I suppose I do. You mean she's too . . . too full of life?"

"That's a good way of saying it. Full of fun, full of laughter. Can such a one escape the criticisms that a preacher and his wife get?"

"I dinna know," Tierney said uncertainly. "Is it like that?"

"I think so," Herbert said, "though Lydia and I try to be thoughtful and supportive. And, for the most part, the pastor is well loved, I believe, and doing a good job. It's just that . . ."

"Just that?"

"Well, there are others . . . other females, who think a good-looking, well-educated young man should look a little farther afield and not settle for a local. One in particular, I guess I'd have to say. Perhaps she has her eyes set on him herself."

"But I thought there were hardly any available women in the territories." Tierney well knew how single women, whether young and unmarried or widows, were actually inundated with offers of marriage.

"Mostly that's true. We just happen to have imported one recently . . . she's visiting relatives, and . . ."

Herbert's voice trailed off, and he gave his attention to the horse, for it was quickening its pace.

"Ah, I've said too much now," the man finished. "Anyway, Parker Jones—that's the preacher—can take care of himself. I think. As for Miss Molly Morrison—never fear but what she can take care of herself, too."

With that Herbert let the horse go and, knowing it was nearing home, it stepped out briskly, causing the buggy to bounce rather alarmingly.

Tierney clung to the side of the seat, silent for the moment, reflecting on the events of the day. First, meeting her prospective employer and finding him wonderfully acceptable; meeting Molly Morrison and finding her friendly and approachable; and last—wonder of wonders—running full tilt into the man who had filled her dreams, waking and sleeping, ever since she had lowered her hemlines. Forgotten for the moment was his final, strange reaction to her presence in Bliss.

It was all too much. Tears, of weariness, incredulity, relief, and inexpressible joy welled up in her eyes.

"Here," Herbert Bloom said kindly—apparently understanding, and sympathetic—and handed her a big red bandanna handkerchief.

4

"Whoa there, Daisy!"

Daisy stopped chewing her cud long enough to look around, perhaps with disgust, at the rather inept fumbling taking place in the area of her nether quarters.

She was a new acquisition on the Dunbar homestead and, if cows have memories, could remember the expert milking of her former owner. And if cows sigh, certainly she heaved a big one. Daisy, it was clear, recognized a novice, had little or no patience with the unskilled bungling she was being subjected to, and shifted again impatiently.

With a sigh of his own, Robbie tucked his head into the cow's flank in proper style, reached again for the turgid teats, and started over.

Why, he wondered, and not for the first time, *did I agree to keep the beast here rather than Allan's place?* It had seemed a novelty, of course, and, craving butter—having gotten by with slatherings of bacon grease on his bread, if anything—Robbie had gladly (poor, foolish lad!) taken the cow into his care when he might just as well have let Allan have the privilege. In fact, he thought now, rather sourly, he should have *insisted* on it.

Ping ping—the milk gave a few splashes into the pail clutched between his knees, even suggested the beginning of a satisfying froth. Robbie flexed his cramping fingers and, with another soothing word to the long-suffering Daisy, continued his task. Chores, morning and evening, for Robbie Dunbar, were becoming routine. What had seemed like a richly gratifying experience in the beginning was fast becoming a tyrannical master.

It wasn't only the milking; it was the further work of caring for the stuff that, in bottles, seemed so soothing and innocent, giving no hint of the work and worry it gave its producer. Herkimer Pinkard, a neighbor, stopping by one evening when Robbie was settling down to milk, had grinned and asked, "Do you know why cream costs more than milk?" and continued, "Because little bottles are harder for the cow to sit on." Oh that it was that easy!

After milking, there was straining the milk and putting it in flat pans that allowed for easy skimming after the cream rose, as it did unfailingly, astonishing as it seemed. Eventually there was enough cream so that mouth-watering, sweet butter could be churned out, worked free of buttermilk, washed, salted, and shaped into acceptable pats or pounds, adding its delightful flavor to meager fare. There was nothing like a good helping of butter soaking into a baked potato, dripping from pancakes, or melting on a warm biscuit.

But the work to obtain it didn't end with the milking and the churning. Milk pail, strainer, skimmer, churn, butter spade, and mold, all had to be washed in hot, soapy water, dried, and covered against the storm of flies that were ever present. Perhaps if one had a wife to turn such chores over to—Robbie's heart missed a beat as he thought of Tierney showing up in this remote corner of the world; and certain dreams came alive.

"Whoa!"

Daisy fidgeted again and quickly brought Robbie from fancy to fact.

With summer just around the corner, he was seriously considering ordering a couple of items from the catalog that would, he felt, enhance his milk and butter production.

Preservaline: "A harmless substance which, when added to milk or cream, will keep same for weeks in an absolutely perfect and wholesome state in any kind of weather—even through thunderstorms—without requiring ice or any refrigerator; absolutely tasteless, odorless, simple and cheap to use; does not affect the flavor or quality of the milk . . ."

It seemed incredible—milk kept sweet for weeks? But the catalog promised it.

Ozaline: "The finest disinfectant for creameries and dairies. Has no smell and gives out none. Removes every offensive smell at once. Positively marvelous in its actions. Prevents flies in creameries [*Would anything actually do that!* Robbie thought, fanning away the usual horde]. Kills all germs in the air, gives off oxygen, and thus keeps the air pure. A small quantity of Ozaline sprinkled on dung heaps and in manure pits, in outhouses, and on anything having a bad odor, will remove all smell at once and for good. It will also prevent chicken lice. Price, in small quantities, 6c per lb."

The trouble was obtaining the six cents necessary to give it a try. And then there had been Herkimer Pinkard's reaction. Herkimer, hearing Robbie through as he recounted the marvels of Preservaline and Ozaline as outlined in the "wish book," had given a great shout of laughter, until the bib on his overalls vibrated with his mirth.

"Milk keeping for weeks! Hahaha! All smell gone from manure! Never heard the likes of it," the large man declared when at last he could restrain his hilarity.

Robbie was in favor of anything that would, in particular, keep flies away. But perhaps he should save his money for the purchase of a churn. Currently he had no choice but to put cream in a jar and shake it vigorously until it separated and butter appeared.

Yes, farming, not to mention housekeeping, was challenging.

While Robbie struggled with the responsibilities of Daisy and her daily output, Allan, for his part, was feeding baby turkeys and slopping the sow they had purchased and that would "bring forth" anytime now (Robbie didn't know the proper term for the birth of a sow's progeny).

He was ignorant about so much, and of course so was Allan. What a pair of greenhorns they were! Herkimer Pinkard's good-natured chortles of laughter over their efforts was often the only sign that, once again, they were doing something all wrong. At that, it was better than severe criticism, Robbie and Allan agreed. Herkimer Pinkard was a sort of measuring stick for them.

Greenhorns or not, they hadn't done badly, so far.

Still, Robbie was dissatisfied. Having gotten a few acres and a few belongings, he yearned for more; Robbie was ambitious. His homestead was the promised quarter of a section; he dreamed of an entire section, 640 acres, one square mile. Only the quarter section, however, was free. The rest would have to be bought, or . . . there were other ways, ways that were in his thinking, even in his planning. It would all come right, given time.

And, in the meantime, he was breathing free! In any moment of crisis, even of discouragement, he had but to remind himself of that and the fact that life could be, would be, what he made it. He had that much power; he had that chance.

He, Robbie Dunbar, was blessed. Looking over his acres, he well knew that many a Scottish highlander, back home, was being forced by the land enclosures to board starvation ships and seek a new life elsewhere; shaking his cream into butter, he knew that the Irish were starved out of their ancient home. Canada's population, it seemed, was derived almost entirely from people whose causes had been lost elsewhere. There was little or no future at home; there was hope and opportunity in abundance here.

Robbie thanked God for the shove—his father's edict—that had thrust him into a place of such possibilities. Here men and women of varying cultures were working together in harmony, united by doggedness and purpose; here a great democracy would arise above the differences of religion, language, or blood. It was exhilarating to be a part of it.

"Le Bon Dieu est Canadien!" was the expression the French Canadians used to express their faith in their country's future, and Robbie shared their confidence. Robbie could feel the expectancy in the very atmosphere, along with the inevitable bowing to bitter sacrifices in order that the dream might be realized. And for those with a will to hold steady, it would come true.

"All right, old girl, we'll call it quits for today," Robbie said, rising from the small, three-legged stool he had cobbled together and giving the tried and tested Daisy a pat on the rump.

Walking with the brimming pail to the house, the cat Whiskers trotting at his heels meowing piteously for his share of the milk, Robbie glanced around with all the satisfaction of a good beginner and all the hopes of a dreamer.

His thoughts turned again to Tierney's unexpected appearance, and his blood quickened. How Tierney would appreciate everything he had accomplished! How he looked forward to showing it to her!

And then, remembering how he had stumblingly put off having supper with her and the Blooms, and the reason for it, his joy faltered.

"She'll understand, when I tell her," he told Whiskers. "She'll understand."

But would she?

W hat an exceptionally pretty young woman, was Molly Morrison's thought as she pulled away from the Bloom buggy and her brief conversation with Herbert Bloom and the new arrival, Tierney Caulder. *Perhaps she and I can be friends. It'll be nice to have another single girl around.*

Not that there weren't a few. And Molly's brow darkened at the thought.

Vivian Condon. Bly Condon's niece. Come to visit with Bly and Beatrice. Come to visit for the summer and already making one and all aware of her presence, and spring was still saying a lingering farewell.

Molly took a deep breath and determined, not for the first time, to adjust her first reaction, if not her opinion. The tall and stately, beautifully coifed and gowned, assured and vastly self-possessed young woman, first turning up at church two Sundays ago, was sending waves of fascination down the lanes and tracks and country roads of Bliss, into quiet backwoods spots where any news was of interest, and this was of more interest than most.

Bly and Beatrice, a reserved couple, had introduced his niece to the community that Sunday with, even then, a hint of apology, as though recognizing and needing to explain the splash her presence made, as though a peacock had settled among the partridges of Bliss. Beatrice had, rather anxiously, explained in an aside to a few people that Vivian had suffered through a painful relationship back home and was in need of recuperation and restoration.

As was the Morrison custom, Bly and Beatrice and their niece had been invited home for Sunday dinner. Kezzie, the Morrison grandmother and "Mam" to many, too frail to stand the jouncing of a buggy or wagon, could rarely make it to church but always tended the stove and the oven's contents, ready for any number of people at the big Morrison table.

<hr>

Of course Cameron, son of Angus and Mary Morrison, was present, and Margo, the girl he was to marry. Present also, this Sunday as most Sundays, was Parker Jones, pastor of the Bliss church, considered by one and all to be a suitor for the hand of their own Molly Morrison.

"Come on in, everybody," Kezzie invited, her eyes still startlingly blue, still alive, loving. Kezzie, though aged and bent, declared she would be around to dance at the wedding of her darling Molly. Of course this brought smiles to the faces of Bliss's believers, whose code allowed for no dancing of the feet but plenty of the heart.

Vivian Condon's first mistake was to spurn the fragile person of Keziah Skye. Not that the gentle old lady showed any offense. And her family, for her sake, absorbed the slight silently, as kind hosts, reaching out with loving touches and smiles to the dear family member tolerating the thoughtlessness of the guest.

"Here, my good woman," Vivian Condon said, removing her cloak and hat and laying them in Kezzie's arms. Kezzie's smile of greeting grew a little fixed but remained just as sweet as she took the garments without a word and laid them aside. This she had been prepared to do anyway, as a good hostess; it was the condescending "my good woman" that showed the true mettle of the one who spoke it and the one who suffered it wordlessly.

If Vivian understood before very long that Kezzie was a treasured part of the family and not a household drudge, no word of apology or explanation attempted to correct the situation. Family and guests gathered around the table, Angus spoke the blessing, remembering to ask the Lord to bless not only the food but the friends who shared it, and then the generous platters were passed around.

It was a bounteous spread. If Mary and Angus Morrison, over the heads of their children and their guests, nodded at each other with thankfulness too deep for words, it was understandable. Having come to Bliss before most of its settlers, they had experienced, and well remembered, the years when their table was not nearly so well nor abundantly supplied. Rabbit, partridge, even venison and bear, sometimes just oatmeal, all had been gratefully received and thankfully partaken of until the land was slowly and painstakingly cleared, plowed, and planted, until the garden began to produce, the hens to lay, the herd to grow.

As available land was taken and Bliss began to fill up with other new homesteaders, the Morrisons had been as a rock in a weary land to many of them. Their hard work and determination had paid off, it was plain to be seen; if the Morrisons could do it, so can we, more than one discouraged newcomer said, settled down, and made it through. But the Sunday meals, offered to them upon their arrival, the words of encouragement and the parting prayer, made the difference in many a situation.

The Condons were comparative newcomers; in their log house Vivian would be comfortable but certainly not pampered. Perhaps that was why her eyebrows seemed to arch in surprise over the starched and snowy serviette at the side of each place setting on the Morrison table. Perhaps that was why her eyes widened over the matching pieces of dinnerware, dinnerware that had—if she but knew it—been purchased only a year ago following harvest. Ordered from the catalog and delivered in a barrel ("We have never heard of a broken piece from any we have shipped") to the post office in Bliss—one hundred pieces had been received for the magnificent price of $7.50. "This genuine English semi-porcelain ware, not first or second grade American, but the genuine English," the catalog informed, "decorated with a delicate spray of anemone flowers and leaves, put on under glaze, which prevents its wearing off, can be furnished in two colors: Blue and Brown."

Vivian Condon ate off the anemone-sprayed blue semi-porcelain ware and seemed properly awed, perhaps surprised, to the amusement of Angus and Mary, and perhaps Kezzie, who had served a notable and ancient family for many years in Scotland before coming to Canada and the West.

Someone asked the guest, politely, how long she would be in Bliss.

"All summer," that young woman said briefly, her interest turned to the slender, dark-haired, fine-featured, intense man across the table from her.

"And you, Reverend," she asked, studying Parker Jones rather too carefully, "aren't you an outsider, too? Have you been in Bliss long?"

"Two years," the pastor replied, helping himself to a generous mound of rice. "And you might as well call me Parker, everyone does, usually. Oh, I get Pastor or Reverend in church, but I think most of these people are my friends, not constituents only.

"But I wouldn't class myself as an outsider; I have been well received by the folks of Bliss. My vision goes only to its boundaries. In other words, I guess you'd have to say I feel that this is my parish."

Vivian Condon's next insensitive move was to ask, as she held the gravy boat in her hand and looked around, "Potatoes—are there mashed potatoes?"

"Rice," Molly said, handing her the bowl. "There's rice."

"Oh," flatly. "Oh. That's fine, I'm sure." And Vivian laid aside the gravy, took the bowl offered by Molly, and helped herself to a few grains of rice. "It's just that I love potatoes . . . mashed potatoes. They seem so right with gravy of this sort."

Mary, at her end of the table, bit her lip, but whether from laughter or vexation was not clear. Her eyes raised to her husband's, however, and it was Angus who spoke.

"Yes, potatoes would be better, I suppose," he said agreeably. "Have you ever lived on a farm, Miss Condon? If not, of course you can't know how all root vegetables—carrots, turnips, potatoes—wither during a long winter. We hope we put enough away in the fall to do us the rest of the year, until a new crop comes in, but when winter is over they are a sorry sight indeed. I suppose if we dug around in the bin in the cellar we'd come up with a few shrunken tubers." Angus smiled at his own description of the few remaining potatoes in the cellar under his feet. "But we'll save them for stew and things like that. We feel blessed, I suppose, to be able to buy rice as a substitute. There were years we couldn't, and subsisted through the last weeks of winter on oatmeal and pancakes and whatever we could manage."

"But," Vivian said blankly, "the store—"

"Yes, the store. But most of us are into it for more money than we care to think of, come spring. We still have a fair supply of rice on hand—right, Mary?—and we'll make it through in fine shape."

"The potato seed is in the ground, and that's good news," Cameron said cheerily. "Margo here, for the first time ever, helped plant a garden."

"Yes, and I loved doing it," that young lady chimed in. "And I can hardly wait until we can reap the rewards of our efforts. The lettuce, very soon now, should be ready to pick. My mouth just waters, thinking about it."

And so the meal progressed along happier lines. But it was quite clear, as the afternoon wore on, that Miss Vivian Condon did her best to monopolize Parker Jones. She had no competition, for Molly, clearing the table, putting Grandmam down to rest and returning to help with the dishes, went about it all quite naturally. Never would this independent young woman lower herself to compete for the attention of any man, even her adored Parker Jones.

But Vivian's conversation was scintillating, clever, even interesting at times. So lately come from "civilization," she was full of news that the community of Bliss was slow in hearing. Molly had been raised in Bliss, and though a self-possessed young lady of considerable charm and plenty of independence, felt herself today, to some degree, to be at a disadvantage. Parker Jones, a city man born and raised, Bible-school trained, had chosen to come to this backwoods corner of the world and had immersed himself in its culture—or lack of it—wholeheartedly. But surely, Molly thought, there must be times when he yearned for wider contacts, for more intellectual conversations, for something more challenging than the people of Bliss offered.

And so it was there, around the comfortable circle chatting amiably in the Morrison home that Sunday afternoon, that the first hint—just a troubling nibble—of concern, raised its head in Molly's thinking.

She had been so sure, had felt so secure in the relationship that had sprung up between herself and Parker Jones. Parker, Molly well knew from their many close conversations, struggled with a sense of inadequacy and was often tempted to feel he wasn't doing the job properly, that the needs of his parishioners were more than he could meet. Consequently he delayed and could not bring himself to face a decision concerning marriage.

"What if I fail," he had brooded. "There are so many needs, such deep needs, and sometimes I don't seem to connect with them."

"Give yourself time, Parker!" Molly had encouraged. "Not every problem is settled overnight. Look at the good being done, the sermons being preached, your life being lived before us all. Think on these things."

"I need to settle this, Molly," Parker had said, more than once. "Can you be patient? Who knows if I'll even be here, in Bliss, the rest of my life. Would that matter?"

"But, Parker," Molly had said in a low voice, "don't you know that I'd go with you, wherever you went, and I'd support you, whatever you did?"

Parker's hand had reached for hers and, she thought, his eyes may have misted.

"Be patient with me, Molly," he had asked, beseechingly.

And Molly was content to wait, though being patient was not in her makeup. Miss Molly Morrison was learning many lessons these days, lessons of curbing her impatience, her tongue, her reactions. To be a good preacher's wife—that was her goal, and it was worth any sacrifice if Parker Jones was the preacher.

Of course it would mean sacrifice. Parker's salary, if such it could be called, consisted of the scant offerings received Sunday by Sunday. "Not enough to keep a bird alive unless that bird is a chickadee," Herkimer Pinkard had declared one Sunday when he was given the task of counting the meager change in the offering basket.

And truly Parker might have suffered if it were not for the generosity of the good folk as they shared what they had. Though money was scarce, food was usually abundant, and many a box found its way to the little parsonage and the pastor's table. And sometimes Parker Jones managed to time his calls to coincide with mealtime and was never slow in accepting a hearty invitation to join the family at their meal. Whatever was served, he partook of it gratefully. Many a cook was rosy-cheeked at his compliment.

Molly had been raised in Bliss and was accustomed to hard times. Enough land was cleared now on the Morrison place to bring in a fair, even good, harvest, but when she was small, the Morrisons had "made do," just as other settlers had done and were still doing. Yes, Molly Morrison would make a fine bush pastor's wife.

Parker knew he needed a wife, knew it badly, knew it particularly when he looked around at the small house that desperately needed a woman's touch. Knew it in the long winter evenings when he was shut in, day after stormy day, weary of his own company. Thinking of his miserable bachelorhood status, Molly smiled now. She wanted to help—like bringing food, tidying up the parsonage at times—but she didn't want to make him *too* comfortable!

Parker Jones, fresh from Bible school and with the true call of a pastor on his heart, had earnestly and passionately promised the Lord that he would serve Him anywhere. Places lowly, insignificant, remote—it mattered not—he, Parker Jones, was ready to spend his life and his strength in the King's service, wherever that might be.

Bliss was all those things; certainly it was remote, almost at the end of the white man's encroachment, except for some loggers and fishermen, and—with the decimation of the buffalo and the depleted supply of beaver—a dwindling number of hunters and trappers.

As for the Indian, the great chiefs were coming to be remembered in the names of the reserves they selected: Sweet Grass, Poundmaker, Red Pheasant, Mistawasi, Strike-Him-on-the-Back, Thunderchild, and others.

But here in the area called "the bush," situated between the north and south branches of the Saskatchewan River, small farms flourished; here God's finger had pointed. Even in his loneliest, darkest moments, Parker Jones was confident of one thing: God had directed him to Bliss.

But as for a wife, God had not spoken.

Molly had made her own commitments, had her own dreams. If, in God's wisdom, they should include Parker Jones—so be it! Amen and amen!

Deep in happy thoughts, wrapped about with spring's fresh mantle, Molly pulled Kip off the road and through the gate into the parsonage yard, careening in her usual vigorous manner up to the door, the box of foodstuff bouncing at her side.

There, head drooping half somnolently, standing on three legs with the fourth resting comfortably—the Condon horse and buggy.

W ith the chores all done—horses curried, watered, loosed to graze, chickens fed and eggs gathered, cow milked, milk strained, strainer and pail washed, dish towel, dishrag, and strainer hung to dry, pail turned upside down on the small porch—Robbie turned his attention to his own dusty, dirty self.

Dipping warm water from the range's reservoir into an enameled basin and removing his stained and sweaty shirt, Robbie gave his face and upper body what was known as a sponge bath, dunked his head into the water, reached for a sacking towel, dried himself, and peered at his reflection momentarily in the small mirror.

It was the same square-jawed, ruddy face he'd seen all his life, but now burned brown. His hair was lightened by the sun; picking up a comb he ran it through the fair mass badly in need of cutting. Running a rough hand over a rough chin, he grimaced, deciding to wait another day before shaving. After all, Alice was accustomed to a farmer and his ways.

Robbie moved to the corner of the room and the twine that was stretched across it on which his scanty wardrobe hung. Selecting a shirt—clean but not ironed—he put it on and buttoned it. Glancing down, he noted the day's accumulation of dust on his shoes and took a moment to rub each one on the legs of his pants. One additional glance into the mirror and, with a rather tentative smile at his own reflection, he turned and left the house.

Briskly he started across the yard, past the barn, heading for the thick bush at the back of the clearing. Whiskers, as usual, trotted close to his heels; he would turn aside before Robbie had gone a hundred yards. Whiskers was a cat to be depended upon. It was the only thing Robbie had acquired that he could truly call his own; everything else was shared with Allan. Whiskers had been given to him by Barney and Billy, Alice Hoy's boys—who had also named him—when he was only a few weeks old.

Mice, everyone told him, were a real scourge; he hadn't been properly introduced to them yet, he was assured. Just let him get some grain on the place, or leave food around in the cupboard. Except for an occasional small rodent scampering quickly out of sight when he reached into a lower shelf for a kettle and a lonely one or two fleeing before him in the barn, he had seen none, thanks to the faithful performance of the cat Whiskers. Robbie reached down now, scratched the gray and white ears, and walked on. Whiskers lingered uncertainly; he had reached his boundary. That is, Robbie thought with a grin, until he aged a little and developed an amatory bent.

Robbie knew a little about amatory bents. His experience with love and desire had all been directed, back home, toward Tierney Caulder, that auburn-maned, amber-eyed, trimly formed sister of his friend James. Having seen her all his life, he had watched her womanly development happen slowly and naturally before his very eyes. It wasn't only her physical attributes that attracted him; Tierney was a girl to be prized in regard to her personality—which sparked at times with a fire that kept him bewitched—and her nature, which was as sweet as her face and figure.

But the love they both came to recognize and accept ripened slowly; slowly but surely. After all, life had gone on for generations, in Binkiebrae, in exactly the same manner, unchallenged and unchanged. As it would for them. Never, in his wildest dreams had Robbie Dunbar imagined leaving Binkiebrae, family, and Tierney Caulder. That she had turned up here, in remote Bliss, seemed so fantastic as to seem fated.

Feeling an elation with life in general and his own in particular, Robbie reached now toward a spray of blossoms, plucked one, and stuck it in a buttonhole.

What the particular bush was or what sort of berries it would produce, he did not know; this was his first season of spring in the bush. But he did recognize the small, blue saskatoon and, as he made his way through the thick growth, snatched off a few to eat; mild, they were, but satisfying to an appetite that had tasted no fresh growing thing in many months.

With regret he recognized that his cellar, come winter, would be barren of all such delicacies. His time wouldn't allow for canning, nor did he have the equipment for canning.

Would Alice pick and can this year? Even as he asked the question he knew that she would not.

The Hoy place, toward which he was making his way, was one of four in the section, the other three being his, Allan's, and Herkimer Pinkard's. It was much easier and quicker to walk across from one homestead to the other rather than going around by the road. And of course a buggy would never make it through the narrow aisle as it twisted and turned through his property onto hers. A horse could make it, but limbs and branches would slap a rider in the face constantly, Robbie knew. Besides, he enjoyed the walk, found it refreshing, and found, too, that he usually pressed on eagerly because of hunger pangs.

Alice was a good cook; there were those days, however, when she simply couldn't stand on her feet long enough to put a meal together. Then Robbie did it, under her instructions, with the boys helping, young as they were.

How would she be this evening? Before too long they would need to talk again, and talk seriously, finalizing their plans, firming their agreement. As it was, Robbie—realizing he was on Hoy property—found himself looking around with a proprietary air.

He could hardly believe his good fortune! To obtain more land and to have it so soon! Robbie's heart sang—if not his lips—and his heart exulted.

Stepping from the gloom of the brushy passageway at last, Robbie let out a shrill whistle, the same whistle his father had used across the years to summon Robbie and his brothers and sisters for some reason or other. Two tow-colored heads appeared as if by magic, one popping up from the yard where he had been romping in the grass with one of Whiskers' siblings, the other sliding helter-skelter from the hayloft, each head bobbing on a thin neck as Barney and Billy raced to meet him.

"Robbie!"

"Wobbie!"

With considerable screeching they reached him, Billy to leap into his arms, Barney to clutch him around one leg and sag there, laughing, defying Robbie's efforts to get him loose, or walk another step. Finally, with a boy perched on one shoulder and the other under one arm like a sack of oats, Robbie continued across the farmyard to the house.

This was no cabin. Barnabas Hoy had arrived with enough money to set himself up in style. The house, every outbuilding, the barn, all had been built from lumber. They were left unpainted, and they had weathered, in the six years or so since they had been built, into a soft gray that blended well with its background—brush on two sides, the road on one side and a field on the other.

The Hoy homestead had been proven up and was well on its way to becoming a producing farm when Barnabas had been gored, just six weeks ago, by an angry bull, bringing all his dreams to an end and leaving Alice to run the place and raise the boys.

But Alice was ill, seriously ill. Something to do with her "innards," Robbie had been told by Herkimer Pinkard, who always seemed to know everything that went on in Bliss.

Some days, when Robbie got there, Alice would be abed, the house uncared for, the boys running wild. At other times she managed fairly well—Robbie had figured out that these times coincided with the days he brought small packages from the post office. He felt sure there was medicine in them; the garbage heap, several hundred yards from the house and in the edge of the bush, had revealed tin boxes, not yet rusted, that read "Dr. Wilden's Quick Cure for Indigestion and Dyspepsia—THE GREAT STOMACH REMEDY." Now these were replaced with bottles—first one ounce, then two ounces, now three ounces—marked "D188 Laudanum (Tinc. Opium)."

Coming across the yard now and seeing Alice watching, Robbie waved; Alice nodded from the kitchen door and smiled what seemed like a bittersweet smile; the boys were still clinging to him like leeches from their own slough.

"Boys," she chided, but not too sternly, "give Robbie some peace now. You can have a romp later on," and reluctantly they slid down, to stand nearby, faces lifted to him like dandelions toward the sun.

The Hoy chores took longer than his own; the reason was simple: Barnabas Hoy had amassed a fair number of cattle; the fowl included ducks and geese and a few turkeys; and besides the work team there was a dandy riding horse. Robbie eyed it with a gleam in his eye. As things worked out, and in time, this treasure, too, would be his.

When Robbie had first come to the Hoy home, to offer his condolences to his bereaved neighbor and to ask, as others did, if there were anything he could do to help, he little suspected the turn of events soon to unfold. And yet he was the logical one, he or Allan, and Allan was even younger and far from inclined to take on the work and responsibilities of another farm, though he, too, could see the advantage of obtaining more land.

Winter had been leaving on reluctant feet when Barnabas had been laid to rest in the Bliss cemetery and Robbie had made his offer of help. Alice, who had simply thanked many another neighbor, realizing their own chores kept them from being any real or lasting help, had seen the possibilities of Robbie's association and had been the one to broach the subject. Surprised, almost speechless, Robbie had only needed overnight to consider her suggestion. Then, with his heart thumping and his hands sweaty, he had agreed.

"Allan," he had said later to his brother, "it will mean that the Hoy place will be mine. Think on't!"

"But those laddies—"

"Of course. They'll be my responsibility."

"But she's sick . . . and gettin' sicker!"

"Well," Robbie said rather impatiently, "that's the reason behind the whole plan, ye gowk! The farm will be mine, dinna ye see? Her sickness is incurable, and she knows it; she's doin' the only thing she knows to do."

Allan had scratched his head, shaken it, and mumbled something that sounded like, "Aye then, do it, and see if I hae any sympathy for ye."

Since the bargain was struck, Robbie had gone over morning and evening. If at times something interfered, Allan, with reluctance, filled in for him. Allan seemed vastly uncomfortable around Alice, though he reached out compassionately to the boys. They responded to him, as to Robbie, with an enthusiasm that hinted of great loneliness, perhaps fear, which was natural with their father put into the ground and their mother so often ill.

"A' reet, laddies," Robbie said now, his stomach growling, and his nose twitching in response to something savory cooking on the range and spilling its good smells across the yard. His supper prepared for him and nicely served—that was another bonus for Robbie, a reluctant housekeeper and a careless cook.

Of course, he excused himself, he had so little equipment—one pot, one bread pan, one baking pan, a can opener, a coffeepot, a teakettle, two enameled cups (no saucers), two tin plates, three sets of flatware, one mixing spoon, a tin washbowl that doubled for washing the dishes and, rinsed well, for mixing bread, a tin pail, a milk skimmer and—that was about all. There was no flatiron, hence the unironed clothes. There was no dustpan; dirt was simply swept out the door. No bathtub; he used the galvanized washtub over which he and Allan occasionally spent miserable hours attempting to do laundry.

Yes, this alliance with Alice Hoy not only had its advantages to come but its advantages now; Robbie knew that. He knew, too, that, unless some sort of miracle happened or science devised a way to safely open the human body and excise tumors and cancers (it was happening some places, but certainly not in the bush), Alice Hoy was not long for this world. And, being a gentle person and dear in her own way, Robbie was not selfish enough to want her farm at the price of her life.

But, he argued, the outcome was beyond his help, the end result was certain. Someone, someone had to take on the task as Alice outlined it, painfully and reluctantly, yet with a certain desperation. And it might as well be him, Robbie Dunbar. In fact, he secretly exulted over the tremendous opportunity providence had thrown his way, like a bone to a dog, all undeserved, but yearned for and dreamed of.

Supper, when the milking was done and the chores finished, was fried chicken, with potatoes and gravy and fresh bread.

"I caught the hen," Barney boasted, "and held it while Mama chopped its head off." You couldn't learn too young, on the homestead. Squeamishness was a luxury that could not be afforded.

"Brave lad!" Robbie praised. "An' was it ye and yer brother been hoein' in the garden the day?"

"Just me," Barney said, while Billy explained, "Mama says I pull up too many veg'bles. But I hunted eggs, didn't I, Mama? Didn't I?" And he looked anxiously toward his mother.

Alice stretched a thin hand and tenderly pushed back a lock of the fair hair that tumbled over the young brow.

"You certainly did," she said, and the little face glowed. "And you fed the chickens, too. You were a great help today."

"And I brought in wood, didn't I, Mama?" Barney, too, looked to his mother for approval and touch.

"Fresh bread," Robbie commented, helping himself to a second slice. "How did you manage that?"

"Molly came today and asked what she could do. Bread making is one thing I dread—it's heavy work for weak muscles," and Alice smiled. "So she got it as far as the pans before she left. It was no trouble then to bake it."

"She's the one that's goin' to marry the vicar?" Robbie, the newcomer and rare-church-attender asked.

"Vicker!" Barney laughed uproariously. "Vicker! She's going to marry Parker Jones—"

"Pastor Jones," his mother corrected, and Barney subsided.

"We don't know that she's going to marry him, Rob. But they both act as if it's on their minds. But Molly would be helpful and kind anyway; it runs in the family. The Morrisons were a tremendous help and encouragement when we first arrived. Molly does have good qualities for a minister's wife."

Robbie refilled his glass (not an enameled cup, he appreciated), and said, casually, "Oh, say, I'll have to get Allan to fill in for me here tomorra night."

"Oh?" Alice asked a little anxiously. Her concern for the farm was great, her concern for the future of her boys even greater. Nothing else, of course, would have persuaded her to make the offer to Robbie that he had found irresistible.

"Aye. There's an auld acquaintance of mine just coom—"

"From Scotland, Rob? How wonderful!"

"Aye, from Binkiebrae, in fact, and I've been invited to eat supper at the Blooms' tomorra and have a guid visit."

"Would you like to have your friend eat supper with us one night?" Alice made the offer hesitantly and seemed relieved when Robbie, quickly, thanked her and declined.

"Perhaps it's best," she said quietly, then offered a small, apologetic smile.

Robbie helped clear the table and he and the boys did the dishes, he washing and the boys wiping, while Alice, at Robbie's suggestion, took the rocking chair and watched, her eyes shadowed, her forehead, even in rest, beading slightly.

The shadows were long when the wood box was filled and the house chores completed. Robbie's last task for the day was to prepare the boys for bed—it saved Alice so much wear and tear, for they were lively and loved to scuffle. He knew, however, that it pained her not to be able to do this intimate thing for them, and so, when they were finally tucked in, he set a lamp by the bedside, and a chair, then handed Alice one of their favorite books and saw her settle for a happy few minutes with her "chicks," as she called them.

Robbie was weary as he made his way homeward. It was too dark to take the shortcut; he went the longer way around, by the road. Soon now it would be light almost until the midnight hour; soon now there would be even more tasks to fill his day, and he would need the longer working hours. The gardens would flourish and need attention, the young calves would arrive, and the baby chickens. The frost was gone and it was time for seeding; there was always wood to get up for the fires next winter . . . and Alice, Alice would do less and less to help. There would come a day when he would have full charge of the boys, when he would care for her.

Robbie drew a deep breath, squaring his shoulders. To have the extra land, to increase his acreage, to move into the larger, better house, perhaps to bring the rest of his family from Scotland—it was a dream come true and worth every effort and sacrifice it called for.

Wasn't it?

7

This girl makes the best cup of tea I've tasted since coming to the territories!" Lydia Bloom declared, holding her bone china cup daintily at chin level and looking over its gold-tipped edge with satisfaction.

There were few luxuries in the bush; teatime, for those accustomed to it and determined to hang onto a shred of civilization, was one of them.

"Not to mention the scones," Herbert added, biting generously into a warm one slathered with raspberry jam—not that the worm-riddled raspberries of the bush were responsible for it. No, fortunately Herbert and Lydia could augment that skimpy supply with store-bought items. Another luxury.

Ordinarily no self-respecting homesteader would be caught having tea in the afternoon; it was a foolish, foppish thing to do. But Herbert had gained a measure of independence through the acquisition of a hired man. It was another luxury, of course, but one Herbert felt he could well consider at this time in his life.

The farm was beginning to produce and, if crops were decent (the growing season was, at best, one hundred days), he would come out ahead at the end of the year.

Herbert Bloom was more fortunate than most; he had sold a lucrative business—a string of three grocery stores—before he made his move west. He might never have done so, of course, if Lavinia, his only daughter, hadn't married a dreamer, a dreamer who put feet to his visions. And where had they taken him? Westward to the vast lands being opened and claimed by others with a like sense of adventure. No matter that it was largely uncharted; no matter that they broke trail most of the way. For all of them, struggle and adversity were accepted as challenges to be met; the tools they used were their own hands, their heads, but mostly their hearts. Herbert, a follower, coming along with his money, felt almost an onlooker, an outsider, warming his hands, so to speak, at other men's fires.

But, Herbert excused himself, why should he struggle and suffer, at his age? He could well afford to be a gentleman farmer, or so he seemed, he supposed, to his hard-pressed, hardworking neighbors.

Luxuries, for them, such as tea with the ladies of an afternoon, were neither expected nor enjoyed; hardships and tragedies, on the other hand, were expected and endured.

So now Herbert sat back, thoroughly enjoying the warm scones so recently taken from the range's oven.

Tierney, who was beginning to feel more like a daughter than a domestic, and in such a short time—she hadn't been in Bliss twenty-four hours!—sat down with the elderly couple for their tea. Though Herbert and Lydia had persuaded her to "Sit! Have a cup of tea with us," she felt a little uncomfortable in the doing, as though Ishbel Mountjoy might pop in at any moment, to gasp and frown at the unacceptable arrangement.

Scones were one thing Tierney knew how to make, and make well. Her thoughts flew briefly to Binkiebrae and the fireplace where all her cooking and baking had been done. Thank goodness the foibles of a cookstove had been learned on the prairie, in the Ketchums' kitchen, before coming to the bush, and under the gentle tutelage of Lavinia, who, like her parents before her, had flouted the employer/employee system, becoming, along the way, a friend.

"We mustn't linger too long, of course," Mrs. Bloom was saying. "After all, that young man, Robert Dunbar, is coming to have supper with us, remember."

As if Tierney needed reminding. Her head was still awhirl from the unbelievable joy of running full tilt into Robbie Dunbar.

Herbert reached for another scone. Though Lydia looked at him sternly and shook her head, he stubbornly persisted. He was rotund already, and the generous jam on the rich scone was as icing on the cake, and thoroughly enjoyed. "Herbert," his wife said reproachfully, "we'll have to restrict our teatimes if you don't show a little restraint."

"But we haven't had tea and scones like these since . . . well, perhaps ever."

"I know, but there will be more tomorrow . . . and the day after that. If we curb our passions, that is."

And that good woman pinked straightaway, having, in the heat of the moment, allowed herself the use of a word that had connotations not at all acceptable when a young, single girl was present. Tierney was gazing modestly into her teacup.

"Now look what you've done!" Lydia said, flustered, having slopped her tea in her distress.

Tierney set aside her cup, took her serviette, and dabbed the damp stain on Lydia's generous bosom, feeling, once again, more like a daughter than a domestic. Everything, to this moment, had been pure pleasure. Pure Bliss? Tierney wondered momentarily if the community would, for her, live up to its name.

When she and Herbert had arrived at the two-story Bloom house—made of lumber and still new enough to have retained some of the original color of the boards, and rising out of the bush like a ship in a green sea—Lydia had stepped outside to welcome them. Indeed, you'd have thought a daughter was coming home. Tierney was to understand more and more, as the days came and went, just how deeply the elderly couple mourned the loss of Lavinia, and to love them for their generosity in reaching out to her, Tierney, and accepting her wholeheartedly into their home and their hearts. And it was hard—in light of that—for Tierney to act the part of a true domestic. Even that first evening, donning an apron and attempting to assist with supper had but seemed as if she were the child, Lydia the mother.

Tierney had fallen quite naturally into helping, and Lydia, into allowing it. Soon, Tierney hoped, she might be the one in charge and Lydia the one assisting, for the older woman's hands were misshapen, and one could tell she was in pain as she used them. Tierney longed to help, to take some of the burden, to make a difference in Lydia's workload.

Obviously the Blooms' need had not only been what Tierney could do for them physically. Deprived of their daughter and her family, isolated as they were so much of the time, getting older and not always in good health, Lydia and Herbert would get their money's worth from the pleasure Tierney's very presence would bring. Responding to this need and sensing the sincerity of Herbert's and Lydia's reaction to her being there, Tierney counted herself blessed and determined to be all that they had expected, and more.

"Now, Herbert," Lydia was continuing, "it's a good thing supper will be later tonight so that this Robert Dunbar can get his chores done and eat with us, because you've had three . . . *three* scones."

"So I have, my dear," Herbert said comfortably. "Do you make anything else, Miss Tierney? Muffins, perhaps?"

Lydia's color hinted at apoplexy. "Herbert!" she said severely, taking up the plate of scones and rising, hurrying them out of reach, "enough of that! Now, Miss Tierney, shall we adjourn to the kitchen and see how the roast is coming along?"

The Blooms were among the fortunate few to have an icehouse, thus keeping meat available even in warm weather. Already Tierney had found opportunity to marvel at the goods and chattels in the well-stocked pantry, and, indeed, the house itself, so well furnished, so comfortable, so generously equipped. The little home in Binkiebrae, two rooms, a loft overhead for sleeping, a scullery for washing up—that was it. Yet it had been cozy, homelike, fitting the Caulders and their simple needs. Tierney thought of it now with nostalgia. But realizing it held James and his bride with little or no room for her, she counted herself blessed to be here, surrounded by the generosity of a couple named Bloom, who, not knowing her, had seen fit to take her to their bosoms. And generous bosoms they were, in all ways.

A little hymn of praise rose in her heart, even passed her lips. With all these blessings the chief one, now and forever, was the faithfulness of the One in whom "all things work together for good to them that love God, to them who are the called according to his purpose."

What safety she felt!—held in the everlasting arms of God and placed in the hands of these good people.

When Robbie appeared, slicked and shined and obviously fresh from a bath, Tierney found herself restrained, bashful. There was, now, none of the heedless rushing into his arms. He, too, looked a little uncertain.

"Hello, Robbie," she greeted him, subdued, remembering her impulsive rush into his arms the day before and his spontaneous response, and blushing a little. Then she excused herself and returned to the kitchen, to fumble ineffectively with the roast and to bumble through the making of the gravy. Lydia Bloom, after a keen look at the younger woman's flushed face, stepped in, and soon supper was on the table.

Herbert stepped to the porch and rang the bell hanging there. Thus summoned, the hired man, Ahab, soon joined them. With little ceremony they sat up to the table. The food was simple but bountiful, and, as appetites were hearty, the meal progressed with few interruptions as they filled their plates, cleaned them, sat back with satisfaction, and awaited the inevitable pudding that Lydia, English through and through, had provided.

Over a final cup of coffee, Herbert spoke. "Ahem!" and everyone perked up their ears. "Ahab told me this afternoon that he is leaving us."

Lydia looked up, surprised. "Oh, I'm sorry. Is anything . . . wrong?"

"Not a bit of it," the hired man assured them, digging into his blancmange after flooding it with thick, golden cream and stirring it thoroughly. "It's just that I've finally saved up enough to get started on my own place. I think I mentioned that to you before—it's been my plan from the beginning. I can't get started any younger," he finished quite seriously.

Lydia nodded, relieved. Her kind heart could not countenance any problem that she and Herbert might have contributed to.

"Of course, I think we knew that. But we've been so satisfied—"

"He has to go, Mother," Herbert interrupted, "if he's to get a cabin up before winter. Just where is this place, Ahab?"

"It's in the Nipawin area."

"There's still some land around here—"

"I know, but my cousin is over that way, and I'd like to be near him."

"Can't say as I blame you. But this puts us in the way of needing to look for someone to take your place. Do you have any suggestions, Robert?"

Robbie thought a moment and then shook his head. "No, I canna think of anybody, but I'll keep my ears open and let you know if I hear of anyone. Say," he brightened, "Herkimer just mentioned a fellow who was looking for a homestead at the Lands Office in Prince Albert and thinking he might need to work a while first, just as Ahab has done. Tha's what Allan and I did, you know, and it was worth the wait, I can tell you."

The men talked it over, and Robbie promised to follow the lead with Herkimer and get back to Herbert Bloom.

Tierney cleared the table and started the dishwashing, only to have Lydia insist she leave the work and spend some time with her friend from Scotland. Going back into the front room shyly, it was to have Robbie look up and suggest, "Can we take a walk, Tierney?"

"Feel free to," Herbert encouraged. "It's not only beautiful over toward the lake but smells good, too."

Fresh grass, spring flowers, breezes over the rippling surface of the water, all combined to bring forth a potpourri that was unique, calling for deep breathing and happy sighs.

Swinging along at Robbie's side, Tierney lost her touch of reserve, and soon they were deep in conversation. Robbie must hear how Tierney came to make the change to Canada; Tierney must learn all that Robbie and Allan had done to get their homesteads and settle in. They must each report on letters from home, Tierney relaying whatever James had written her, Robbie with news of his family, and both talking of Binkiebrae and home in general.

"We've not given up thinkin' the whole family will coom over," Robbie said. "We could put 'em up, Allan and I, atween us. Build on a room or two, if we need to."

"Your hoosie, Robbie, your very own hoosie! I can hardly wait t' see inside it." Truth to tell, Tierney could almost see herself as mistress of it. Dreams do come true after all!

It was then Robbie said, "Tierney," and if his voice sounded strained she had no reason to notice it; she could barely restrain herself from slipping her arm through his as they walked, or, more daring yet, taking his hand. Modesty prevailed, and she waited for Robbie to make such a momentous decision.

"Robbie . . . do ye remember our farewell, there on the hill? The pain of it, the mortal misery? I said—to mysel', o' course— that I'd hae gone wi' ye anywhere, e'en to the ends of the earth. Anywhere, and yet I couldna follow to Canada." In her earnestness she slipped into the Scots dialect, forgetting all her efforts to speak more plainly. "And yet, here I am. Dinna see the hand o' Someone bigger than us in a' that?"

"Tierney—"

"Oh, Robbie, I'm jist so happy—"

"Tierney!" Robbie spoke, this time, more urgently.

"Aye, Robbie, what is't?"

"I . . . wanted to tell you aboot my plans . . ."

"And I want to hear. Aye, Robbie, you talk, and I'll listen." She was looking at him, contentment on her face.

"Y' see, I've a chance to get more land. Tha's not easy to do, believe me. I thought I'd have to wait years and years before I had the opportunity. But this land I'm talkin' aboot is available to me now, and best of all—" Robbie's face was tight with his concentration, his need to make her understand, "it's right next to mine. Can you believe that? It seems like the hand o' fate, or something like that. I can hardly believe it meself."

"But, Robbie, you can only file for one quarter section of free land, reet?"

"Tha's what's so great aboot it—I wouldna have to file for it."

"Well, what then?" Tierney was clearly puzzled, clearly interested, alert now.

"You see," Robbie said, speaking quickly, "it's my neighbor's land, my neighbor that died just a short time ago. His homestead had been proved up, so it was his own. And his wife's, I guess you'd say. Well, she's alone now, an impossible situation; she can't handle it by herself, no woman could—"

"And you'd take it on for her? But how would that make it your own, Robbie? Or is she wantin' to sell? Would you have the money to buy it, Robbie?" Tierney was attempting to work this out in her thinking.

"Na na, she dinna wants to sell; she wants to keep it for her boys."

"Her boys?"

"Two of 'em—Barney and Billy. Just sma', they are."

"I guess I don't understand, Robbie. What else?"

"She's sick, Tierney. Verra sick."

"How sick d'ye mean, Robbie? Won't she . . . get well?"

"Dyin' sick, that's how sick."

"Oh, Robbie!"

"Aye. And she hasna got long to live. And she—Alice, that is—needs someone to take over the farm and to raise the bairns after . . . after she's gone."

"Tha's a big responsibility, Robbie. But we . . . you could do it, for the sake of the farm. Is it settled, then?"

"Aye. It's all settled. Signed and settled. I'm to do it."

Tierney drew a big breath. Well! It was a surprise, but nothing she couldn't handle, for Robbie's sake.

"You see, Tierney," Robbie said, staring rather desperately out over the lake, "there's only one way to do it, if I'm to have the place."

"Robbie?" Tierney asked slowly.

"Aye. I'm to marry Alice."

At first Molly was astonished to see the Condon buggy in the parsonage yard, knowing that Beatrice rarely felt up to driving herself around, and that Bly would be in the fields this time of year. Perhaps there was a serious need of private counseling . . .

Vivian! The thought struck, quivered, panged.

Molly's next thought: *What right has she got to be here!*

Immediately, shamed, she admitted that Vivian Condon had every bit as much right to be here as she herself did. *After all,* she confessed reluctantly, *I don't own Parker Jones!*

With this thought in mind and determining firmly that she, Molly Morrison, would never, *never* compete for the attention of any man, even Parker Jones, she urged Kip back, step-by-step, until she was clear of the Condon buggy and could begin a tight turn out of the yard.

Too late. The door, which had been left—discreetly—partly ajar, opened, and Parker Jones, calmly and sedately, stepped outside and called, "Molly! Come on in, Molly."

"I'm off to the store, Parker," Molly responded, pulling Kip to a halt. "I'll stop by on my way back."

"Molly—*please!*"

Anyone else, not knowing Parker Jones well, might not have caught the appeal in his voice. There was a definite cry for help in his tone and in his eyes, though his words were ordinary. Caring as she did, there was only one thing to do.

Turning Kip's head once again toward the hitching post, Molly automatically hauled back on the reins and stared as a superbly fitted and outfitted feminine figure stepped through the doorway to stand by the side of the man.

Not only was Vivian Condon's ensemble in the latest style— or so Molly supposed, having only the catalog and rare visits to Prince Albert stores to instruct her along these lines—but richly so. Vivian Condon's clothes exuded affluence; her demeanor was that of a person who considered herself, who *knew* herself, to be a person of superiority. She was superbly confident.

Molly's calico, though sprigged with tiny blue flowers, edged with ribbon, freshly laundered and crisp, seemed, in comparison, just what it was—a homemade, second-best dress. And at that moment, particularly, Molly seemed just what she was—a hometown girl. Hometown, perhaps, but never *second-best!*

In spite of good intentions, Molly found her jaw tightening just a little. With finesse she pulled Kip into place, turned, and reached a small foot below a neat ankle toward the buggy's iron step, finding Parker at the rig's side and his hand outstretched to help her down. Unless she was sadly mistaken, there was a look of desperation in his dark eyes.

"The box—" she said, a little breathlessly, and Parker reached to pick it up from the seat of the buggy.

"I'm afraid it's rather shaken up," she offered as they turned toward the house.

"Molly, Molly," Parker said, shaking his head and smiling, "when will you ever slow down? It's a good thing Kip likes to run."

"He's lucky he's not hitched to a seeder this lovely morning," she answered in her defense. "Maybe he was so thankful, he just stepped out."

"And maybe you just like to hurry through life," he said, smiling down at her. "Well maybe not *through* life," he amended, "but *into* it."

Yes, and eager to get there, she might have responded, recognizing and loving the light in his eyes. But Vivian still lingered on the porch steps, her lips fixed in a half smile that had no humor in it and no welcome.

Nevertheless, "Good morning, Vivian," Molly said in a friendly manner, first names having been decided upon around the Sunday dining table.

But Vivian was preceding her into the house, and her response, if any, was lost in the rustle of what Molly supposed was the taffeta lining of the four-yard sweep of her skirt.

Sitting in the middle of the table, beside the sack from which it had apparently been removed, was a loaf of bread and a pound of butter, Vivian's offering and excuse for coming. The incongruity of it—the society belle and the plebeian foodstuff—wasn't missed by Molly, who might have laughed under different circumstances.

Over the back of a chair, as though she intended to stay a while, was Vivian's cape of silk brilliantine, its collar trimmed with fine black lace and satin ribbon, and its lining made of changeable silk. A Monday costume! Even Molly's second-best calico would be changed, as soon as she got home, to something worn and serviceable in preparation for Monday's laundry, which her mother was sorting even at this moment, while water heated on the stove.

Biting her lip, Molly restrained herself from asking, brightly, of course, "Your Aunt Bea? She's doing the wash—by herself?"

Immediately stricken, Molly reproached herself: *Molly! Behave yourself!*

And so she spoke more humbly than was normal, for Molly, and spoke honestly, "You look very nice this morning, Vivian.

Are you off to the one and only store of our wee hamlet? Or," she added, growing more uncomfortable as she saw the long-suffering look on the other's face, "the mail—I'm sure you are looking for mail from home. We still look forward to hearing from family in Scotland—"

It was beyond her. Somehow, Molly sensed, she was missing the mark, and her attempt at conversation faded away. What a mumble-mouth! And she had dared to think she would make a pastor's wife!

The day, which had been so bright and full of hope, turned dismal for Molly. She wanted only to get out of there, make her run by the store, get back home in time to help her mother, and find normalcy in her household's routine tasks.

"Sit down, ladies," Parker was saying, having deposited the box on his round oak table. "The coffeepot is still on, and I'll be happy to serve you. I think I have three clean cups here—"

Ordinarily Molly would have laughed good-humoredly at Parker's often-inadequate attempts at housekeeping, counting the days until she should be in residence to do these things for him, and happily so. But Vivian was seating herself at the side of the table, spreading her skirts with a fine and satisfactory rustle, leaning her chin on her ringed hand, and having every semblance of making herself at home.

What must she think of the rude, two-room house, barely more than a cabin? Most of the furnishings were donated; a few were handmade. The stove dominated the living quarters, as it did in most bush homes where, day by day it ate its way through cord after cord of wood. Even in summer it blazed; not a cup of tea could be made without it. Bread had to be baked weekly or oftener; water for anything and everything was heated either on the top of the stove or in the reservoir at the side.

At the side of the stove were a couple of rocking chairs. The round table, set in the center of the room, was covered by a patterned oilcloth; the cupboards were without doors, and Parker's skimpy supply of household goods were on open display. A cord across one corner held a couple of tea towels and a dishrag, obviously drying; a few battered pans hung on nails on the white-washed walls. There were books scattered and piled everywhere. The room beyond was, obviously, the bedroom.

As sharp as Vivian was, there was no way to suppose she hadn't taken it all in at a glance. Molly watched as Vivian's eyes turned thoughtfully toward Parker Jones.

Feeling stifled suddenly, Molly wanted to be gone from this young woman's scrutiny, from her evaluation.

"I really must go—" Molly began her excuse, but realized she wasn't speaking truth. To feel second rate was one thing; but to dissemble, to be drawn into pathetic untruths, was another thing and quite outside the realm of what Molly would allow of herself. So she checked herself and her stumbling excuse, and tried again.

But neither did she want to put down the other person. So, "It's wash day," she began, only to falter again, hesitating on the brink of intimating what any well-brought-up girl should know: Monday was wash day, and washings were a monumental task. Vivian obviously was not involved and apparently not concerned.

"Mum," she diverted herself into explaining, beginning to perspire, realizing she wasn't handling the situation well, and feeling the amused eyes of Vivian Condon on her, "is waiting for me to go to the store and bring back some Fels Naptha—"

Fels Naptha! Could anything be more mundane, more uncalled for than a reference to the bar of brown soap that, shaved by hand with a good sharp knife, was added to wash water?

And, sure enough, Vivian's eyebrows were rising, and her curling lips were asking, "Fels Nap—what?"

Half hysterical—from a mix of emotions, one of which was sheer hilarity at the lunacy of the conversation—Molly caught herself in time to refrain from trilling *"tha, tha, tha*—Fels Nap*tha!"*

Who could blame Parker Jones if the coffeepot trembled in his hand, and if his usually firm lips threatened to do the same?

"It's wash day, Miss Condon," he said hastily. "Even so, Molly, please stay long enough for a cup of coffee? No? Well, here, let me empty the box—"

Boxes were as treasured as paper bags or wax paper or writing paper . . . so many things were in small supply, in the bush, or no supply at all, and were used and reused until every shred of usefulness was wrung from them. Except for that, Molly would have fled the premises. As it was, she waited, carrying on some sort of feeble but safe conversation with Vivian, until Parker had emptied the box of its contents—bread, a pound of butter, enough meat from yesterday's dinner to make a meal, leftover cake.

"I wish you'd stop a moment," he said again, and Molly, who knew him well, recognized again the urge in his word.

But the too-patient face of Vivian Condon spoke otherwise; it was obvious she was simply out-waiting Molly.

Molly—if she could help it—would be no hindrance! Molly would do battle for nothing, nor for anyone, even Parker Jones.

"Mum's waiting," she said quietly, and Parker Jones, just as quiet, followed her to the buggy.

Helping her up into the rig, untying Kip, and stepping back to her side, Parker spoke in a low voice, "I hoped you'd stay until . . . that is—"

"This is something, Parker, that you'll have to handle yourself."

Though much of what had happened inside was laughable—and Molly could feel a sort of hysterical giggle struggling to erupt—still she knew beyond all doubt that it was not her place to rescue Parker Jones from Vivian Condon or any other female.

"But—"

Molly left Parker Jones standing looking after her and had to harden her heart. Much as she wanted to fly to his aid, to clean—as a ruffled mother bird—her nest and make it her own again, she felt it was not hers to do.

Her last glimpse back, as Kip whirled the buggy out of the yard and in the direction of Bliss and the general store, was the face of Vivian Condon in the doorway of the parsonage, a small smile on her lips.

9

Tierney crept into the house not the same vital, spirited, winsome girl who left it not more than an hour ago with Rob Dunbar. Even Lydia, who knew her very little as yet, could tell something was terribly amiss with her new "help."

Tierney hesitated inside the kitchen door, still a stranger to the house and its occupants, and uncertain of herself and her responsibilities in this moment. Needing to seek the privacy of her own room, her right to do so was in question. She was, after all, the hired girl, a "domestic."

Lydia had been hanging up the last damp tea towel. Turning to look at Tierney, her plump face showed its shock. Here was this bright-faced young woman—girl, really, for she couldn't be more than nineteen—with the happiness blighted from her face, and her lips taut and white. Lydia, a mother and a grandmother, couldn't let this go, she simply couldn't.

"Oh, my dear," she said spontaneously and gently, her loving concern evident in her tone.

It was almost more than Tierney could take and retain her last bit of self-control.

"Ma'am," she began, and it was a pathetic attempt at normality.

But her new employer's arms were around her. Her new employer was saying things that only mothers and grandmothers say, or very dear and close friends. It was too much for Tierney. The tears, which had been held sternly in check, spouted and ran.

This is wrong, all wrong! her common sense cried. *What would Ishbel Mountjoy say!*

To come to a new place, be on the job no more than twenty-four hours, bring your special friend into their midst to be fed, skip doing the cleanup and go for a walk with him, only to come back in a collapse of tears, was most unacceptable. Tierney made a brave but futile effort to get control.

It was the arms of Lydia Bloom that were her undoing; it was the crooning comfort of her murmured words. It was the tender pats on the back. Tierney, taller than Lydia by a good six inches, sagged helplessly against the motherly bosom.

The sound of buggy wheels going past outside, fading quickly away, brought Tierney's head up. Then, with a desperately white and resigned expression on her face, she took a deep breath, stared over Lydia's gray head, and spoke.

"He—Robbie—is to marry . . . someone else."

Lydia's eyes widened, but without saying anything she guided Tierney to a chair at the side of the kitchen table, handing her a nearby serviette that she had been going to toss into the laundry. Tierney took it gratefully.

There were a few quiet moments as Tierney mopped her eyes and drew several more deep and shaky breaths. Lydia, standing at her side, waited patiently.

Lydia wanted Tierney to be able to talk, but to pry was not in her. So, "I'm sorry," she said gently, leaving the way open if the girl cared to confide in her, but asking no questions.

"It's his neighbor, Alice—"

"Alice Hoy, of course," Lydia supplied and was not surprised. Deaths and remarriages, on the prairie and in the bush, were a way of life. Mates died, and the remaining partners turned to anyone who was available, especially if there were children. Barnabas Hoy had died a few weeks ago; Rob Dunbar was near and, everyone had supposed, available.

"Aye, Alice. With two bairns. Robbie is willin' . . . is willin'," the tears threatened again and were choked back. "Robbie is goin' to marry her and raise her two boys."

It's her land, of course, Lydia said to herself. *He wants her land.*

"You mustn't blame Robbie," Tierney said, and though it was a generous thing to say, the need to say it made it pathetic.

"Y' see, he issna promised to me," her lips explained.

But I was promised to him! her heart cried.

And she had thought he was promised to her. The bonds between them had been that tight, that solid, that real.

Lydia was wise enough to offer no platitudes. Nothing like "You'll feel better in the morning," "He'll think it over, and things will change," "Alice won't hold him to it, now that you're here, if he'll explain."

Neither did she—wise, wise woman—offer the dreadful consolation of the truth that Alice Hoy had not long to live, and then—

Still, later, when she was in bed, wrestling with heartbreak and trying to accept it, it was that thought—that Alice was not long for this world—that kept occurring to Tierney, troubling her greatly.

Robbie—with face averted and obviously shame-faced—had brought up that very thing.

"Tierney," he had said, having seen her first look of disbelief turn to dreadful realization, her astonishment to anguish, "she—Alice, that is—canna live more than a few months, a year at the most. She's told me that hersel'. Then," though his eyes couldn't meet hers, he said it; doggedly he said it: "Then we could marry. Then, Tierney, I can offer you a decent place to live, a working farm, and—"

"And do ye think I care aboot all that!" Tierney had cried, breaking into Robbie's words almost with horror. "Dinna say sich things! Dinna think them!"

"Tierney," he had said then, taking her hand in his and speaking pleadingly, "I had no idea you were anywhere on the continent. As far as I knew, we'd niver see each other again."

Tierney knew it was true. Still, no matter where he was or how long it would be until she might hear of him again, her heart had been irrevocably given to Robbie Dunbar. And his heart, she had thought with every fiber of her being, had been pledged to her.

"Robbie," she said, "I think I could bear it better if you were to tell me you were in love . . . I could understand that. But this—this cold-blooded marryin' for what you can git out of it—"

"It's not like that, at all, at all," Robbie defended quickly. "She needs me, Tierney; dinna y' see the difference that makes?"

"Are there not many bachelors lookin' for wives? Isna it a well-known fact that there's not nearly enough lassies to go aroun'? Why ye, Robbie?"

"Why not me? I'm the lucky one," Robbie said and couldn't keep the note of triumph from his voice. "Think on't, Tierney! Jist a few months, a year maybe, and then I'll be a landowner of some account. What an opportunity! Think on't, Tierney! Did ever sich a chance come along in a thousan' years?"

And Robbie gave Tierney's hand a little shake, his eyes alight with his great good fortune and his tone pleading with her to understand, to be glad for him.

Tierney's eyes, in the fading light, were becoming large and shiny with her effort to hold in the storm of tears that threatened. But she knew, if she gave in to it, Robbie's arms—his *dear* arms—would go around her, and she would be lost.

"Ah, Robbie," she said, in a low voice, "what am I supposed to do now? Stan' by and see you—" her voice thickened and her tone wobbled, and sure enough, Robbie's arms came out toward her.

Quickly Tierney stepped back. One thing she knew: Robbie Dunbar was pledged to someone else; he was not free to take her or anyone else in his arms.

"Don't, Robbie," she said quickly, stopping him. "Dinna y' see, your arms are not mine anymair. I canna coom into them—"

"Tierney," Robbie pleaded in a low voice, "it's not a love match atween Alice and me. There's no love atween us. In fact," even in the dim light she could see the color mount in his sunburnt cheeks, "it's t' be a marriage in name only. Tierney, do y' under-stand what I mean?"

It sickened Tierney to even think on the subject. Alice—ill and dying, and Robbie planning—na na, it was not to be coun-tenanced, what he was explaining.

And that's what she finally managed to say: "Na na, Robbie. I canna let y' talk this way . . . I canna even think on sich a thing."

Robbie looked miserable. "Please, Tierney," he begged earnestly, "please wait for me. It won't be long. You'll be busy workin' for the Blooms for a while, y' need to keep your part of the terms y' made with them. We'll jist be a few miles apart . . . we'll see each other often."

"Nae, Robbie!" Tierney cried, "I couldna stand it! We'll not—"

"Will ye think on't? Promise me ye'll think on't, Tierney, and wait and see. Please, lass!"

Thoughts and emotions whirled through Tierney's head, thoughts of good sense and proper procedure, emotions of pain and longing and desire.

"When, Robbie? When is this weddin' to take place?"

"No date is set," Robbie replied. "She's no more anxious for it than I am. Her husban' has been dead less than two months, after all. As long as she feels she can keep goin', we'll carry on as we have, me doin' the chores, helpin' with the boys, helpin' with the hoose when she can't do it."

A spasm of pain crossed Tierney's face. It was all too personal, too intimate, to think about—Robbie and *someone else* keeping house!

"I'd like you to meet her, Tierney," Robbie said now. "You'd see what I mean. After all, you can't be jealous of a . . . a shadow. An' that's about all there is to her now. You'd like her, Tierney. I think it would help, to meet her. Would you? Would y' let me take you over there someday, to meet Alice and the boys? See the place? Help me dream, maybe?"

It had a sick sound to it. Something in Tierney rebelled at the very thought of what Robbie was describing so earnestly. But Robbie!—hadn't she promised to follow him to the ends of the earth? And wasn't he worth any price to have, at last, as her own? Would a few months matter? A few vows spoken but soon obliterated by death?

"I'll see, Robbie," was the best she could promise.

Then, with the long-checked tears threatening to overflow at last, she had turned away, picked up her skirts, and run toward the house—and Lydia.

Lydia's last words, before Tierney went upstairs, were wise ones: "We'll pray with you, lovey. We'll pray, and it'll work out right, you'll see."

Tierney, so recently come to the One who invited, "Come unto me, all ye that labor and are heavy laden, and I will give you rest," knew she should do just that; it was what her heavy-laden heart cried out to do.

"Lord, help me!" The timeworn plea, so simple and so full of unexpressed meaning, came from a heart that felt the better for having uttered it. Tierney, so new to praying, even newer to believing, did her best to "cast her burden" on the Lord.

On the buggy ride home, Rob Dunbar found himself drenched with sweat, though the evening was cool. With no one to hear, he groaned. What a fix to be in! Had he reached Tierney with his explanations, his pleas? Had he helped her see the reasonableness of his argument? If not, there was nothing to be done but try again, for he was irrevocably committed to the plan as he outlined it to her.

Oh, he might have backed out, explaining about Tierney and helping Alice find another man, capable, and willing to take on the marriage and the boys for the prize offered—the Hoy homestead. It would have been a bit embarrassing, perhaps, for the widow who had not found it easy to approach him. But she was desperate; she would have no other choice but to find a substitute if he, Robbie, backed out.

But the homestead! A neat, lumber-built house of five rooms—three down, two up—a roomy barn, two small granaries, chicken house, coop for other fowl, shed. As for stock, Barnabas Hoy had assembled a fine team, a riding horse, five cows with three of them calving this spring, a bull . . .

Counting these assets over and realizing how easily they might slip away from him, Robbie's sweat increased. He had to, he *just had to* persuade Tierney. To know that she was waiting for him would see him through these next months, would lend strength for his weary days, would supply purpose for all of it.

How great she looked! How his heart had leaped to see her! His feelings—other than sympathy—toward Alice had never been involved; it was strictly a business arrangement. His heart, now as ever, was fixed on the Scottish lass of his choice—Tierney Caulder, once lost to him and now so miraculously restored.

"Wait for me, Tierney, lass," he muttered now and turned his thoughts toward the material things he would be able to give her. As always, when he thought of this opportunity to gain new acreage, his heart leaped.

Had it leaped more for Tierney or for the land? he wondered, briefly, and a trifle uncomfortably.

He had barely unhitched and cared for the horse when Allan arrived, on his way home from the Hoy place and evening chores.

"You can have it!" he said disagreeably. "Thass a lot of work over there, Robbie!"

"It'll be easier when I get all my belongin's over there," Robbie answered. "There won't be all this traipsin' back and forth."

"She looked bad tonight, Rob."

"She does, at times. She's fatally sick, y' know." Robbie was defensive, for some reason.

"Nice lady," Allan said, "but ye wouldn't catch me takin' on sich a job, thass for sure."

"Nae, and ye'll end up wi' yer original quarter section, and thass all," Robbie said, still belligerent, though he didn't know why.

"But happy. I'll be happy, Rob. You got yoursel' a problem, thass for sure. Alice and the land on one hand, Tierney on the other. Think ye can pull it off? How'd it go tonight, anyway?"

"It went a'reet. She'll wait," Robbie said more confidently than he felt. "Tierney'll wait for me. You'll see."

"But are ye breakin' her heart, lad?" Allan asked keenly.

"It'll all coom right, when the land's mine; you'll see," Robbie insisted, closing the barn door behind him and turning toward the cabin, Allan following, and Whiskers at his heels.

"Gowk!" Allan muttered and marched off toward home.

With his books and papers spread around him on the old oak table that occupied the center of the room—a contribution of someone in the Bliss congregation—Parker Jones dropped his head on the pages of the open Bible and groaned.

So often, searching for something to bring to his people, he found his own soul being exercised and corrected. Today was such a time it seemed.

Reading the sixth chapter of Second Corinthians, Parker had been contemplating a portion of the moving sixteenth verse: "Ye are the temple of the living God; as God hath said, I will dwell in them, and walk in them; and I will be their God, and they shall be my people." It should have been heartwarming . . . it would be good for the people. But Parker, in considerable turmoil, was in need of something pointedly reassuring regarding his private battle.

Perhaps it was because he was feeling a bit anxious about a certain young lady who had appeared on the local scene and the impact she was having on Bliss in general, and him in particular. Perhaps, feeling *un*comfortable, he wanted comfort; perhaps, feeling uncertain, he wanted approval.

As his eyes ran over the chapter, his attention was caught and held by something far different: "Giving no offense in any thing, that the ministry be not blamed: but in all things approving ourselves as the ministers of God . . ."

Oh, oh! The affirmation that Parker needed seemed questionable in light of this verse. Always fighting a battle concerning his worthiness anyway, and now uneasy about *something* in regard to that new young woman Vivian Condon—Parker found his eyes settling rather apprehensively on additional verses in the same chapter. In their light, was he, could he claim to be what he desired above all: "a workman that needeth not to be ashamed"?

The Word seemed clear as it outlined what was expected of a minister of God, and as he read it, the feeling of insufficiency that troubled him in the best of times now beat a drumroll in his heart. But he read on: ". . . approving ourselves as the ministers of God, in much patience, in afflictions, in necessities—"

Better, much better, he thought cautiously. Here he qualified, undoubtedly so. Afflictions, particularly physical afflictions, had been few; what there were, he had borne with fortitude. As for necessities, he certainly qualified; the life of a bush pastor was one sacrifice after another. Hadn't his few white shirts, laundered week after week and worn continually, begun to show wear? Hadn't Sister Dinwoody, just the other day, offered to "turn" the collars and cuffs for him? Weren't the pants to his one good suit beginning to bag at the knees? Didn't he eat his meals mainly at the doled-out generosity of his parishioners? Didn't he subsist, at times, on a diet of beans and oatmeal and pancakes?

". . . in distresses, in stripes . . . in tumults, in labors—" Now, finally, Parker could draw a deep breath of relief. All these things he was faithful in, or would be, if called upon to so endure.

But there was more: ". . . in watchings, in fastings—" Yes, Lord, yes, he agreed quickly—some watchings, some fastings.

". . . by pureness—" And now again, arrows of uncertainty struck his sensitive spirit. How pure? Parker groaned again; sometimes he wished he weren't so introspective.

Going on—". . . by longsuffering . . . by evil report and good report—" I'll suffer long, and gladly, he cried silently, and do it patiently. But—evil report? Lord, let there be no evil report!

Parker knew that his life, words, and actions were under the intense scrutiny of the entire community; he guarded his reputation as his very life.

When women of the parish stopped by the parsonage, coming inside, perhaps to leave their "offering," he always saw to it that the door was kept discreetly open. And if there needed to be a conversation of any length, they stepped outside, onto the small porch. Parker deemed it a wise thing to do.

This rule applied even to Molly, especially to Molly, for the eyes of the congregation, though turned on the couple with a certain tolerance, were keen, too, and ready to condemn any indiscretion. Molly was as aware of this as he and played by the rules. Even on their walks, though there might be a discreet holding of hands, further intimacies were curbed, all for the sake of the congregation who looked to him as their spiritual example. Only in the confines of the Morrison home were the young couple allowed any semblance of intimacy; and even there it was always with prudence.

Parker Jones was a cautious man, and though Molly Morrison was all his heart longed for or desired, something restrained him and kept him from doing more than talking in generalities about marriage plans. Molly, sensitive to his hesitation, controlled her natural tendency to impatience, and waited. The good people of Bliss, imagining their pastor was near to finding a wife, which the Bible called "a good thing," waited tolerantly. And, through it all, the proprieties were observed.

Yes, a good report was important.

But Vivian—usually managing by some means or another to make Parker feel like a perfect stick—had, this very day, breezed past him after knocking at his door. She had sailed, uninvited, into the house, laughing, tossing her head as she left him standing at the entrance feeling like a stiff and stilted theologian rather than a living, breathing male.

Once inside, Vivian had removed her short cape and made herself at home, demanding a cup of coffee. Before Parker—having entered the house reluctantly—could do more than clear his throat and begin an explanation of why she would have to leave, Molly had showed up. And left again, almost as summarily! How awkward it had all been! No wonder, Parker thought now, he was uncomfortable in his spirit.

He read on: "... as deceivers, and yet true—" Was there such a mix in himself?

"... as chastened, and not killed—"

Chastened indeed. Sometimes he thought it would be better to be killed outright than suffer the pangs of chastisement.

Parker hurried on and felt his battered spirits lifting a trifle as he came to "as poor, yet making many rich ..."

How apropos for a bush pastor. Hadn't Brother Dinwoody, just last week, assured him that the sermon was enriching? The dear people of Bliss were kind and responsive to his sermonizing, urging him on with hearty amens, shaking his hand warmly at the close of each service, and "God-blessing" him faithfully. Yes, he dared to believe that not only his sermons, but his very presence in the barren homes of Bliss, brought a measure of enrichment.

Parker continued to read: "... as having nothing—" He turned his eyes from the Book in front of him with its curiously timely applications to himself and looked around his living quarters.

If ever a man had given up everything, Parker Jones was that man.

He saw with new eyes the poor pieces of furniture, the almost empty cupboard, the old stove that seeped smoke at times, the linoleum that had seen better days, the collection of ragtag items that furnished his living quarters. The bedroom beyond was no better; it held a sagging, cast-off bed, an ancient chiffonier, a single chair, and a wire across one corner to hang his scanty wardrobe on. The single window had a dark green blind.

True, someone had made curtains of red check for the windows in the room in which he now sat and covered the seats of his battered chairs with cushions of the same material. Even now the Morrison men were working on a hand-turned settee, and Mary and Kezzie were preparing to pad it, making a comfortable and attractive seat. Herkimer Pinkard had pledged a new stove after harvest, depending, of course, on how bounteous the harvest was this year. One dear lady came weekly to scrub his floor, clean his cupboards, and gather up his bedsheets and take them home, returning with clean ones. It was kind of her, but again it was evidence of his total dependence on the charity or the parsimony of his parishioners. Parker Jones, a proud man once, had become, of necessity he supposed, a humbled man.

At least he had his privacy. Lonely as it was, at times, and skimpily as the small house was provided for, still it was better than the arrangement for his keep the church had made when he first came.

Stepping from the train in Prince Albert, Parker had been met by Angus Morrison and taken directly to his home, with an explanation that permanent quarters were in the planning stage, that a "parsonage" would be forthcoming. Until then, the plan for his board and room was that he spend a month in various church homes.

One good thing had surfaced right away: The new pastor had come into immediate and rather intimate contact with that black-haired, blue-eyed dynamo, Molly Morrison. Molly's obvious enjoyment of life in general, her abounding energy along with her good humor and laughter, all mixed with a generous, loving heart, had won Parker over from the beginning.

A month later he had packed up his things and moved to his second assignment—the Dinwoody home. After a month there it had been on to the Condons, Platts, Mudges, even the bachelor quarters of Herkimer Pinkard. Month by month he had shifted his clothes, his books, his belongings, from the home of one parishioner to another. At the Mudges he had shared the unfinished upstairs with the three Mudge sons. It had been the dead of winter, and the upstairs was heated only by a single stovepipe that passed through the floor from the room below and out through the roof, and from which only a faint heat radiated. Occasionally, during a storm, he had watched the tin pipe trembling in the wind, at the same time freezing his fingers as they tried to set down his sermon thoughts. The boys, housebound much of the time, roughhoused and cavorted nearby while Parker attempted to study.

At the Platts', Jacob had taken ill, and Parker had spent most of his month chopping wood, filling the wood box, hauling water, milking and feeding cows. The Platts were apologetic but helpless, and Parker hadn't really minded. Until, that is, Sunday rolled around and he was sure that his congregation, looking to him with expectant eyes for their week's spiritual food, were disappointed in the skimpy hash of a message he served them.

Yes, if ever a man had little or nothing of worldly goods, it was Parker Jones. And, as an offering to the Lord, they were a very small gift indeed; how much of *himself* had been given up?

Dreading further painful revelations of his role and his inadequacies concerning it, Parker Jones's eyes returned to the Scriptures. Returned, opened wide, blinked, misted: ". . . as having nothing, and yet possessing all things."

Had he not, in forsaking home and parents and siblings, found a home in the heart of the bush, in the hearts of its people? Had he not, in giving up an opportunity to amass this world's goods, made an exchange for true riches? In seeking the will of One higher than himself, had he not set his feet upon a path that had brought intense satisfaction and fulfillment?

Present temptations should not, would not, turn him aside from his chosen calling.

With fingers that trembled from the assurance that warmed his heart and the relief that flooded his troubled spirit, Parker Jones scrabbled through the thin pages of his Bible until he found the very consolation he needed: "I know thy works, and tribulation, and poverty, (but thou art rich).... Fear none of those things which thou shalt suffer ... be thou faithful unto death, and I will give thee a crown of life" (Rev. 2:9–10).

God would show him; God would be patient while he, Parker Jones, struggled with the troubling question of His will.

There was considerable excitement at the Bloom home: The new hired man was to arrive today.

True to his word, Rob Dunbar had searched out the man he had met at the Lands Office in Prince Albert, still hovering over possible moves on his part.

Wanting to file on a homestead, Quinn Archer lacked the cash to do all those things necessary to prove it up in the allotted length of time—erect living quarters, buy certain pieces of equipment, clear the bush—and was pondering his options. Should he, he wondered, file for a homestead now, leave the land sit idle and get a job for a while, or get a job, save some money, and then file?

"I'm afraid," he told Rob, "all the land in the vicinity of Prince Albert—that is, within reasonable driving distance—will soon be gone, and I'll be stuck out in some remote hinterland where it'll be hard to get the crop to the railroad, or get mail, or supplies."

Robbie Dunbar was quite at sea concerning where or what the hinterland might be, but he supposed it was a poor place and to be avoided.

Quinn Archer, from whose tongue the word had rolled effortlessly, was, in spite of rough clothes and a seeming lack of this world's goods, a man of some education and, perhaps, of some polish, though this remained to be seen.

"Aye, it's fillin' in, I guess," Robbie responded, grateful again that he and Allan had the great good fortune to locate on some of the last land in the Bliss area. "I know there are places at Carrot River. And of course much, much land farther oot. It's still an untracked wilderness in many places. Or there's always the possibility of findin' someone who for one reason or another hasna been able to stick it oot, and he'll sell his homestead, and probably cheap, jist glad to get oot."

"I've had a chance or two like that," Quinn Archer said, nodding. "A couple of men were hanging around the Lands Office, wanting to dump their homesteads. The wife of one man had died and he couldn't make it alone, and the wife of the other one was slowly losing her mind, or so it seemed. Anyway, that poor man said she was stubbornly refusing to go through another winter in the bush."

"Thass hard, for sure," Robbie said sympathetically, thinking of his own cheerless cabin, "especially when winter cooms, and a man is hoosebound a lot o' the time."

Robbie's winter, probably, would be spent in the comfortable quarters of Alice Hoy and her sons. Just thinking of it brought a stab of condemnation to his heart. What had seemed, in the first place, to be a fine opportunity, had now taken on more than a hint of ugliness.

And why? Not because the plan was not a worthy one with Alice desperately needing help, but his eyes had been opened—when he saw Tierney Caulder again—to the crassness of the venture from his viewpoint. Suddenly the proposed marriage took on an almost obscene aspect. To marry—without love! To marry—for the reason of obtaining the bride's property!

Until the arrival of Tierney, Robbie had felt few, if any, qualms about the proposed marriage. Alice had presented the arrangement so sensibly.

Sensibly, and bravely. "Robbie," she had said one evening when he had stepped into the house with a brimming pail of milk to be strained, "sit down, please. I . . . I have something I'd like to talk over with you."

Puzzled, Robbie had sat. "Aye, Mrs. Hoy, an' is there somethin' I can do for you? You've jist to ask."

Alice immediately looked relieved. "I truly hope so . . . once you've heard my proposal—" And then, in spite of her calm demeanor to this point, Alice had blushed and stammered.

"Proposal?" Robbie had asked slowly, totally in the dark but intrigued by the word and Alice's reaction to it.

"Aye . . . that is, yes," Alice had continued, still flustered. "It's really . . . really a business proposal, Robbie. You see, it's this way—"

And Alice Hoy had, steadily and clearly, spelled out her astounding offer: They would marry, Robbie would take on the care of the homestead and of the boys, would, in fact, raise them. For she, Alice, was certain she was not long for this world.

And certainly she didn't look well. Even Robbie, with a man's eyes, could see that. She was frail, pale, and often clutched her hands over her . . .

Robbie hesitated. Even in his thoughts, he hesitated, reluctant to so much as *think* the word stomach in regard to the female anatomy. And belly seemed degrading when applied to the gentle sex. So he settled for midriff. Alice often pressed her hands to her midriff.

She spoke delicately of another aspect of the arrangement. Though natural reticence kept her from mentioning the matter specifically, it was Robbie's understanding that it was to be a relationship without intimacy. It would not be a true marriage, but a business affair; no word of love was ever mentioned between them.

Until that moment, Robbie, to do him justice, had not thought, even remotely, of marriage with Alice Hoy. Having heard of her illness, he had gone over to the Hoy place after the death of Barnabas simply to be a good neighbor, knowing there was a great need of a man on the place. After all, there were chores every day, the seeding hadn't been done or the garden planted. He and the other men—and women, too—of the district had taken on these responsibilities, though it meant some neglect of their own places in a very busy season of the year.

Yes, Robbie's one thought had been to help—that was his purpose in going, his only purpose. Realizing that he had not harbored cunning thoughts or had any devious plans concerning the Hoy property, was the only comfort Robbie had at this time when, at last, he saw the entire situation through another's eyes— the eyes of Tierney Caulder. Now it seemed wrong, all wrong.

Again the image of Tierney's stunned face rose before him, stamped on his heart from the moment he had tried to explain. Stunned and anguished then, it had not been much different each time he had seen her since that dreadful night.

When he went to talk to her, Robbie had thought that he and Tierney would be comforted by the realization that all would yet be well, that the present circumstance was for a purpose, and that he and she were, in truth, bonded in heart and mind, now, as ever.

It had not turned out that way. Tierney had staggered as from a physical blow, her face desolate, her eyes brimming with a pain that she did not, probably could not, express in words. Instantly Robbie knew he had done a terrible thing.

And she had avoided him from that night on. The first time or two that he had gone to the Blooms to see her, her white face and stricken eyes had struck panic to his heart—had he irrevocably destroyed their chance of happiness together?

Tierney had sat on the step with him, wringing her hands helplessly, and talked, or tried to talk, of his plans.

"I'm happy for ye, Robbie," she had said, "if that's what ye want sae bad—more land. I'd hae thought y'd be happy as a king wi' your ain wee homestead."

The Scots accent and the muffled words told of the misery of her heart.

And then she had said, "Ye canna keep coomin' o'er here, Robbie. I'll nae see ye again . . . it's not reet . . . right. Dinna coom, Robbie."

And Robbie knew she was right; he stayed away.

He had seen her next at church. Though Robbie had not made church attendance a practice, he went the first Sunday Tierney was in Bliss, knowing she would be there with the Blooms—faithful members. Sitting behind her, watching the sun through the window as it rollicked among the glints and gleams of her ravishing head of hair—his heart turned over. He had, indeed, done a terrible thing. Perhaps a final thing.

Then, remembering Alice, too ill to come to church, he felt that he was being unfaithful, in some way, by hungering for Tierney, and he groaned within himself over the strange turn of events that had brought him to this painful moment. Promised to one woman by words, pledged to another in his heart—Robbie, quite naturally and for the first time in his life, felt guilt-ridden. Perhaps a prayer . . .

But Robbie Dunbar was not a praying person. Perhaps, if he had been, he thought grimly, he wouldn't have gotten himself in such a fix.

He had erred. He had erred greatly. Not only to Tierney but to Alice. Alice deserved better, if only for the short time she had left.

It became clear to Robbie, as he thought on the entire sordid situation, that he had placed himself in as unprincipled a state as could be imagined. Loving Tierney, marrying Alice—and accompanying this was the unspoken thought that he was waiting for Alice's death.

When this realization sprang full blown in Robbie's mind, he almost gasped aloud, so stricken was he by the truth, the miserable truth. It had sounded so good on the surface: help Alice; be there for the boys; be bighearted; do a generous act of kindness. But even the kindness aspect faded when he thought further about the boys, who were, he admitted, beginning to turn their affections toward him, looking to him as a father figure in their lives, and who might yet be disappointed. Surely there was more selfishness than wisdom in what he was doing.

Under the sound of the gospel message as delivered by Parker Jones that morning, arrows of conviction struck and stayed and quivered in Robbie Dunbar's heart.

The sermon was based on the thirteenth chapter of First Corinthians, "The love chapter," Parker Jones called it, and faithfully pointed out the "more excellent way."

"Charity [or love, Parker substituted] . . . doth not behave itself unseemly."

In the light of the Scripture and the sermon, what Robbie had done was not only unacceptable but reprehensible . . . unseemly! And try as he would to think calmly about it, the idea that he had behaved toward Alice, and toward Tierney, in a most unacceptable way, could not be excluded any longer from his thinking.

What a fix to be in! What could he, honorably, do? Alice was innocent, needy, depending on him. And he had given his word. By agreeing to marry her he had done one dishonorable thing; he'd not compound it by another.

Shaking hands at the close of the service, smiling, talking, heart beating heavily all the while, Robbie thought he was, after all, just "sounding brass, or a tinkling cymbal," and no real man. And certainly not a man of God, a man of principle.

Bowing his head over the mane of his horse as he rode home—with Tierney quiet and reserved in the Bloom wagon, her eyes hurt and avoiding his glance—Robbie Dunbar prayed what was probably the first serious, earnest prayer of his life. It was preceded by the thought "Only God can get me out of this mess that I'm in." And not himself only; Alice Hoy and Tierney Caulder were deeply affected by his actions, by his choices.

O God! Please solve this terrible situation . . . please show me what to do, he prayed.

⌐————⌐

Well, that's ready, Tierney said to herself, stepping outside the small shack that was the quarters of the Blooms' hired man. She had spent an hour cleaning it thoroughly after Ahab's departure, sweeping the board floor, shaking the rag rug, plumping up the pillow on the rocker beside the small heater, stripping the bed, turning the mattress, and putting on clean sheets and blankets. Any moment now the new man, Quinn Archer by name, would arrive. Arrive in time to do the evening chores. Without Ahab the last few days, Herbert had roused himself to unusual activity and had milked and watered and fed the animals by himself, though with a good deal of "Ahemming" sprinkled throughout his conversation all day long. Herbert felt put upon, doing his own work.

In the house, where the hired man ordinarily took his meals along with the family—though he could, if he wished, do so on the small stove top in his shack—special preparations were underway. First impressions were important! One needed to impress the hired man, after all. Good help was hard to find! Or so Lydia told Tierney every once in a while, with a solemn shake of the head followed by a kind smile.

"Whatever would we do without you . . ."

"It wasn't nearly so good before you came!"

And just flat out "I'm so glad you came to be with us!"

Lydia saw the two horses and their riders from the kitchen window. "That must be him—that Quinn fellow," she said to Tierney, who stopped beating the cream for the top of the pie and came to stand beside her.

"And that's Herkimer with him," Lydia continued. "You met Herkimer at church, you may remember, my dear. He's a bachelor, of course. He knows right well it's suppertime. And he knows Lydia Bloom never turns anyone away hungry. Might as well," she warned, "be prepared to set another plate on the table. No doubt about it—Herkimer will eat supper with us."

"Those're the Bloom cows over there," that worthy gentleman was saying, pointing to a dozen or so cattle in a nearby pasture as he and Quinn Archer came down the road at a comfortable pace. "Say, Archer, do you know how to calc'late the number of cows in any herd?"

"I thought I did," the stranger said, with a wry glance at his loquacious companion, a man of considerable girth and as full of fun as of talk.

Herkimer Pinkard had attached himself to the newcomer in the hamlet of Bliss, offering generously to show him the way, personally, to the Bloom homestead, and already Quinn Archer had an understanding of the sort of fellow Herkimer was—neighborly, open, given to great good humor.

"But I'm sure," Quinn continued now in response to Herkimer's question, "if there's a better way to figure the number of cows in a herd, you're about to tell me."

"It's this way," Herkimer said, settling himself comfortably in the saddle and watching Quinn Archer closely to see what effect his explanation would have (Herkimer liked an appreciative audience). "It's this way—you count their legs and divide by four."

Quinn Archer grinned enough so that Herkimer was satisfied and cast about in his mind for another such sally, in order to bring about the good cheer and enjoyment that, to Herkimer Pinkard, made life worth living.

"This is the Bloom farm?" the stranger asked, nodding toward the buildings that had appeared in an opening in the bush. "A prosperous appearing place."

"If it don't grow, Herbert can buy it. If it runs away, Herbert can replace it. If it lays down and dies—"

Just what Herbert would do in such an instance, Quinn Archer never knew. A young woman had stepped from the shadow of the porch, to walk to the clothesline and pin up what seemed to be a damp tea towel. Young, shapely, her hair glowing vividly in the late afternoon sun, she caught the attention of both bachelors, who automatically dug their heels into the sides of their horses, hurrying them into a trot.

Even the garrulous Herkimer found himself curiously silent, intent on the girl's graceful passage. "Marriage is a great institution," he said, finally, more thoughtful than anyone would have supposed him to be, "but I didn't know, till now, that I was ready for an institution."

And now Quinn Archer gave the former wag the accolade he had wanted—he greeted Herkimer's philosophy with a shout of laughter.

"Good luck!" he called, his excellent mount already nearer the final goal than the accompanying plow horse carrying the big, bumbling form of Herkimer Pinkard.

On this good-natured exchange they turned in at the gate, made their way to the farmyard, and were greeted by Herbert Bloom, who reached up to the stranger, shook his hand, and welcomed him.

"Take the horses to the barn, Herk," he suggested, "and you'll earn yourself as good a supper as you're liable to find hereabouts."

"Well, the price is right," Herkimer said agreeably, took the reins to Quinn Archer's horse, and did as directed. After all, everyone knew Lydia Bloom was an excellent cook and, moreover, there was variety, tasty variety, at the Bloom table. Herkimer was mighty weary of fried potatoes and onions, his recent experiment with change in his diet. What had seemed novel at first had quickly changed to surfeit.

Herbert guided the new man through the kitchen door—the only entrance used by any home in the territories—and presented him to the ladies of the household.

Because the Blooms were among the fortunate few to have an icehouse, there was roast beef for supper rather than the ubiquitous chicken, ordinarily the only fresh meat available on a farm home. Unless, of course, someone went out with the rifle and brought back a rabbit or two. Partridges, in season, were relished. But beef or venison—there was none of it, usually, in the warm months, aside from the little that might have been canned and put on the cellar shelves for later enjoyment.

Tierney opened the oven door and rich beefy flavor filled the room; Quinn Archer was not too well-bred to sniff the air, nod, and smile engagingly. Herkimer, that poorly fed bachelor, when he came in, closed his eyes in pure bliss, and inhaled deeply and often.

Lydia greeted the newcomer warmly. Quinn Archer, gentleman that he was, waited for her hand to be presented before offering to shake hands. Then it was a firm, brief grip, along with a small bow of the head, his hat held casually in his other hand; Lydia was impressed immediately. Tierney, a hired person, as he was, turned from the stove and nodded.

"Tierney," Lydia directed, "dip some warm water from the reservoir for this gentleman—"

Quinn Archer found a nail among those beside the door, hung up his hat, and turned toward the washstand. Tall and well built, he bent gracefully enough over the low stand, washing his face as well as his hands.

"It's been a long ride," he explained as he reached for the snowy towel, "and this is refreshing. Dinner [not supper!] smells enticing."

In spite of herself, Tierney found herself studying this man who, in just a couple of minutes, had proved himself to be a person of quality. This was no Ahab; this was no Herkimer.

This was a man who felt perfectly at ease sitting up to the table, whether it was supper or dinner. He seemed comfortable with the bowing of the head for the blessing; he conducted himself well in the matter of the table service and of eating and drinking. He was, Tierney and the Blooms concluded, that rare find— a gentleman, even as Lydia had surmised right away.

"I'm grateful to that friend of yours—Rob Dunbar—for looking me up," Quinn Archer said, helping himself to the small, fresh carrots, "and giving me the opportunity to take this position."

Position!

"You understood," Herbert said uncertainly, "when he talked to you, that this job is for a hired man—"

"Certainly. Entirely suitable, too. I need to work for a while, then look into getting a place of my own. I'm grateful."

"Well," Herbert responded, ahemming, gratified with the response, "we're happy to have you, I can tell you. Our other man left right at the busy season, I guess you'd have to say. Summer keeps us hopping if we're to be ready for winter."

Quinn Archer explained that he had been raised on a farm in the States, then had become a teacher, only to become dissatisfied with that.

"I need a place to call home, a place of my own. A place I can put something of myself into," he explained, and they all understood. "The more I see of Bliss, the better I like it. The more I learn of it, the more I think I'll be happy to settle in the area. The name alone is descriptive of everything I'd like to incorporate into my life."

"Well," Herbert said reflectively, "it won't come without a lot of hard work, some disappointment, and lots of prayer."

Thus spoke the man who had arrived with enough money to almost buy his way to ease. The felling of the trees, the grubbing of the stumps, the erection of the buildings—all, all had been accomplished with paid help. And still it had been almost more than Herbert Bloom could weather. How a man, alone, might accomplish all that was necessary to prove up his land, was almost too much to comprehend.

But Quinn Archer was not the only man to make up his mind to do it. "I know you're right," he said. "But less equipped men have made it, and I will, too. I have my strength, a little money, and a lot of determination."

"And," Herkimer interjected, "if you'll just pass the homemade butter and the homemade jam, made by some woman of determination I'll be bound, I'll put them on this homemade bun and recover a little of my strength, and all without money and without price. For this one meal, at least," he added, more seriously than jocularly.

Herkimer could recall skimpy rabbit-stew suppers with bannock, huge bowls of oatmeal yellowed with brown sugar and cream and more bannock, and the recent fried potato binge and was well aware that, if he didn't stir his stumps and get a garden underway, a long winter of such meals stretched ahead, and not too far off. In the middle of summer the specter of a

Saskatchewan winter breathed on the back of sunburnt necks with a chilling reminder of tough days ahead, and little enough time to get ready for them.

Lydia's comfortable "Save room for saskatoon pie," was music to the ears.

M olly saw Parker Jones as he walked past, looking a little hot and already fatigued, with another mile to go. If Molly had been a vindictive person, she would have muttered "Serves him right!"

As it was, along with a pang of what she supposed was jealousy—and wasn't proud of it—she felt a certain anger.

Beatrice Condon knew full well that Parker Jones had no rig of his own and no barn in which to keep a horse, had anyone loaned him one, and must walk everywhere he went. She had really done an unreasonable thing when she had asked him to call. If the situation had been desperate, with someone ill or dying, hurt or even lonely, Parker would have gone willingly, of course, and Molly—noting his devotion once again at the expense of his comfort—would have added her blessing.

But Molly had been standing within hearing distance, following the morning's service, and had listened in on Beatrice's stumbled request of the pastor, with Vivian—guileless eyes and half smile at her shoulder—prodding her on.

"Brother Jones," Beatrice had begun tentatively, glancing again at Vivian's face, "do you suppose . . . that is, we would like it if . . ."

"What is it, Bea?" Parker had asked kindly, turning from shaking the hand of old Mrs. Finnery.

"We'd like it . . . that is, Vivian, my niece . . ."

Vivian's face flushed ever so slightly, and she had interrupted smoothly, "I think Aunt Beatrice is trying to say that we'd appreciate the honor of your presence tomorrow evening at dinner."

"Dinner?" Parker Jones asked, obviously with his thoughts still engaged with Mrs. Finnery, and making the transition with difficulty. "Dinner . . . tomorrow?"

"Supper, she means, of course," Beatrice, a true bush pioneer, corrected. It may have been dinner back in England, but it was supper in the territories, and this she well knew. Ordinarily there was nothing "dinner-ish" about the evening meal, and everything "supper-ish."

"Supper," she said again, adding, "we'll try and eat at six. That way, you can stay and talk a while and still get home before dark. I think . . ."

Beatrice paused, sounding dubious. Perhaps she knew her niece well by this time. And Vivian, at her aunt's elbow, was looking very expectant and pleased.

"I think Bly can work around that time. Yes, I think he could be counted on to join us by six," Beatrice continued, thinking aloud. "Anyway, do say you'll come," she encouraged, apparently recognizing a moment's hesitation in the pastor's response. "You see, there are some matters . . . that is, a pastor's advice would be appreciated. Perhaps a prayer . . ."

"Of course, if I'm needed," Parker Jones was quick to say.

The strange thing about it all, Molly thought now, watching Parker trudge past, was that, at dinner following the sermon, eaten as usual at the Morrison table, Parker had made no mention of the invitation.

Of course there was no need to, Molly reminded herself crossly. He had no obligation to her, Molly, for heaven's sake! But still it rankled. Why couldn't he talk naturally about it? Why did he avoid the subject of a pastoral call on neighbors who lived just beyond the Morrisons?

And why, for goodness' sake, didn't he stop in for a cold drink of water!

But no, Parker Jones, kicking up a trail of dust—it had been some days since rain—walked on past the Morrison place.

Molly toyed with the mad idea of quickly hitching Kip to the buggy and whirling alongside the plodding pastor, sweetly offering a ride. But she curbed the impulse, which was, after all, only a passing one and not worthy of consideration.

Molly resumed her work, wishing for a task that called for her full attention rather than the mindless churning that allowed for foolish and vain imaginations. On the other hand, it seemed good, after the week's wash was completed, to sit and turn the crank to the "Improved Cedar Cylinder Churn," containing two gallons of cream (but holding three, when necessary), its double dasher and crank locked into place, and guaranteed against leakage. The barrel, or cylinder, was made of white cedar, banded with galvanized iron hoops, and it sat on the table rather than on the floor in the manner of the old dash churn. Oh, the shoulder and arm aches that had caused!

Molly's thoughts turned, at last, from Parker Jones and his visit with the Condons, to the fascinating possibility of turning a churn with dog power. And not dogs only but goats or sheep. "A thirty-pound animal," the catalog stated, "will do the churning; if you keep a dog, make him 'work his passage.'"

Or, if you had a really large barrel with as much as ten pounds of cream, a *double*-dog churn was available. The animal was led onto a treadmill (with a frame around it to keep it from abruptly deserting its post), encouraged to keep walking, and a device, made up of a balance wheel and a belt, turned the churn. In spite of the sketch in the catalog, Molly wasn't exactly sure how this new-fangled contraption worked, but the idea was intriguing.

She was, she thought, a modern woman, and forward looking; anything that would improve the quality of life, she was in favor of. But just thinking about old Jock's reaction, should he be persuaded by some means to get onto the treadmill, brought a smile to Molly's face. She could imagine the ancient animal simply lying down on the job, the cream going sour . . .

"What's so funny, Sis?" Cameron asked, passing through the kitchen.

"Just thinking . . ."

"That's a dangerous habit to get into. By the way, where do you suppose Parker is off to in the middle of a hot afternoon? Poor guy, we should finish up that little barn we've been working on over at his place and see that he gets the use of a rig and a horse. Maybe just a horse would do; he can ride, can't he?"

"Well, of course he can ride. Can't every man or boy?"

"I dunno . . . not city fellers, sometimes. Still, he could learn, and it would save him a lot of walking. Yes, I'll bring up the subject to Dad and see if we can't do something. It would mean keeping him supplied with straw and hay and oats and whatever. It sure is a busy time to be taking on a job like that . . ."

And musing on the workload and the tasks to be done, always pressing heavily from spring's first blush to fall's finally fading brilliance, Cameron went back to work.

Parker Jones, plodding past the Morrison place, had stubbornly resisted the impulse to stop in. How simple, how restful, just to end this trek here! But no, his appointment was with the Condons. And hadn't he spent yesterday, Sunday, here, with Molly and the family? And hadn't he, once again, relaxed wonderfully in the friendly atmosphere?

And hadn't he said his good-byes, once again, struggling with his right to enjoy such fellowship, to even think of pursuing a closer relationship with Molly? With his own future so uncertain, how could he settle down to serious plans of marriage?

Passing by, thinking on these things and his insecurities concerning his call, Parker Jones sighed deeply and strode on.

His present perplexities had been triggered a few months ago by the sudden death of one of his parishioners. Subsequent revelations had caused Parker to feel that, as pastor, he had not been in touch with the problems of that home and the needs of that particular man. Crushed by what he felt was a failure on his part, Parker had been thrown into a spiral of questioning the effectiveness of his ministry, wondering about his original call, and full of uncertainties.

Still, in response to needs like this one today, he faithfully carried on.

There was no doubt about it, he concluded now—he needed a horse. Parker's feet hurt! Knowing the reason why, he looked down sourly. It was these ridiculous "coin" toed shoes, so dubbed because the tip of the toe was shaped to fit nothing larger than a dime! The catalog offered a good three dozen different styles of dress shoes, and all with the long, tapered toe, for men as well as for women.

Parker's choices, when it came to ordering, had been such numbers as Hard Cash Jewel Toe; Cordovan Lace Opera Toe; Fine Needle Bals; Russian Colt Lace New Coin Toe; Fine Kangaroo Congress Needle Toe; Caska Calf Needle; Satin Oil Lace Razor Toe; and many more, all coin-, razor-, or needle-toed. His remaining options were Moose Hide Moccasins (smoke-tanned by the Indians); Shoe Pacs (made from an oil tanned pac); River Shoes (laced, with bellows tongue making them very warm and practically waterproof); Oil Grain Creole (guaranteed to be the best wearing shoe on earth for the money—$1.25); mining or lumbermen's shoes, men's extra heavy police shoes, or two-buckle plows.

Pondering on the "Men's Police Congress, made from selected satin calf stock, with heavy dongola tops and hub goring, with soles made extra heavy so as to be practical for hard wear," his attention had been drawn to the "Corn Cure Shoe."

Now there was a sensible shoe! "The chief feature of this shoe is the toe, as it runs extra wide, being almost the same width as it is across the ball of the foot, giving the toes abundance of room to lie in their natural shape without being cramped as they are in a too-narrow shoe. This shoe will create no corns but on the other hand will cure them."

The trouble with the corn cure shoe was that it gave the appearance of a paddle going out ahead of your foot. Parker Jones was certain he would feel like a duck, paddling along in the corn cure shoe. And as he had no corns to cure, Parker made the decision that was to cost him his comfort for as long as the "Men's Plain Buff Lace" shoe, which was his choice, should last.

Yes, pride had piped her alluring, entrancing tune; he had heeded her siren call and ordered the handsome but narrow pointed shoe; the prideful dance had turned into painful plodding, and he was paying the piper for sure. Parker Jones felt that, without a doubt, a corn was in the dreadful making.

And what's more, the Buff Lace shoe—which referred to laces rather than elastic sides or buttons—would be dusty and dirty beyond recognition when he arrived at the Condon home. He might as well paddle up to the door in the corn cure shoe, for all the fine impression he would make!

Consequently, Parker Jones was not in the best of moods when he walked—limped—into the Condon yard. His spirits weren't lifted any by the baying dogs that rushed to meet him, sniffing his feet and licking his hands as he attempted to dissuade them from their friendly overtures. Dirty of feet and wet of hand, he stepped up onto the split logs that formed the steps to the Condon house.

"Oh, do come in, Reverend!"

It was Vivian herself, cool and perfectly groomed, holding out her hand in welcome; if she had helped with Monday's wash, she showed no sign of it now.

Aware of the dog slobber on his hand, Parker Jones hesitated. How was it that this particular young woman made him feel so unsure of himself, so backwoodsy, so bucolic? What was wrong with him anyway? There was nothing belittling about being associated with the good people of the backwoods. These people, from all walks of life, including teachers and leading citizens of other places, felt no less of themselves because they had chosen to homestead. For the most part they were fine, upstanding, hardworking, even ambitious, people, and ordinarily Parker was proud to be associated with them, to encourage them in their struggle to populate and tame this land that was theirs by choice.

"I think I need to wash—the dogs, you know," Parker Jones said rather lamely, sure his grin was lopsided and uncertain.

But Vivian seemed to find it endearing. And this disturbed Parker Jones even more. He felt at sea, unsure of himself and aware of forces at work over which he seemed to have no control, understanding them not a whit.

Vivian directed him to the washstand, herself dipping warm water from the reservoir and handing him the soap, ever so capably, as if to say, "See what a homey, woodsy girl I am."

Beatrice turned from the stove, her face perspiring, her hair damp, and smiled her greeting. After all, it wasn't the first time she had entertained the pastor. Every other time, however, it had been "potluck," as he sat up to the family's simple meal. Under the eyes of her husband's niece, however, even the placid Beatrice was flustered.

The Condon log-built house was the usual large kitchen/living room, with the remaining third of the structure divided into two small bedrooms. Such homes were not built randomly but with the express purpose in mind to heat them as easily as possible. Though some were larger than others, not really qualifying as cabins—which were ordinarily one room—still the pattern was the same. Dominating, and the first thing installed—the range for cooking and the heater for warmth.

Now Vivian seated Pastor Parker Jones in a comfortable chair at the side of the heater where it reigned, summer and winter. There was no fire in the iron-bellied monster now, of course, but the range, out of necessity, was blazing hot at the other end of the room.

The door to the outside was open, allowing some movement of cool air; fortunately the Condons had been able to afford a screen door. Fortunately—because the outside of the screen was almost black with the flies that were drawn by the cooking odors and that would have swarmed in, given a chance. In many a homesteader's cabin, tea towels covered every morsel of food, at all times, against the invasion of flies that plagued all flesh, human and animal alike, from dawn to dark. The mosquitoes were almost as bad. And even after dark, whining around beds and cots and pallets, they made their obnoxious presence known. And felt.

The northland was a land that offered much—but reluctantly. It was a place of great opposites: the biggest and clearest sky you ever saw and the shortest growing season—so green in the summer, so golden in the fall—void of any color whatsoever all winter long; so fragrant, so full of birdsong, yet so silent, so odorless aside from wood smoke about nine months of the year. So promising—so threatening.

So the flies were held at bay at the Condon house, and those that made their way in whenever the door was opened for a moment were enticed to their death by the fly traps—sticky, twisting paper—that hung here and there from the ceiling. One had to learn to avert one's gaze from the sight of dead and dying flies just above one's head, though the desperate buzzing of the struggling insects, in a quiet room, was unsettling. Chances were better for a bear to come face-to-face with a housewife in the woods than a fly in that same woman's home!

"Now, Pastor, just be comfortable," Beatrice said, fussily. "Sup . . . dinner is as good as ready, and we'll sit up and eat as soon as Blystone comes in. We gave him strict instructions—"

"I'm in no hurry, I'm sure," Parker reassured, wishing the ordeal was over. *What was it about the young woman Vivian that caused him to feel like such an inexperienced boy, all thumbs and big feet! And those feet, just now, in wretched, pointy shoes!*

Parker calmed himself and tried to think back to the days he was in Bible School, fulfilled and content. What good days they had been—learning, sharing, growing, filling pulpits round about the area, confirming the call in his spirit, eager to be out into the harvest field. What had happened along the way? Where had the eagerness gone, the satisfaction?

Sorely troubled, Parker laid his concerns aside and greeted Bly Condon when he came in from the fields. Bly washed himself, dunked his dusty head in the basin, scattering water hither and thither as he shook his great shaggy head and reached for a towel, all to the tightened lips of Vivian and the nervous glances of his wife.

Finally, shining of face and hands and dusty of garb and shoes, Bly, with total satisfaction, bellowed, "All right—come and get it!"

Though he had said those same words each time Parker Jones had eaten at the Condon table, eliciting no more than a fond smile from his wife, she now looked apologetically at Vivian and twittered her way to the table.

"Oh dear, yes, let's sit up to the table. Come, Park . . . Pastor."

It seemed that Vivian's presence and influence reached even to Beatrice's regard for her friend Parker Jones, elevating him to the lonely rank of pastor.

Pastor Jones was invited to bless the food, which he did with simplicity and grace. That at least hadn't changed!

Unfolding the serviette and placing it on his lap, Parker asked, "How's the field work going, Bly?" Strangely, he found himself biting back an impulse to call his parishioner and friend "Brother Condon."

"Pretty good, Parker." No nonsense from Blystone Condon, Vivian or no Vivian. But, at dessert time, Bly rather reluctantly gave up the fork he had retained, to be handed a clean one for the chocolate cake mounded with whipped cream that was placed before him. Bunch of nonsense! his expression seemed to say.

Even Bly Condon was coming under the influence of the visitor. But was Vivian a visitor?

Beatrice, over coffee and after a meaningful look from Vivian, broached the subject that had, apparently, been waiting in the wings for the appropriate moment.

"Pastor, we need you to help us pray for . . . for something, er, important. Vivian here is seriously considering whether she should stay on in Bliss over the winter, maybe even making it her permanent home."

Here, with the Condons, in their small house? Locked in here all the winter long? Attending church every Sunday, in Bliss? Casting her strange spell over those she contacted—Bly and Beatrice, Parker Jones . . . ?

"Well, Pastor?"

It was Vivian who spoke, her large gray-blue eyes fixed soulfully on his, her delicate eyebrows raised, her rosy lips parted over her white, rather large, teeth, her expression curiously watchful.

Parker Jones was aware that his mouth was open. His mind was working furiously—how to respond and be honest?

"You see, Pastor," those full, rosy lips were saying, and who could refute or deny the importance of what they said next: "This is the first time I've felt I was getting any spiritual food. I believe I could embrace everything that you preach, given an opportunity to stay, to hear, to learn, to respond."

I need you to go to the store this morning," Lydia said as she and Tierney sat at breakfast, the menfolk already dispersed to outside work.

Womenfolk got away from home very little—in summer the workload was too heavy and too unremitting, in winter travel was often impossible, and home fires had to be kept going at any cost. A trip to Bliss, anytime, was enjoyable, a real break in either the wearying round of work or the pressing loneliness. In distance it was about four miles from the Bloom place, and when she was feeling well, Lydia enjoyed the outing thoroughly. Lydia and Tierney had gone together on numerous occasions; Tierney had even taken the reins from the more-practiced Lydia a few times and was beginning to get a feel for driving the buggy.

But go by herself? The very thought of it made Tierney uneasy. At home, in Binkiebrae, her family had never owned a horse. Her da had spent his life—as boy and man—on the sea, fishing, and her brother James had joined his father when he was fourteen years old. There was no horse, and they walked wherever they went, catching a ride to the nearby Aberdeen when a trip to the city became necessary.

"We're out of a lot of things," Lydia continued, "not the least of which being new rubber rings for the jars. What we've canned so far—strawberries and rhubarb and saskatoons—isn't a scratch on the canning we'll do before the season is over. We'll miss the pin cherries completely if we don't get at it. They're hanging thick and ripe along the edge of the pasture."

"Aye, I've seen 'em. And tasted them, too. Good!" Tierney responded, already having learned the importance of taking advantage of the local wild fruit and, having sampled some, caught the homesteader's passion to preserve them for the winter season.

"Did you notice—your last trip down into the cellar—if there's any more of this chokecherry syrup left?" Lydia asked, pouring a generous supply over her pancakes, watching the purple-black concoction flow over and around the pancakes and down onto the white plate—a lovely sight to the critical and satisfied eyes of the canner.

"This's the next to last jar," Tierney said, following her mistress's example and helping herself to last year's chokecherry syrup. "I've seen chokecherries all along the road—at least I think they're chokecherries. I tasted 'em." Tierney made a comical face. "Never again till they're ripe!"

Lydia was sympathetic. "I guess not. Now you know why they were named *choke*cherry. Leave them alone until they are almost pure black and getting soft; that's when they're best, and that's when they're full of juice. Syrup, from any berry, is simple to do—just boil the juice and pulp until it's thick and bubbly—adding the right amount of sugar, of course—then put it in the jars, and it will keep indefinitely. It doesn't last long around here, though."

"Ahab used to put chokecherry sauce over his fried potatoes. He called it fruit soup."

"High bush cranberries can be used the same way as chokecherries—they make wonderful sauce, sort of orange in color and simply delicious. We have to go to the river for them. Whatever fruit it is, it goes fast. That's why we need plenty, and it certainly keeps us busy. No matter how hot the day, we have to fire up the range and keep something going into the jars—fruit, or vegetables, even meat.

"Some families," Lydia continued after pausing for a sip of coffee, "don't can like they should; perhaps they don't have the jars, maybe they can't find the time, probably they don't have the sugar. It's pitiful to see them doling it out skimpily to the family, using it mostly when company comes. What a shame. I've eaten strawberries in homes where we've been for supper when the pinched faces of the little tykes just glowed to see a sauce dish of those sweet gems set before them." Lydia sighed. "But—back to the jaunt to Bliss—do you feel comfortable going by yourself?"

"By myself?" Tierney squeaked, her worst fears realized. "You aren't going then?"

"Kay Mudge is coming over to get me to help her cut out her new dress pattern. How I'll manage that," Lydia said ruefully, flexing her swollen fingers, "remains to be seen. Maybe I can just point out where to cut, and she can do it. Poor woman—never made a dress in her life before she came west. Too bad she can't afford what the catalog offers—"

"I know," Tierney said, nodding, having studied the "wish book" diligently herself from time to time. "There's a 'handsome Persian Percale Wrapper in the verra latest style,' at least that's what the catalog says—with those big puff top sleeves and all gathered full as full can be—for ninety-eight cents. Why's a simple dress called a wrapper, anyway?"

"It's just the term right now. It's a morning dress, if you ask me, maybe nothing more than a housedress, though why anyone would want that 'Watteau' back is beyond me."

"Aye! What is't?"

"Just what the picture shows, I guess, though I've never seen it on any dresses around here—it's just a long piece of goods that seems to hang down straight, from the neckline to the floor, rather like a train—silly, if you ask me. It must get in the way dreadfully. And yet so many of the wrappers have it. I hope Kay Mudge doesn't want to incorporate that feature into her dress today. It's going to be tricky enough without that."

"That Vivian Condon—I s'pose she'll have it on her dresses. If she wears housedresses, that is."

The ladies spent a few minutes discussing Vivian Condon's advent into the district and the fascination of her wardrobe.

"She probably makes all our women feel like little brown wrens by comparison," Lydia said. "We dress for practical reasons, I guess. Some of the ladies are wearing the Sunday clothes they brought with them when they came, two, three, even four years ago. And happy to be decently covered."

"But she—Vivian Condon—looks so lovely." This from the little Scots lass with her best outfit still the travel "uniform" worn by all the domestics—a dark serge skirt and white shirtwaist. No wonder Tierney eagerly studied the catalog with its tempting array of goods. No wonder she admired the wardrobe of Vivian Condon.

"Well," Lydia said, referring again to Kay Mudge and the dress to be cut out and partially put together today, "this dress of Kay's, of course, will be cut from flour sacks—the ones with the little roses all over it. But flour sacks mean a lot of piecing." Lydia sighed, seeing her day slip away when there was this great urgency to *work*. "I can't understand how Kay can take time out, this time of year, to *sew!*

"It's a good thing we put those cucumbers to set overnight," she went on. "Kay and I can have some for lunch. These are the first ones, and though they are small yet, we got enough for a good meal along with some cold roast. Herbert will love them. Food from your own garden—it can't be beat for satisfaction. He feels the same about his breakfast eggs—his own chickens, doing what they're supposed to do. There's a good feeling goes along with reaping the reward of your efforts."

Tierney was learning so much. It had been a whole new experience to take the tender young cucumbers, slice a quart of them, add a cup of vinegar, a cup of water, a cup of sugar, and a tablespoon of salt, and set them aside, to "marinate," as Lydia said. The succulent treat was tantalizing to starved taste buds.

"Soon as the sweet onions are big enough," Lydia had said, directing Tierney in the process, "we'll slice one or two and add them. That's really special. When we eat these tomorrow," she concluded with satisfaction, "we'll have a quick pickle. More of a relish, I guess. Anyway, they'll be fine, and they'll satisfy our hunger for fresh stuff. My mouth fairly waters to think about it."

Finishing up her pancakes, Lydia suggested, "If you'll mix up the bread before you go, my dear, it'll probably be risen when Kay gets here, and I'll have her do the punching down. I can get it in the pans and bake it, though you may be home by then. I know you love a slice of good, hot bread."

Lydia spoke fondly, as to a beloved daughter of the family. "If you'll buy some Roger's Golden Syrup—we're completely out, I see—you can have a treat fit for a king: syrup and hot, crusty bread. It's as good, maybe even better, than the quick cucumber pickles."

Tierney found her mouth watering. She had been in Bliss long enough to know that meals could be a horror or a celebration. "Especially in winter," Lydia had told her. "Shut in as we are, mealtimes are high points, or they are if you have sufficient food. I guess even the oatmeal eaters look forward to mealtime . . . anything to break the monotony of a long, dark day. The family gathers together, sits up to the table, and solemnly—and often silently, especially if they're specially hungry, maybe half-starved for certain things in their diet and they don't recognize it—and it's almost a ceremony. Nobody turns up their noses at meals, in the bush and, I assume, on the prairie. I've never heard a parent have to tell a child 'Clean up your plate!' It's done willingly, even happily, I suppose, if it's all you have."

"Well, I certainly have enjoyed my meals since I came to Bliss." Tierney stated a fact; the food on the Bloom table was bountiful, though simple and somewhat limited as to variety. And with the garden coming on, the future—for mealtime—looked bright.

Tierney's thoughts turned again to the proposed trip to the store, and though she loved the satisfying feeling of doing the shopping, she felt more than a little nervous about making a trip by herself. What if she met another rig on the narrow road? What if the horse shied? What if she got in a tight corner and couldn't turn the buggy when she was ready to come home? What if the horse wouldn't obey her commands?

Lydia seemed to recognize Tierney's sense of unease.

"I think," she said now, "it might be a good idea to have Quinn go along. After all, you need him for the heavy things—we should get a couple bags of flour, and those are one hundred pounds each. And he needs you along to pick out the assortment of staples and so on that I've got listed. Herbert never was any good at that sort of thing; I doubt if Quinn Archer is either. How those poor bachelors—Herkimer, Allan, Robbie, and others—manage, I don't know." Lydia shook her gray head over the undeniable ineptness of men to shop properly.

And so it was decided. Though Quinn was hard at work at a job Herbert had lined up for him, Herbert was too fond a husband to deny his wife her requests.

"Ahem!" Herbert said, having received Lydia's request through Tierney, and Quinn's busy hands quieted as he turned from the roll of fencing wire he was untangling, "the missus needs you to take Tierney to town. I don't suppose," he added, twinkling, "you'll mind a little break. And I don't suppose you'll object to the company. Eh? Eh?"

"Not at all," Quinn Archer said politely and went to his shack to clean up a little.

With list and money carefully stowed in her handbag, Tierney climbed—an old hand at it by now—up into the buggy, always unsteady for a moment while the springs righted themselves. The seat, less than two feet wide, accommodated her trim hips and the almost equally narrow build of the hired man. For Quinn Archer, a manly figure, was broad of shoulder and slim of hips, with capable hands, and with a fine face under a neat head of hair.

"Now then," Lydia said fussily, tucking a portion of Tierney's serge skirt up and away from the wheel, "you have the list . . . the money? All's well, then. Remember, if you see something you know we need or are out of, and I haven't thought to put it on the list, get it. Within reason, that is." And Lydia smiled, calling her last few words after the buggy as Quinn slapped the reins on the horse's broad bay back, chirruping a signal that the horse well understood and obeyed.

"It's a beautiful day," Tierney offered, looking around as they rode along, her tone hushed, and her words inadequate of course, for she hadn't the ability to express the effect the bush had on her. Not only the green shroud but the blossoms it harbored and the fragrance it exuded. Not only the sky but the clouds that graced it, moving lazily to a rhythm of their own. Not only the countryside but the rough fence posts that bordered the fields, with meadowlarks perched on them here and there, the vivid green sprouts of grain laced across the black soil of the fields like stitches in a crazy quilt, the many sloughs that rippled and sparkled in the morning sun and frisky breeze.

"At home," she explained, "we'd say it was all too muckle—much—to take in, to experience. Already," she added softly, "I love it."

"It's easy to do," Quinn agreed, settling himself more comfortably. "Especially at this time of year."

"Lydia says it's just as beautiful, in another way, at every season."

"Yes, but it depends on your circumstances, whether you can bring yourself to appreciate it or not. If you're freezing, for instance, with the cold whipping in under the door and around the windows, and you have to go out in the storm to chop wood, or milk cows, or feed chickens, you might have trouble celebrating the beauty of the snow. If your back is tired and your neck sunburned, you might not see the beauty of a big garden, at least at the moment you're hoeing it."

"I know," Tierney admitted. "I haven't gone through all the seasons yet, at least not here. I lived through a winter on the prairie, though. And winter on the prairie is worse than here, I ken."

"We're protected some, of course, by the very bush that frustrates us when it comes to clearing our land. But I haven't lived through a Bliss winter, either. I'm not sure I'm looking forward to it. Still, I've chosen this area and plan to stick it out. One of these days I'll have my own place; it'll be home."

"Our nearest neighbor, on the prairie, was aboot eight miles away. We dinna see anyone for days, maybe weeks, at a time."

"Well, then," Quinn said, quirking Tierney a small smile, "when you get ready to settle down—'doon' to you—it'll be here in the bush, right?"

Tierney was quickly serious, her face gone still. "I dinna ken," she answered quietly. "I don't know. It would be hard, loving Bliss as I do, to leave. But—who knows where God will lead, or how He'll work things oot."

"Yes, who knows," Quinn agreed. "It's like that hymn said Sunday, remember—?"

"Lead on, O King Eternal," Tierney quoted instantly,
"We follow—not with fears!
For gladness breaks like morning
Wher-e'er Thy face appears . . ."

"Aye," she said, "I'm glad you reminded me of that. If I were a singer, like that bird over there warblin' his heart out, I'd sing it for ye. But it's true . . ."

Tierney's thoughts were interrupted as a buggy appeared on a side road. The driver, a woman, was engrossed in handling the reins and barely had time to give them a nod before she, the horse and buggy, and two small boys made the turn onto the road ahead of Tierney and Quinn.

"Who lives doon that road?" Tierney asked. "I dinna remember seein' her at church, do you?"

"No; and I think I'd remember. Wouldn't you?"

And she would have. For the woman's hair, spilling out a little from beneath a small hat, was thick and fair, her face was distinctively fine featured, well-molded in sharp but quite lovely lines, her form was slim and her movements graceful.

And the two little boys, as fair as their mother, as fine featured. Tierney could see them clearly over the ears of the horse. One was seated beside the woman, nothing but his blond thatch showing over the buggy back, and the other, bigger and older, was sitting in the box at the rear of the buggy, looking back, his feet dangling, his cap pushed on the back of his head, his eyes studying the Bloom buggy and Quinn and Tierney in particular.

Quinn raised his hand in a salute of sorts, and the boy quickly grinned and waved, saying something to his mother and to the other, smaller boy. That child turned himself around on the seat, climbed up onto his knees, and leaned on the back of the buggy seat, watching solemnly.

Even without catching a glimpse of the thin blue-veined hands on the reins, Tierney had no doubt about who was driving the buggy, two small boys accompanying her and the family dog trotting alongside.

Alice Hoy.

Pulling up in front of the general store and leaping out with characteristic vigor, Tierney turned to see Alice Hoy working her way off the buggy seat, between the wheels, stretching a foot to the iron step, and almost staggering when she made contact with the ground.

"Quinn," Tierney said quickly as Alice reached a hand that could be seen—even at this distance—to tremble, toward the small boy standing in the buggy and holding out his arms to be lifted from the rig. "Quinn, could you help? I think that woman needs help getting that child down."

"Of course," Quinn answered quickly, after a glance in the direction of the other buggy, suiting action to words.

Quinn's long legs took him to the Hoy rig in a matter of four or five strides.

"Here, let me help. C'mon, young 'un," he said jovially and swung the tot up and over the wheels to the ground, where he immediately clutched his mother's skirt with one hand, the thumb of the other going into his mouth and his big eyes staring up at the stranger.

"Thank you," the woman said, a little breathlessly. "That was very . . . kind of you."

"Glad to help," Quinn said, only then removing his hat and giving his quaint and gentlemanly half-bow.

"Name's Quinn Archer," he said.

"I'm Alice Hoy," the woman said, two bright pink spots on her cheeks adding considerable attraction to her face, unhealthy though they were.

Now, Tierney thought, *if her eyes would sparkle, she'd be quite a beauty.* And she felt her heart pang even as she thought it.

But there was no sparkle in the eyes. The woman turned toward Tierney, waiting at the side of the Bloom buggy. "Your wife?" she asked.

"No, ma'am," Quinn said, "though she'll make someone a good one someday. This is," and he included Tierney in his glance, and she could do nothing but move closer, smiling a tentative greeting, "Tierney Caulder—"

If Tierney had any doubts about the identity of the thin young woman, they were dispelled when Alice Hoy acknowledged the introduction with, "Robbie Dunbar's friend from Scotland."

"Reet . . . right," Tierney murmured and wondered why it hurt to have that dear name casually spoken on the lips of this woman.

"These are my boys," Alice Hoy said. "Barnabas—Barney, and Billy. Say hello, boys."

"Hello"—brightly from the older boy Barney.

"Hewwo"—shyly from the little, half-hidden boy, not much more than a baby.

Together the three adults and two children moved toward the store. Alice hesitated at the step to the porch, and Quinn's keen eye noticed, and his strong arm came out to help.

"Thank you," she said again simply, her light blue eyes glancing up appreciatively, though perhaps with a little embarrassment. "I'm just fine, really. I haven't been very well since the death of my husband, but I'm sure I'll gain in strength any day now."

It was a gallant, optimistic thing to say. Quinn's eyes filled with sympathy.

While Tierney presented Lydia's list to the man behind the counter, eventually taking a few turns around the store and the fascinating array of goods, Quinn loaded the sacks of flour, keeping an eye on the frail form of Alice Hoy the entire time. Medlin Stover, new proprietor of the Bliss store, and postmaster, talked all the time, getting acquainted with his customers, both Alice and Tierney, and offering the boys each a lemon drop.

"Mr. Stover," Alice said finally, delicately, "would you be kind enough to check and see if I have any mail . . . especially packages?"

"Well, ma'am, I know right well you do," the garrulous shopkeeper boomed, and Alice winced.

"I been keepin' them for you for several days now," he continued. "Faithful as you've been to send for 'em, I knew they was mighty important."

Medlin was pawing through numerous items just behind the small glass partition sectioning off the post office from the store. "Yep, here they are!" And he produced and held up three identical packages. "The first one came a few days ago, then this 'un, then the last one. Looks like they are all in good shape. Nothin' broken, I'm proud to say."

The pink spots brighter on her cheeks than before, Alice Hoy took the small packages and quickly stuffed them in the string bag hanging on her arm. Turning away, she called in a shaky voice, "Come, boys, it's time to go."

"Aw . . ." they each resisted, loving the strangeness of the place and enjoying wandering around the piles and stacks of goods, sucking their candy.

"Have you forgotten that Robbie will be over for supper? All right, then!"

Stricken, Tierney saw the pleasure leap into the eyes of the boys, and they turned, happily enough now, to leave. Going home—to Robbie Dunbar.

14

A nation, a democracy, was being born from a sense of adventure. It was in the very air. The pioneers—those who trekked across country by prairie schooner, Red River cart, bumboat, wagon, or on foot—breathed free and found it exhilarating.

The population—growing slowly at first, then with greater impetus—was made up almost entirely of people whose causes had been lost elsewhere. Most had faced injustice, degradation, hopelessness; almost all bore wounds of bitterness and scars of despair. These wanderers—of widely differing nationalities, with strongly held religious convictions and greatly divergent ideologies but bonded at heart by experience and understanding—were slowly but strongly being welded into a united people.

These people knew that the real tragedy of life was not in living where men differed sharply but rather to dwell where differences of opinion were forbidden. In Canada there was room enough to absorb the differences—the backgrounds, the characteristics, the idiosyncrasies, the ideas of all; enough room to fulfill the dreams and the desires of all, and sympathy enough to know that your neighbor had suffered even as you had, dreamed as you do, and both of you need tolerance and brotherhood.

Their very northern-ness was significant, settling them a long way from ease and warmth and softness. It made them tough; it made them tenacious; it caused them to work hard. It made them know their need of each other.

Their satisfaction came from rare experiences: biting a plow through sod that had lain virgin ever since time began; clearing away bush whose tangled resistance gave ground reluctantly but promised much; throwing up living quarters from sod or logs that were captured in their nativeness and tamed or tussled into obedience and usefulness; building their own churches . . . electing their own school boards . . . educating their children.

For them all—their Canadian beginnings were full of harsh suffering and adversity; it was what they had in common. It welded them into a people unique—proud of what they were accomplishing, proud of what their children would become.

For all of them, the church was central, vital. Usually it began in a home that was a simple soddy or cabin—people gathering together for worship, for fellowship, for the strength they needed, and received—from the Word and from each other.

The church was the one institution that gave hope when, to all appearances, there was no hope. It gave encouragement where there was sheer, almost insurmountable discouragement as people struggled to keep body and soul together. The body might know great deprivation, but the soul—thank God!—would be fed. And weary shoulders, having come bent and bowed into God's house, would be lifted; faltering feet would turn back, with renewed strength, to the seeming impossibilities of the task.

Most of their social life was within the church—all-day meetings, revivals, church suppers, Sunday school picnics, youth programs, children's Bible-memorization competitions, quilting bees.

Song fests! Was ever singing heard to compare with the sounds—musical or tuneless, tremulous or sepulchral, harmonious or strident—that swelled within the sanctuary of God? Be it log or sod or green lumber, it reverberated to the lifted voices of the people of the prairie and bush as they gave vent, in song, to their joy, their pain, their longings, their strivings, their victory.

In the community of Bliss, as in many other districts, the schoolhouse did double duty—it was both the place of learning and the place of worship. A white frame building, it had four windows down each side, placed high to discourage the day-dreaming of children seated at desks but yearning to run free. The entire front wall was blackboard. In front of it stood the teacher's battered desk, the children's scarred desks. The entrance area was an open space; here the young ones donned and removed cumbersome wraps and bunglesome pacs or overshoes, here was a cupboard for lunch pails—syrup pails with their names scratched on them; just inside the door was a wood box, and on a shelf nearby sat a water pail with a communal dipper hanging beside it.

Between the open cloakroom area and the school proper, a black and nickel monster reigned—the massive Radiant Sunshine heater. "By closing the upper sliding mica doors," the catalog advised, "the stove can be used as an airtight surface burner." This was important, because in the winter, large kettles of milk were heated there and either canned tomatoes were added to make soup for the children to have with their noon lunches or a mix of cocoa and sugar for the favorite drink of all—hot cocoa.

The engineering that had gone into this stove was a marvel: "Thoroughly mounted. Elaborately ornamented. It has full nickeled skirting and nickeled swing dome, an elegant and expensive urn, nickeled and tile door ornaments, nickel foot rails, nickel nameplate, two check dampers in feed doors and one in collar. Vibrating grate with draw center, and sheet iron ash pan." This burning, belching, wood-guzzling blast furnace stood on a "Crystallized Stove Board," made of wood, lined with asbestos, and covered with tin. Here the children, in winter, spread their wet mittens to dry, and the room reeked with the combined odors of barn and wet wool.

When fed with poplar and roaring its pleasure, the Radiant Sunshine parboiled those seated nearest to it while, on the coldest of days, children in the far corners of the room rubbed chilblained hands together and attempted, with stiffened fingers, to sensibly record the day's lesson in their scribblers.

An hour before church or schooltime, someone had to start the fire, shaking down the grate, perhaps emptying yesterday's ashes, crumpling paper, striking a match to it, and blowing on the first few flickers, carefully feeding in the kindling, chunking in ever larger sizes of wood, adjusting the drafts for proper draw and a minimum of smoke. This task fell to the teacher during the week and to the pastor on Sundays.

Accustomed to going early—even though it was summer and no fire was needed—Parker Jones found himself arriving at the schoolhouse long before his parishioners; it was a fine time to meditate and pray, to go over his sermon, to make any last-minute changes, to wipe the road's dust from his shoes, his coin-toed shoes. In summer, between rains, it was easy to see why footwashing had been a practice in the Lord's day, and a blessing.

Parker Jones had no trouble with the concept. In all honesty he could think of no one in the Bliss congregation or in the entire area whose feet he would not willingly have washed, should he be called upon to do so. Parker Jones felt, essentially, humbled by the task set before him.

Was it possible to be too humble? And was humble the term? Was he, instead, uncertain?

Now, with this thought presenting itself, Parker Jones had new fuel for his doubts. Standing in the center of the room, he spent a long time gazing out the window at the motionless treetops surrounding the school yard, his mind full of conflict and his heart wrestling heavily with the same old problem: Was he worthy of the responsibility charged to him? Was he, indeed, *called?*

The Mudges were the first through the door. With a start Parker came to himself, turned, and greeted Kay and Woody.

Woody was shiny of face and slick of hair, and his Sunday suit strained over his big arms with their hardworking muscles, and his shoes (no coin toes here) squeaked on the oiled floor. Kay was self-conscious in what seemed to be a new floral-patterned dress, which sported, Parker Jones noted, a strange train, of sorts, down the back, from neck to floor. The Mudge boys—all three of them—could be heard outside shouting and tussling over the teeter-totter. Momentarily Parker harked back to the month spent in the Mudge home and the close quarters with these same rowdy boys and was able, from this distance, to smile at the memory of the constant hubbub in the small house.

Sister Finnery tottered in, quarterly in hand and Bible under her arm, her creased old face softened in anticipation of the blessed experience that awaited her, and all of God's children: Parker Jones's sermon.

The Popkinses arrived, and the Zumwalts, finding their favorite seats and settling down happily, glad it was Sunday and the day of rest—there was very little arguing, on Bliss homesteads, with the Scripture advising a workweek of six days.

With the arrival of the Dinwoodys, their organist had appeared. Florence Dinwoody looked at the list of hymns Parker Jones had prepared and frowned or smiled as the difficulty or ease of each became known to her.

"You'll do just fine," Parker encouraged, as he did each Sunday.

And when the service opened, with the congregation on its feet singing, soaring into blessed heights, Sister Dinwoody, with no hesitation at all, thumped out the melody, having pulled out the Dulciana, Bass Coupler, Principal Forte, and Vox Humana for maximum effect. Her generous hips churned, and her feet pumped magnificently, and perhaps the Lord looked down and said, again, "Behold, my servants shall sing for joy of heart" (Isa. 65:14).

"O sometimes the shadows are deep," they sang with great feeling, "And rough seems the path to the goal;

And sorrows, sometimes how they sweep
Like tempests down over the soul!

"O sometimes how long seems the day,
And sometimes how weary my feet;
But toiling in life's dusty way,
The Rock's blessed shadow, how sweet!
O then to the Rock let me fly . . ."

Oh, the meaning, the feeling, the cry that lifted from tested souls, troubled hearts, burdened spirits, weary bodies. And oh, the surcease, the rest, the assurance!

Standing before the group, leading the singing, Parker Jones felt his questions and concerns lift on wings of faith and fly away. And he sang with true fervor the ancient hymn, "I love Thy kingdom, Lord!/The house of Thine abode—/The Church our blest Redeemer saved/With His own precious blood."

With no spire, no stained glass, no robed choir, no swelling pipe organ, in an insignificant building in the heart of the bush, with a few wildflowers in a mason jar at his elbow, and before him a congregation of work-worn, hard-pressed homesteaders, Parker Jones felt himself fulfilled, blessed, content.

"Take your Bibles," he said eventually to his people, "and turn to Romans, chapter eight, starting with verse thirty-five."

And to people—who went home to a chicken dinner from a flock they had first nurtured by hand in a box by their range; potatoes and vegetables from a garden patch of ground they had dug out of the bush with painstaking effort; bread baked from their own field's hard-won grain, all earned by backbreaking work, sheer grit, and determination—he read, triumphantly, "Who shall separate us from the love of Christ? shall tribulation, or distress, or persecution, or famine, or nakedness, or peril, or sword? . . . . Nay, in all these things we are more than conquerors through him that loved us."

Old Sister Finnery whispered "Glory!" and her hearers—knowing that she had lost her husband to a winter's blizzard and hobbled around on feet crippled by the same storm—nodded earnest agreement.

Anything Parker Jones said was an anticlimax; good, true, precious though it was, the singing of the hymns and the reading of the Scripture had worked their miracle. What they had come for, they had already received. Sensing this, Parker Jones spoke simply and briefly; the Word and Spirit did the healing.

And people who knew firsthand about "all these things" experienced long ago by the apostle Paul, tightened their spiritual belts and lifted their heads one more time, and knew themselves to be, with divine help, "more than conquerors."

"Haw there, haw!"

Stupid creatures! Robbie Dunbar sawed on the reins until the oxen were into approximately the position he wanted. Then, in a passion of weariness, frustration, and despair, he dashed the reins to the ground, staggered to the shade of a nearby poplar (poplars—wherever you were—were nearby!), flopped down, spread-eagled himself on his stomach, buried his hot, sweaty face in his arms, and gave himself over to the misery that had walked with him, step for step, all day.

The oxen, borrowed for today's task, simply dropped their heads where they stood and endured this mortal's idiosyncrasies patiently, as they endured all else. Pulling stumps in the middle of summer! They flicked their tails against the flies that swarmed them, heaved their sweating sides, and waited.

It had been a foolish idea in the first place—to pull stumps. They were too green, the trees too lately chopped and cleared away. In a season or two, Rob had been told, the stumps would be dryer, ready to loose their hold on the earth, and would come out rather readily for piling and burning. But so torn with feelings had Robbie become—turning to first one thing and then another, with little rhyme or reason and wanting, needing, something to occupy his mind and his body totally—he had opted for the challenge of the stumps.

For the task, he borrowed Herkimer's oxen—ideal for such a job, supposedly—but soon found out the task wasn't accomplishing what he had hoped for: blankness of mind, easing of the pain that twisted his heart, the erasing of the realization that—in agreeing to marry for financial gain—he had acted as . . . as stupidly and as mindlessly as the oxen.

Burying his sunburnt face in the leaf mold, Robbie Dunbar groaned. Such groaning was ordinarily reserved for the night seasons when he was turning and tossing sleeplessly on his bed, with the knowledge that, just a few miles away, the lass of his dreams and desires lay wrapped in uneasy slumber, or tossed, as he did, wakeful and wretched. The few miles of bush in between might as well have been the heaving ocean between Canada and Scotland, so inaccessible was she. And all due to his own crassness, his blind desire to increase his acreage!

Why, oh why, had he agreed to Alice Hoy's offer? Not for a day, hardly for an hour since he had sailed away from Scotland and Binkiebrae, had Tierney Caulder been out of his thoughts. If he'd been a praying man, he would have been constantly beseeching God to—somehow, someway, sometime soon—make it possible for her to sail to Canada and join him. And, having prayed, he would have believed.

Not praying, not believing, it had seemed such a remote possibility, that when Alice approached him with the reality, the urgent reality, of the present—her land for his strong arms and care of her boys—he had seen no farther ahead than the next few months and what they would bring.

Again Robbie tried to defend himself; pride sought a way to explain his predicament: It had been Alice's idea. It was a business arrangement, pure and simple. An arrangement that would be a benefit to her.

But the comfort he sought escaped him, and rising up before him was the face—the dear face—of Tierney Caulder.

Again he went over the sweet memory—he saw her coming to him across the furrows of his homestead. He saw the unbelief that widened her eyes when she recognized him, the joy that flooded her face. That same joy gave wings to his own feet as he leaped the plowed ground to meet her, to take her in his arms.

He had not held her since. Never before, and not since.

Realizing almost immediately that he must go to Tierney, must tell her of the arrangement between himself and Alice Hoy, he had hoped against hope that, when he did, she would take it gravely, with understanding, willing to wait patiently until—

This was when Robbie's dismay erupted: Until—until Alice Hoy died. That was what it came down to. What a ghastly thought, and how it cleared his vision and caused him to see the plan for what it really was. It all turned on the death of a woman.

Why—when Alice broached the subject—hadn't he suggested Herkimer Pinkard? Herkimer's homestead was on one side of the Hoy land, Robbie's on the other. Herkimer, a bachelor, with no heart-ties to anyone, would have been the ideal choice to take on the Hoy responsibilities.

Under honesty's glaring searchlight, Robbie Dunbar admitted that he had been thinking of himself, not Alice and the boys. Or at least he thought of them second, himself first.

Robbie rolled over and stared with unseeing eyes up into the heavy growth of a black poplar, its leaves quaking green and silver in the slight breeze—a beautiful sight. And so meaningless. Robbie's pleasure in his homestead and in his accomplishments had fled. The purpose for his efforts, his plans for his future— all were gone.

His dream had centered on Tierney more than he knew; with her unattainable, the dream was a faded remnant of the bright possibilities that had accompanied him and buoyed him all the way from Binkiebrae to Bliss.

The sound of a rig passing on the road brought Robbie to a sitting position, ready to spring to his feet. To be found, like a child, sobbing into the damp leaf mold of the bush, was not a manly thing, and not one he cared to try to explain to anyone.

Half risen to his feet he paused, recognizing the Bloom rig, the Bloom horse.

On the narrow buggy seat, jaunting home from what had obviously been a trip to Bliss and the store—Quinn Archer, the personable man he had searched out and sent to the Blooms as hired man, and at his side, Tierney Caulder.

<hr>

Tierney had made the same trip enough times by now to recognize where she was and whose land was passed along the way; she had been well indoctrinated by Lydia, who felt a responsibility to introduce the young woman to the district. From time to time they had stopped to deliver mail or an item purchased on request for the lady of the home who was out of sugar, or soda, or yeast, and, with the horses engaged in fieldwork, had no way to get herself to town.

"This place, I believe," Quinn Archer said as they passed by, nodding in the direction of the buildings, "is the homestead of Rob Dunbar. He's the man who advised me of the opening at the Bloom place. I'd say he did me a favor."

"I believe ye're reet . . . right," Tierney said, but she kept her gaze from wandering in that direction. To see Robbie and not be able to run to him, to see him and not be able to call to him, to see him and ignore him—it was hard, so hard.

Without looking she knew every aspect of the place, every animal, every fence post, the small granary, the log barn, the cabin. In imagination she had scattered feed to the chickens, watching them come running to the sound of her "Heeeeere, chick, chick, chick!" She had drawn water from the well, tipping the pail into the trough, watering the brown and white cow; she had pinned overalls to the clothesline—and they were Robbie Dunbar's. She had picked peas from the vines in the garden and cooked them— for Robbie Dunbar. She had baked scones and sat down beside the fire and eaten them—with Robbie Dunbar.

She had, in dreams, watched children running around the cabin and the yard—and they called her Mither and Robbie Dunbar Da.

She had, in sad reality and with wrenching determination, put the dreams away and watched as they shriveled and died.

"Aye," she said now, fixing her gaze on the horse's ears, "thass Robbie Dunbar's homestead. And thass," looking ahead and pointing to the next cabin, the next set of outbuildings, "the homestead of his brother, Allan."

"And back of them, I understand, making the final two in the section, are the homesteads of Herkimer Pinkard and Alice Hoy—that charming lady we just met."

"Aye."

"You and the Dunbar men," Quinn asked casually, "aren't you from the same place in Scotland?"

"Aye."

"Did you know each other there?"

"Aye. We knew each other—there."

Wise Quinn. Perhaps it was her clipped answers, after they had been engaged in cheerful conversation; perhaps he had heard rumors; perhaps he was suspicious. At any rate, Quinn Archer said no more, but chirruped to the horse, and without a backward glance at the Robbie Dunbar homestead, hurried the rig on past, toward whatever the future had in store.

For himself, he was more certain than ever that his plans were fixed on Bliss and a place, one of the remaining few available, of his own.

As for the girl at his side—Quinn slanted Tierney a quick glance and became aware, once again, of the abundant life that seemed to emanate from her, the vigor restrained in that slim body. Even her hair, lively and vibrant, testified to it. Her face—lovely but strong—was set now, her gaze fixed resolutely on the road ahead.

Quinn Archer's eyes narrowed thoughtfully. "Yo! Giddap!" he commanded the horse, as though eager, even anxious, to move on into whatever future Bliss held for him. And for the girl.

16

I declare!" Lydia exclaimed with vexation. "I've had about all of these flies that I can abide!"

The harried housewife looked up from her work—washing canning jars in a dishpan of hot, sudsy water—brushing futilely at a particularly obnoxious pest that was hovering around her head.

"The regular flies I don't mind as much," she gritted, "as these horrible blue bottles! Horseflies! Listen a minute, Tierney—"

Tierney let her hands come to rest in the pan of beans she was preparing to string and snap, cocked her head, and listened. Sure enough, clearly, in the quiet kitchen, could be heard the droning and buzzing of flies on the windowpanes, the angry, useless buzzing of those caught in the dangling fly traps, and the insistent cacophony of those outside thronging the screen door, jostling for place, hoping for a way in.

"The music of the northland, Herkimer calls it," Lydia said despairingly and shuddered.

"Pity the homes without screens when we are this bad with screens," Lydia continued, sighing. "There's no way a house can be kept shut up, as hot as it is today, and so doors hang open, screens or no screens. And in those without, the flies are thicker'n sandhill fleas. And those are thick enough, goodness knows!"

"They certainly are a terrible plague," Tierney admitted. "The flies, I mean. I thought they'd drive me crazy out in the garden pickin' these beans."

"You know what, Tierney? It's time for fly patrol!"

"Fly patrol?" Tierney asked, intrigued. This was just one more new experience among many since she had come to the Canadian bush.

"First," Lydia said, drying her hands, "we pull down all the blinds and darken the house as much as possible."

Mystified, Tierney hurried to comply.

When the dark green shades were all pulled over the windows, Lydia handed Tierney a large dish towel.

"This won't work unless the door is open, as of course it is, and the screen door shut. Now, you and I—we go back here . . ." Lydia led the way to the rear part of the house, stumbling a little in the dark.

"Now we're ready. We start flapping the dish towels—"

Lydia suited action to words, swinging her towel in a mighty arc, back and forth, up and down, all around.

"It doesn't work unless you keep it up," she panted, "and you have to walk toward the light, shooing as you go."

Side by side the two women flapped, flapped until their faces grew red in the heat of the day and their arms weary. Flapped, and approached the door letting in the only light in the darkened house.

The flies, as is their wont—and urged on by the dish towels—had made a beeline (fly line?) toward the screen door. Soon the inside of the screen was as loaded with flies as the outside.

"Keep flapping!" Lydia urged, laying her towel aside and reaching for the broom.

Standing at a distance from the door and with the broom handle held before her like a sword, she pushed open the screen, Tierney behind her, flapping all the while, urging the swarmed pests toward the light. With one final flap on Tierney's part, Lydia yanked the screen door shut and—wonder of wonders—the house was comparatively free of flies. For the moment. Whenever anyone went in or out, they well knew, more would slip back in, and eventually the whole procedure would need to be done again.

"Now then, my dear," the determined Lydia said, "you'll need to get up on a chair and get those fly traps down—they're full up. I suppose I should be grateful for them; at least they are doing their job. It's getting them down that's disgusting."

Once again Lydia was grateful for Tierney's young strength and her willing spirit. With her crippled hands, many tasks were beyond her. One of numerous nice things about Lydia was that she never hesitated to express her appreciation. "There! That's it!" "Good job!" "Whatever should I do without you!"

Ridiculous as it seemed, Tierney almost felt privileged, given the most odious tasks—liming the toilet, emptying the slop bucket, gutting a chicken—to be the one to do them, so genuine and unfailing was Lydia in her gratitude.

Tierney stepped lithely up on the chair Lydia steadied, reached gingerly for the thumbtack fastened in the ceiling, and took down the traps, holding them at arm's length until she could get down and walk with them to the stove. Here she lifted a lid with her free hand and flung the revolting twists of sticky paper and their graveyard of flies into the fire.

Then, of course, new tubes had to be opened and untwisted and hung. About this time Quinn Archer appeared on the stoop. About to open the screen door, he was stopped by Lydia's screech.

"Wait! Wait, Quinn!"

Lydia left Tierney to her own devices in the hanging of the last fly trap, snatched up her dish towel once again, toddled to the door, and began flapping.

"Now," she said, "come ahead."

With the towel swishing over and around him, Quinn made his entrance, ducking his head against the attack and putting a protecting arm over his face.

"See," a deep-breathing Lydia said with satisfaction, "it's ever so much better in here. Now, Tierney, if you'll just come on down—"

A gallant Quinn was holding out his hand. Tierney took it and stepped lightly down to the floor. Tall, she was, for a woman, but Quinn Archer, standing closely beside her, was much taller. He smiled down at her.

"We could use your help with the flies out in the barn," he said. "I often get bitten when I'm milking and both hands are engaged." He rubbed his neck ruefully.

"You can help Tierney pull up the blinds again," Lydia, who loved to be in charge of good help, suggested, and soon the house was restored to normalcy.

"Herbert has decided," the hired man said, "that he can let me off tomorrow, and if you can do the same for Tierney, we'll take a turn at helping with the garden and the canning at the Hoy place. He says he agreed to tomorrow."

Quinn had made reference to Sunday's announcement concerning the church's responsibility where the sick widow woman was concerned. Immediately hands had gone up and a schedule of sorts worked out whereby the various households would leave their own work for a day to help Alice Hoy get ready for winter. In spring, soon after her husband's death, volunteer help had plowed the Hoy fields and planted the grain and the vegetables; summer had seen the weeds chopped, the garden tended, and now the rampant growth was ready for picking and canning or storing in the cellar. Soon the grain would be ready for harvesting. All of it was necessary if Alice and the boys were to survive throughout the long winter months. And all of it was accomplished by the callused hands, the strong backs, the weary forms of concerned neighbors who were never quite sure when they themselves might need a helping hand.

When Parker Jones made the announcement from the pulpit, calling for a concerted push to get the Hoy garden harvested, there had been a general nodding of heads, Herbert Bloom's among them. The good people of Bliss would lay aside their own work, if need be, to assist the needy neighbor. If it wasn't for Rob Dunbar looking after the chores each day, they all agreed, the situation would be hopeless indeed.

If the widow weren't so sickly—dying, perhaps—a husband would have been forthcoming immediately. Why, she had three bachelors living on her own section: Rob Dunbar, his brother, Allan, and Herkimer Pinkard. The Dunbar brothers were a little young, perhaps, and Herk a little . . . well, heads were shaken as Herkimer's assets and liabilities were totted up, and all concluded that Herkimer was . . . Herkimer.

"You know vat he said d' udder day?" Gebhard Popkin reported when caught in the midst of such a discussion. "It was the day d' skunk did his bizness 'roun' our place, and Herk come by: 'Vat kills a skunk is d' publicity it gives itself.' That's vat he said!"

"My land! What next?" someone offered, with more of the head shaking that seemed to affect all in general when Herkimer was mentioned. "Where'd he get such an idea?"

"He said it vas dat American president—Lincoln—dat said it."

"Well, who knows enough about it to argue with him?" No one, it seemed.

"It would take a saint to put up with that Herkimer Pinkard!" more than one woman was heard to mutter. And yet, when asked just what the problem was, they fell silent, with more muttering and very little substance. And the conclusion of all was that Herkimer was, after all, a fine man . . . in his way.

But husband material for Alice Hoy? No one even suggested it. Alice was a gentle lady, Alice was refined, Alice was *sick*.

"I went by the other day," more than one Bliss homesteader or his wife reported, "and she could barely get to the door. All glassy-eyed, she was."

Other times she seemed quite normal, like herself, except that she had grown excessively thin, even frail, with blue veins showing in her temples and on the backs of her hands. Her white hands. For Alice spent more time on her sofa than at her tasks.

So, "Yes, of course," Lydia said now in response to Herbert's reminder through Quinn, that tomorrow was their scheduled day to help at the Hoy place. "Tierney can be free whenever you can, Quinn. I wonder if Alice has cleaning materials or if the ladies take their own . . ." and Lydia was off and running, planning the next day's activities.

"Of course, Tierney," she concluded, "after you whisk through the house—and no doubt it needs it, what with Alice being so sickly and all—the main thing is to get at the canning. Hopefully she can help; it's a terrible task for one alone, as you know."

After the canning sessions in the Bloom household, Lydia felt confident that Tierney, by herself, could do the job, but the workload would be heavy, hot, and wearing to the extreme.

"Quinn can pick and gather," Lydia continued, "and you, Tierney—and hopefully Alice—can get the jars to boiling, the vegetables chopped and ready for the water bath. For heaven's sake, Tierney, wear your coolest cotton! It's going to be a scorcher. I'm sorry to do this to you, dear. It isn't a day to anticipate, that's for sure."

Anticipate? Tierney dreaded the experience, getting to know, to see, to watch, the woman Robbie would be marrying. Cleaning *their* home, putting up the vegetables that *they* would enjoy next winter, touching the items, the household equipment, that would be *theirs*.

In bed that night, desperately in need of a da's comfort and a mither's loving arms, Tierney found them both in her heavenly Father.

"Dear Father," she wept into her pillow, "Ye've brought me sae far, sae verra far, from home, and I know Ye'll no' forsake me. Niver, niver! Help me tomorra, gi' me grace for tomorra. In Jesus' precious name . . ."

17

Parker Jones looked up from the books spread before him on the dining table—his place of study—his attention caught by the sound of a rig.

Usually, a rig passing by on the road was enough to call any member of a household to the window or to the barn door, simply to see who was passing by. It wasn't because curiosity was so great; what was almost overwhelming at times, particularly during the winter season, was the loneliness. Shut into a small enclosure with only yourself for company or the well-known members of your family—so well-known, in fact, that there were no surprises remaining—a new face, a fresh train of thought, some outside interest, was enough to brighten the darkest and longest of days. There was life, after all, on planet Earth! The small satisfaction of a glimpse of another living, breathing, toiling human, with perhaps a wave, a smile, a halloo, gave encouragement and uplift that was often much needed.

Even so, Parker Jones, during his sermon-building sessions, would not be roused and turned aside by a passing rig. But this one, on this particular day, had turned off the road, was pulling up to the house, was stopping.

Reluctantly Parker turned from his notes, sighing at the interruption. It was, he supposed, someone bringing an offering—of baking, cooking, canning.

And he was always grateful; such donations kept the proverbial wolf from the parsonage door. At times, for meals, the pickings were slim. Last night's supper, for instance, was a pot of soup made from a jar of canned tomatoes—curdling when the milk was added, to Parker's dismay and disgust but not changing the taste greatly—and a few great slabs of bread and butter. There was plenty of it, but sometimes the lack of variety in his diet was wearisome. When it became too hard to take, or when he was tired to death of his own cooking (or when he had burned his meager meal past redemption), he simply turned his coin-toed shoes in summer, his overshoes in winter, in the direction of the home of a parishioner. And local hospitality was such that he had never been turned away. The fare might be just as simple as his own, but it was shared with goodwill and friendliness, never apologies, and Parker went home blessed in spirit and tight of belt.

Of course he was always welcome—almost as a son of the family—in the Morrison home. Here the fellowship of the dignified Angus and the gracious Mary were reminders that, outside of this remote corner of the world, life went on with civilized people engaged in everyday affairs and with no worries whatsoever about what the weather was doing to the crop. Angus and Mary had been among the first to settle in Bliss, but traces of a better life were clear, with touches of other days, other places, remembered niceties.

And Molly—Parker admitted that Molly Morrison was the chief attraction. With her vivacious face, lively hair, and equally lively ways, yet knowing when to be gentle, when to be thoughtful, when to be quiet, she was a pearl among women, to Parker's

136

way of thinking. And to the thinking of others, for bachelors continually showed up at the Morrison home and, Parker noted, with some embarrassment for his own similar practice, always at mealtime. In spite of their persistence, Molly had remained heart-free until those vivid blue eyes of hers had turned seriously upon the new minister, and the independence that marked her ways gave place to a passion for Parker Jones that was only guessed at, except perhaps by Parker Jones.

Even so, there was a restraint about Molly, a cool exterior that belied the depth of feeling within, except when she chose to let it be glimpsed. And, since the arrival of Vivian Condon, Molly had been restrained indeed, cool indeed. Not cold, never cold. Quick to respond, to smile, to listen, but with something . . . something that Parker Jones was at a loss to explain but felt, instinctively, uncomfortably, that it was related to the arrival of Vivian Condon.

Now, with a sense of dread, almost a premonition, Parker Jones rose, stretched himself, and went to the open door. Immediately he recognized the Condon horse and, hitched to it, the Condon buggy. But it was not Blystone or Beatrice holding the reins, looking expectantly toward the parsonage door.

Stepping outside onto the stoop, closing the screen door behind him, Parker nodded to the driver of the rig—Vivian herself.

"Good afternoon, Miss Condon," he said, his heart sinking.

Every time Vivian Condon appeared on the scene something dramatic happened, something that made him uneasy, almost guilty. And there was no reason, no reason whatsoever, to feel guilt! He had done nothing reprehensible, nothing to reproach himself for, not in the least. If Molly was disturbed by the other young woman's presence—

Parker Jones found himself on the verge of anger with Molly for—he could find no reason. He realized he was being unreasonable, and it pulled him up short, astonished that he should blame Molly Morrison for the tension he was feeling over Vivian's effect upon him.

But it was happening again: Vivian Condon had no more than driven into the yard and here he was, on the spot again, flustered again, at a loss again.

"Good morning, Pastor!" Vivian's expression was pleasant, her words ready, her smile smooth.

Parker Jones stood indecisively on the porch, his hands in his pockets, his tie awry, his dark hair slightly mussed, and was not aware of the picture he made. Was not aware that his very air of reluctance was fuel for the fire of this woman's interest.

Vivian Condon was not accustomed to disinterest. But this, she figured shrewdly, was not disinterest; it was hesitation. And hesitation was a challenge, especially at a time in her life when she was cut off from her circle of friends and their round of pleasures.

Only once in her lifetime had Vivian been thwarted: Ted Kingsley had wooed, and won, and flouted. Not so much brokenhearted as chagrined, Vivian had hastened to escape the pitying glances of her friends and had fled to her father's brother and his wife in the heart of the bush. Here, she was not long in realizing, life was much different, much more serious.

The occasional social times enjoyed by the people of Bliss were rare in the summertime, and when they occurred they were, to Vivian, so bucolic as to be heartily boring. The Sunday school picnic with its long tables of food that seemed to be the chief attraction—its children racing and leaping and yelling, its youth awkwardly flirting with members of the opposite sex, its men sitting in one group, talking, the women doing the same in another, the seeking of shade from the hot sun, the fanning of the face, the perspiration—was a trial for the city born and bred girl. The talk, of course, was mostly of crops and rain—too much or too little—cows freshening and chickens laying, garden stuff and canning. And it was so interspersed with mosquito-slapping and fly-shooing and featured refreshments as heavy as pie or as tasteless as pudding, that Vivian had great difficulty suffering the entire event without displaying her contempt of it all.

Yes, Vivian, if she were to make it through the summer, needed diversion.

She settled on the pastor: good-looking, educated, *single*. Parker Jones's devotion to spiritual things—God, the congregation, sermons, visitation, not to mention the girl Molly—was so single-minded that it was almost a game to Vivian to try to distract him, turn him aside, set his thoughts ajumble—a challenge worthy of her attention!

Sitting in a dusty buggy, impatient, Vivian could see the conflict in the eyes of the man on the parsonage porch, the pathetic parsonage's excuse for a porch, which was made with split logs laid side by side for a floor and a small overhang of the eaves for a roof. Surely a man of refinement, of some education, could not settle for this forever. Vivian suspected that, even now, she could see the doubt in his eyes. It was a good beginning.

"Parker Jones," she caroled. "What are you doing inside on a fine day like this? How about taking a little time away from the books? I'm sure you'll be much more effective for it."

Opening his mouth to respond fittingly, refusing her offer, Parker was checked when her voice, gaily importuning, continued.

"We'll all be better off for it—you, me, the congregation—if you just take time to clear your head a bit, get a new perspective. Catch a new vision, perhaps?"

The last was in the form of a question, and Parker Jones found his armor pierced.

A new vision. Was it so obvious, that even this outsider recognized his problem, understood the uncertainties gnawing at his spirit?

Opening his mouth to speak, to say . . . what? Once more she was ahead of him.

"I had in mind a run . . . well, a trot, to Prince Albert. Are you game?"

"Not really," he finally managed. "This is prayer meeting night, and I'm working on my talk."

"Work, work, work! Talk, talk, talk! Is that all you do? Take a look around—doesn't the bush call, doesn't the sky beckon?"

In spite of himself, Parker's gaze followed her sweeping hand. Summer was fast fleeting away; soon winter would be upon them, and buggy rides would be a thing of the past. And not available again until the far future, for the snow came early and stayed late; sometimes they had snow as early as September and as late as June.

"Besides, I have something I want to talk to you about . . . something important."

In spite of himself Parker Jones was beguiled. After all, it was too nice to stay inside. The blue sky did indeed beckon, the birds' sweet calls enticed, and the girl . . . the girl offered an hour or two away from the routine cares of the pastorate.

"I'll get my hat," he said, turning to the house and missing the triumphant look that sprang into Vivian's eyes.

"I don't think it can be as far as Prince Albert," he said, climbing into the buggy and taking the reins she handed to him. "As I said, I have a service tonight. But we can take a spin for an hour or two."

Clip-clopping around Bliss—there was no need to hurry—Parker began to relax. The prayer meeting message he had been struggling over was put aside, his meager supper menu lost its importance; even Sunday's sermon was forgotten for the moment.

"Now see," Vivian said archly as Parker Jones settled back, his hat tipped rakishly and his lean face, exposed to the merciless rays of the sun, showing to wonderful advantage, "you needed this—the afternoon off, the buggy ride, me, to help you get your priorities straight."

"I'm not sure I have my priorities straight," Parker hedged, "but it won't hurt, for once, to take some time off in the middle of the week. 'Six days shalt thou labor' is the commandment, and I work on the seventh day. There's no reason to feel guilty over these couple of hours off."

"Of course not! I hate sermons that make me feel guilty. It's so . . . old-fashioned, so archaic, to preach that way.

"Tell me, Parker, about why you are in the ministry, and why in the world a young man would choose such a vocation anyway." Vivian gazed earnestly at Parker Jones, giving him her full and rapt attention, an absorbed congregation of one.

Now here was a topic that related to the ministry. Answering her, Parker had a small feeling of relief—see! the time wasn't totally wasted, at all.

"It's hard to explain. Men and women who preach the gospel or go to the foreign field as a missionary refer to what they sense is a 'call.'"

"And do you have such a call? Did you hear a voice or something like that?"

"No," Parker Jones said rather haltingly, not a bit sure he could explain it and already struggling with this very concept. "No voice. Just a growing conviction—"

"But is that enough to build a lifetime on—a growing conviction?"

"I thought so—"

"What if the conviction, as you call it, stops growing?" she asked shrewdly.

"I only know," he said, rather too heavily for Vivian's preference, "that I had it. It was like a gleam. It isn't anything one can give up . . . easily."

"See what I have," Vivian said abruptly, bringing out a slender box from under the seat and opening it. "Chocolates! Have one . . . have several, and see if the day doesn't sweeten up a little for you."

The anticipated hour or two spun out into the remainder of the afternoon. Up one road and down another, across Bliss and into the neighboring district of Home Park, back again for a stop at the store in Bliss and a bottle of Wild Cherry Phosphate paid for out of the meager coins in Parker Jones's pocket. Finally, they turned the buggy back toward the parsonage.

"You said you had something important to talk to me about," Parker Jones finally managed to interject into the flow of chatter.

"It can wait," Vivian said, tossing her head until her hair, loosened by the breezes, whipped across his shoulder, so close to hers. "After all, you need this time to unwind, I'm sure of it. Such a hardworking minister I never saw!"

No mention of the fact that her association with ministers was limited to Easter and Christmas services. And so the "important" item was tabled for the time being.

"You can come to dinner again soon," Vivian said, "and that would be a fine time to talk about it."

Parker agreed; supper out was never refused.

"Now see," Vivian said, as they turned in at the parsonage driveway, "you're home in good time for your prayer meeting—"

"What—" Parker interrupted. There was a buggy in the yard, pulled up to the fence.

A man sat on the edge of the porch, his head in his hands.

Pulling the horse to a halt, Parker Jones handed the reins to Vivian and reached a foot for the ground, his eyes fixed with apprehension on the bowed figure, a picture of misery and despair.

"Jake? Is it you, Jake Finnery?"

The craggy face of old Sister Finnery's son, raised to Parker Jones, was twisted with pain and runneled with tears.

18

It seemed forever before anyone came to the door. Tierney, having knocked, stood by with numerous things in her arms—paraphernalia that Lydia had suggested she bring for the canning process at the Hoy home—feeling more strange by the minute. Quinn was heading toward the barn to unhitch the horse. He would find numerous things to do there, or so it was assumed, and would stand by to give Tierney a hand if she needed it, another suggestion of Lydia's.

The lace curtain stirred at a window, catching Tierney's attention. She recognized the small face that appeared, chin just higher than the sill. The child—Billy, Tierney recalled—gazed at her solemnly.

Tierney smiled. The small boy blinked, but his expression remained unchanged.

"Can you let me in?" Tierney asked, raising her voice.

Billy continued to gaze at her soberly, silently.

"H'lo."

The door had opened, and Barney, the older child, stood in the opening, as solemn as his brother if not as speechless.

"Hello, Barney. Remember me?"

The boy nodded. "Mama's sick," he said.

"May I come in?" Tierney asked, already stepping forward, gently pushing open the door that had been ajar just enough for Barney to be seen and heard. Willingly enough, he stepped back.

"She's over there," and the boy pointed across the room.

Struggling to sit up, Alice Hoy was the picture of disarray. Clutching a robe about her with one hand, with the other she pushed at the back of the sofa on which she had been lying, attempting to come erect. The sofa's mix of vivid colors offered a startling background for Alice's frail, pale outline. In a room that was well furnished, the tufted sofa was one of three pieces in an overstuffed parlor "suit"; it was ornamented with fringes and featured tassel valances around the bottom and arms. At another time Tierney might have admired it. The material, she knew, was called "crushed plush," and if it hadn't been crushed before, it was now: Alice had slept there.

The boys, standing to the side and watching Tierney, were big-eyed and still. They were dressed, but carelessly, as if they had put on the same clothes they had removed the night before. Or perhaps they had slept in them.

On the table were two bowls with the remains of what had been servings of oatmeal. The pot in which it had been cooked was on the back of the stove, dribblings of oatmeal drying down its side. A breakfast made by a man, Tierney deduced promptly—a woman would have filled the pot with water. A woman would have dressed the boys more capably, would have combed their hair.

So thinking, Tierney felt a sadness tinge what was a grudging admiration for Robbie's efforts. She felt certain his had been the only attention given, on this morning, to the boys and their needs. He was keeping his part of the bargain.

As of course he would. Having given his word, Robbie was bound. Though the cords used by the sick woman were as fragile as spiderwebs, they were as binding as chains.

"Wha . . . who is it?" Alice asked now, making an effort to focus her gaze toward the light coming in the open door.

Tierney closed the door behind her, laid the kettle and other canning materials on the table, and approached the woman who was struggling to rise.

"Dinna get up," she said kindly. "It's me—Tierney Caulder."

"Scotch," Alice murmured. "Robbie's friend . . ."

"Aye. I've coom to help wi' the cannin' of the day."

Alice put her face, momentarily, in her hands. "I'll . . . I'll be all right . . . in a minute. Sometimes I have trouble . . . getting going . . ."

"I'll make you a cuppa tea," Tierney said, speaking cheerily. "Me mither always said a cuppa tea would put the curl in your hair, the light in your eyes, and the bounce in your step."

Alice attempted a wan smile, putting a hand to her own head of hair and combing it with shaking fingers.

"Now, let's see," Tierney said, at a loss in a strange kitchen, tea-making escaping her for the moment. "Laddies, hae you had enough to eat?"

They nodded, sidling over to their mother. Alice pulled them to her, a child on each side. Burying her face in Billy's hair, she grimaced faintly. Apparently it had been too long since heads had been washed.

"I'll go get dressed," she said, and it was obvious she had regained enough of her poise to feel a certain embarrassment, perhaps humiliation, over having been found in a state of disorder. She got unsteadily to her feet, and as she did, a bottle fell with a thump from the folds of the blanket to the floor.

"My medicine," she said quickly. "Barney, pick that up for Mother; that's a good boy. It's empty . . . toss it into the wood box."

Tierney was clearing the table, putting the bowls aside to be washed later, getting a dishpan of hot water from the reservoir, adding soap, making a suds, and preparing to wash, then sterilize, the jars that would be needed for today's canning. In a large kettle of water, she put the clean jars on the stove to boil.

"I understand," she said to Alice, "Mrs. Dinwoody was here yesterday and left things ready for piccalilli, reet? Lydia said she would hae chopped up the green tomatoes an'—"

"Yes . . . they're in that big pan. Have you made piccalilli before? You have, with Lydia, of course. We . . . all of us, I guess . . . have such an abundance of tomatoes this year. Somebody picked those—I think it was Hazel Trumbell—oh, I don't remember—"

On the verge of leaving for her room and the task of fixing herself up, Alice hesitated, troubled over her faulty memory.

"Aye," Tierney reported, looking in the kettle, "they're all ready—one peck of green tomatoes, eight large onions, all chopped fine, with one cuppa salt stirred in. I'll jist build up the fire, and as soon as it's hot I'll get to the boilin' part—twenty minutes, the first time."

With Alice gone and Billy with her, Barney staying behind, kneeling on a chair, elbows on the table, watching her, Tierney went about the job of draining the "liquor" from the green tomato mixture, breathing a sigh of relief when that was accomplished with no mishap.

"Add two quarts of water," she murmured aloud, checking the notes she had placed on the table, "and one of vinegar. Now where in the world would she keep vinegar?"

Gravely the small boy climbed down, marched across the room, and pointed to a corner cupboard. Sure enough, just inside—a gallon jug of vinegar.

"What a smart lad! Thank you, Barney!"

The small boy looked modestly pleased with himself.

"Once Robbie made some chips and put vinegar on them," he said, speaking up suddenly. "A little vinegar goes a long way, Robbie says. Robbie isn't a very good cook."

In spite of herself, Tierney laughed at the picture of Robbie Dunbar trying to cook. Indeed he was taking on many tasks and responsibilities here in the new land that he had never tackled in the old. If only she were at his side to help.

Fighting down a lump in her throat that she thought to have conquered weeks ago, she turned to timing the boiling process. It didn't take long, this first boiling. Before the next step—draining the entire batch once again through a colander, a touchy undertaking because it was so hot—Quinn stepped into the house.

"How are you doing?" he asked. "Need any help?"

"Aye, and I'm happy to see you aboot now—"

At that moment Alice reappeared, Billy in tow. Both had been cleaned up, and Alice was in a fresh dress, with her fair hair restrained in a thick knot at the nape of her neck. Blue was her color. If only her eyes had been alive, full of sparkle! But they were dead, dead. And her hands, as she took an apron from a nail and cinched it around her slender waist, shook badly.

"Good morning, Mr. Archer," she said. "It's so nice of you to come today. You and Tierney."

"Quinn, please, ma'am."

"Quinn, if you'll drop the ma'am," she responded with what passed for a smile. And almost, almost a cheek dimpled.

"Now where are we?" Alice asked in as businesslike a tone as she ever used, for she was a person of gentle speech.

"I was aboot to drain the piccalilli again," Tierney explained, "and Quinn is jist in time."

"Then we'll need—let's see," and Alice bent over the recipe, not certain of the measurements where the spices were concerned.

Standing at the side of the table in her clean gown, her fair hair neat, her exposed neck slender and somehow vulnerable, Alice appeared fragile indeed. As the eyes of Tierney and Quinn were turned on her, and into the silence that fell, perhaps the thoughts of the man, as well as of Tierney who knew the story, were *What a shame that one so young, so . . . delectable, should be so obviously fading away.*

Alice sighed, and the spell of the moment was broken. Quinn, with masterful hand, lifted the heavy, steaming pot, and poured the piccalilli through the colander and into another large kettle.

"Now we add," Alice read from Lydia's recipe, "two quarts of vinegar, one pound of sugar, half a pound of white mustard seed . . . I hope I have that . . . two tablespoons of ground pepper, two of cinnamon, one of cloves, two of ginger, one of allspice, and half a teaspoon of cayenne pepper."

"If you'll locate them, I'll add 'em," Tierney offered, looking helplessly at the unfamiliar cabinets, and together the spices were soon measured and added, mustard seed and all, and the mix put to boil again.

Quinn was filling the wood box, drawing out and holding in his big hand the small, dark bottle.

Neutralizing Cordial.
Composed of Rhubarb, Peppermint,
Golden Seal, Cassia, Brandy, etc.

With his back turned to the others, Quinn uncorked the bottle, put it to his nose, sniffed, and grimaced. *Whew!* his lips formed soundlessly.

"Stir often to prevent scorching," Tierney was reciting, suiting action to words.

Already the day was hot, and Tierney's upper lip was beading, and her hair, which had been fastened up snugly, was escaping in small, curling tendrils. Turning to her with the bottle in his hand, gesturing toward it, shrugging his shoulders, Quinn would have been blind indeed had he not recognized the womanliness, the grace. And if he recalled his first glimpse of her, hanging something on the clothesline, trim and slim and pert, he may be excused if he slipped the bottle in his pocket without further reference to it and the one who had emptied it, and said, "Here, let me. I've had enough experience with cooking in my life to keep piccalilli from scorching. You sit yourself down for a few minutes."

Tierney, surprised, turned over the big wooden spoon with which she had been stirring the contents of the kettle, and said, "I promised tea. The kettle's boilin', and Alice hasn't had any breakfast, near as I can tell. At home in Binkiebrae t'would be porridge for sure, but I've an idea she's had her fill o' that. Maybe scones, while the oven's hot."

While Quinn stirred the stringent green tomato mixture, Tierney put together the ingredients for scones, and Alice languished at the side of the table, lackadaisically removing jars from the scalding hot-water bath, lining them up, preparing them for filling and sealing. Little Billy knelt on a chair at his mother's side. Barney had gone outdoors, possibly to feed the chickens, for a cacophony of cackles broke loose from the direction of the hen house.

Tierney's chief thoughts—rather than dismay, disgust, or derision, all reactions she had felt previously for Alice—were, rather, those of pity. Pity for the young woman who, obviously, was in grief from her recent bereavement and yet felt compelled to make arrangements for her land and her children, pity for the broken figure she presented—both in body and spirit. For her form drooped, and it seemed her thoughts were not on the task at hand. Life, for Alice Hoy, had lost its savor.

Tierney looked down at her own healthy young body, thought of her future, as bright and big as the Saskatchewan sky, considered her trust in the goodness and guidance of her loving heavenly Father, and could not find it in her heart to hate—no, not even dislike—Alice Hoy.

"Thank You, Father. Oh, thank You!" she breathed, tears starting into her eyes, needing to be brushed quickly away lest they be noted and misunderstood.

Tierney was about to put the scones in the oven to bake, Quinn was about to ask if the boiling process was completed, when Barney returned to the house, a pet chicken in his hands.

Stepping inside, both hands engaged in keeping the squirming hen steady against his body, the little boy allowed the screen door to slam shut behind him. *Bang!*

Startled from her thoughts and her lethargy, Alice screamed and jumped. In the act of withdrawing a jar from the near-boiling water with a pair of tongs, her hand jerked. The bottle, full of piping-hot liquid, slipped from the tongs, hit the table, broke, splashed.

Splashed on the arm of the small boy at her side. Splashed up into his face, into his eye.

Alice's startled cry had been nothing compared to the sound that shrieked from the throat of the child.

19

Somewhere, afar off in the wide blue Saskatchewan sky, a meadowlark trilled its spontaneous song. But as Parker Jones looked down at the face raised to his—a picture of misery—the sweeter sound was lost in the broken cry of the man seated on the edge of the parsonage porch, his feet dangling, his gnarled hands hanging, empty and somehow pathetic. It was as though those hands, accustomed to grappling with tough emergencies and bitter hardships, were helpless in the grip of grief.

"Jake," Parker said, "what's wrong? Can you tell me?"

The anguish on the face of the middle-aged man seemed to lessen, and as he looked up into the face of his pastor, the light of reason returned to eyes that had been glazed, seeing nothing, lost in their private pain.

"It's Ma," he managed.

"Your mother? What's wrong with her, Jake?"

"She's dead. She's dead!" And again the head bowed, and the massive shoulders, accustomed to heavy burdens but finding this one more than they could bear, shook uncontrollably.

Helplessly Parker Jones watched. Until Jake Finnery gained control, there was little he could do but wait. But his heart had lurched and was now beating heavily.

Parker Jones had left his responsibilities for an afternoon of frivolity, or so it seemed now, remembering the frothy and vapid conversation and laughter he had engaged in with the young woman still seated in the buggy and watching the proceedings on the parsonage porch. He had filled his troubled heart, for a time, with talk and thoughts far removed from the momentous decision he was struggling with, he had fed his dissatisfied spirit with Vivian's attention, and had, in return, done nothing to minister to her, or to anyone, nothing at all. It had been an afternoon wasted.

And still she sat in the buggy—a part of the little drama unfolding on the porch, yet apart from it—an onlooker.

Parker Jones left the side of Jake Finnery for the moment. Stepping to the buggy, he spoke to Vivian.

"There's no need to stay—"

"What's wrong? Who is that?"

"It's Sister Finnery's son. Jake Finnery. He says his mother has . . . died."

It seemed such a cold word, such a final word. Dead! Dead, and he not at the bedside. Another death, and once again he, Parker Jones, pastor, had been derelict in his duty.

At the very root of the questions that burned in his heart about his call, was the death of another parishioner soon after his arrival in Bliss.

After Henley Baldwin's death, when Parker began to realize the problems that had existed in the Baldwin home and the silent humiliation and belittlement the dead man had endured across many years, Parker blamed himself sorely for having been too detached from the lives of his people, this troubled family in particular. He might have helped! He could have counseled! He could have prayed, had he but taken time to get involved.

Now here was another parishioner, bowed, broken, hurting. And where had he, Parker Jones, pastor, been? Gallivanting.

Parker took hold of the bridle, about to turn the horse and rig toward the road.

"Hadn't you better wait?" Vivian asked pointedly, glancing at Jake Finnery. "You don't have any way to get to the Finnery place, do you? Isn't it possible that you might need to go?"

Parker's hands dropped uselessly to his side. She was right, of course.

"Thank you," he muttered, turning back toward the cabin, "if you'll just be so kind as to wait a bit—"

"I'll wait," she answered smoothly. "I'll get down and come in—if I can help."

"No, no," Parker said quickly. "There's no need—"

At that moment the clip-clop of a horse was heard, and a rider turned in toward the parsonage—Herkimer Pinkard.

Herkimer pulled up beside the buggy and looked down at the rather intimate little scene—the pastor, the young woman, engaged in close conversation. Eyes less shrewd than Herkimer's could see the distress on the face of the pastor and the smooth satisfaction on the face of the girl. Tongues less controlled than Herkimer's might have asked, "What's going on here?"

As it was, Herkimer politely doffed his cap for a second and offered, "Herkimer Pinkard, at your service, ma'am.

"Hey, Parker," he said, settling the disreputable, shapeless cap on his mop of hair and turning to his pastor.

Parker Jones made a wordless gesture toward Jake Finnery, but before he could make explanations, Herkimer spoke up. "I've just come from the Finnery place. Came to see what's keepin' ol' Jake. See if he's doin' all right."

"I just got here myself," Parker Jones said in a low voice, as though every word hurt, as indeed it did. "I need to get back to Jake—"

"I'll wait," Herkimer said imperturbably.

Parker Jones turned back toward the porch and its silent, grieving occupant. Herkimer sat on his horse, his eyes fixed speculatively on the young woman in the buggy. When, after a few moments his gaze hadn't shifted, but seemed, rather, to probe past the fancy hat, the modish outfit of linen crash blazer with its large sailor collar, into the very heart and soul of the girl, Vivian looked up, met that narrow gaze, and flushed.

"What?" she asked sharply.

"Just thinkin'."

A few minutes passed. Herkimer's gaze never faltered; Vivian's fidgeting grew pronounced.

"Why don't you get down!" she said finally. "You can't be all that comfortable." Unspoken was *and neither am I!*

"'The thunder god went for a ride,'" Herkimer began, and Vivian's gaze narrowed—*What is this clod up to?*

"'Upon his favorite filly.

"'I'm Thor,' he cried.

"The horse replied,

"'You forgot your thaddle, thilly.'"

There was no laughter, no, not even a smile, on Vivian's face. But then, there was none on the face of Herkimer.

<hr />

Parker Jones had made his way back to the side of Jake Finnery.

"Come inside, Jake," he urged, needing, somehow, to get away from the watching eyes of the girl in the buggy. Taking the man by the elbow and helping him to his feet, Parker led Jake, who moved almost blindly, toward the door and eventually into a chair.

"Now tell me," he said, seating himself, "surely I didn't hear you correctly. Your mother—"

"Is dead," Jake Finnery croaked baldly.

Parker Jones was silent before the news that, truly, grieved him deeply. He had been fond of the ancient woman, admiring her gallantry in spite of life's blows.

Testimony time at last Wednesday night's prayer meeting had been an example of Sister Finnery's indomitable spirit.

"It's been a hard week," she had begun, getting to her feet, and everyone had listened sympathetically. "First off, a skunk got in the chicken house and killed four of my best setters . . . a jar broke, cannin', and chokecherry juice spread everywhere. Then I found where a mouse had eaten into the bag of flour. Oh, the devil he was doin' his best to get me down. Trouble . . . trouble! I've had it this week. But—"

Here old Sister Finnery's voice had lifted, her eyes lighted, and she concluded triumphantly, "like the good Book says—'It came to pass'!"

Thinking of the note of victory and of Sister Finnery's habit of applying Scripture, whether fitting exactly or not, brought a mist to the eyes of Parker Jones.

"Tell me about it, Jake," he said, his voice cracking under the depth of emotion he was feeling for the loss of this "sheep" from his flock.

Jake Finnery heaved a sigh and sat up. Accustomed to life's blows and having bent for the moment under another one, like a good, strong bush poplar he was straightening and facing the elements.

"Seemed like she felt good all morning," Jake said, hollowly. "Of course, like always, she overdid it. I couldn't get her to take it easy, not ever. This morning she was butchering chickens and canning them. After dinner she complained of a burning in her chest, sort of. Said it was indigestion. I told her to lie down for a while, but it got so bad she was sweatin' and groanin,' and I went fast for Gramma Jurgenson. As soon as she saw Ma—well, she got sorta white-faced herself. 'It's her heart,' she said, scarin' me like everything, and gettin' Ma's attention.

"Then Ma sorta got herself together and turned to me and said, desperate-like, 'Get Parker Jones, Jake! Go get him quick. I need for Parker Jones to come pray with me—'"

Parker stifled a groan, his face in his hands.

"I hurried on over, fast as I could. I guess I sat on your porch for an hour or more, waitin'. I knew you'd be along . . . but just before you came, one of the Jurgenson boys came by to tell me . . . to tell me—"

Jake—big, strong, bull-of-a-man Jake Finnery—broke down. Parker Jones found himself on his knees, but this time not praying. His arms—as far as they would reach—were around Jake, and the two men wept together.

"You'll be wanting to get on back, Jake," Parker managed eventually. "Gramma Jurgenson will be needing to do . . . whatever it is she does at times like these. Herkimer came to escort you, I think. I . . . I'd like to go, too."

Leading Jake out onto the porch, closing the door behind them, neither Jake nor Parker heard the voice of Herkimer Pinkard as he said thoughtfully, staring off into space the while, "A mousetrap never pursues a mouse." If they noted the open mouth and outraged flush on the face of Vivian, neither gave it a serious thought.

Finally, Herkimer dismounted. Leading his horse to the Finnery buggy, he tied it behind. Then he helped the dazed Jake up into the rig, climbed in himself, took the reins, and headed toward the road and the Finnery homestead.

Without a horse of his own, never had Parker Jones felt more helpless. Whether he wanted her assistance or not, he needed Vivian and the Condon rig at this moment.

Parker Jones knew he could walk, if nothing else. It wouldn't be the first time.

Had he walked the path of duty for the last time?

This grim question was in the mind of Parker Jones as he and Vivian followed Jake and Herkimer. His dereliction—being unavailable when a parishioner needed him—seemed to spell finish to the pastorate for him.

Not only did Parker feel his own failure deeply, but he was confident that God, whose word adjured ". . . that ye walk worthy of the vocation wherewith ye are called," considered him a failure also.

Weighed in the balances, and found wanting. These ancient words rang like a death knell in Parker Jones's heart.

At the Finnery place, Parker followed Herkimer and Jake into the house. Numerous people were there, having picked up the word from Herkimer as he passed, and from the Jurgenson boys who had come checking on their grandmother who, though not young, was the nearest thing to a doctor—or undertaker—the district boasted, and who was called upon in every emergency.

Sister Finnery, by this time, had been bathed and dressed, and lay in state on her bed until such time as a coffin could be obtained.

There was no grandchild, no daughter. No one except the burly Jake, whose wife had died years ago in childbirth, and who had not remarried but who had taken the care of his aging mother on himself, finding that she did as much for him as he did for her.

At one time there had been other Finnery children—three of whom had died in infancy, two as youths. There had been two grandchildren. A daughter and her two children had perished with Jacob Finnery in the blizzard that had crippled his wife. It was one of the horror stories of the bush—a family far from home and not properly dressed, a blinding storm, horses given their head to find their way home, drifts too deep to stagger through, two children and their mother and their grandfather dead when found. Sister Finnery, piled high with bodies and blankets, had somehow survived, but never quite forgave her Jacob for his sacrifice in saving her life at the expense of his own.

And now—to have died without the comfort and consolation of her pastor! No knife, thrust into a beating heart, could have been more murderous than the guilt that slashed through the bosom of Parker Jones.

Still, a devotion to duty kept him going through the paces. He knelt at the side of the makeshift bier and prayed; he comforted, as best he could, the bereaved son; he spoke proper and fitting words to grieving friends. And felt it all to be a mockery.

It was one of the Finnery horses, after all, that took Parker home. Jake had roused himself, shaken his great body, blinked his reddened eyes, and lifted his head.

"The Lord giveth and the Lord taketh away," he said, in much the same manner his mother might have spoken, and friends, listening, nodded and agreed that Jake, with such a heritage, would pull through, pull through one more tragedy.

"Take one of our . . . my horses," he said to his pastor. "Just tether it out back of your place, and I'll be by sometime later to get it. We should," he said, glancing around at fellow church members, "get on with the task of putting up a barn for our preacher, and gettin' him a rig of his own."

Already Jake Finnery, with the spirit of the true pioneer, was looking ahead, doggedly looking ahead. Present circumstances should not triumph. There was a tomorrow for the longest day, there was a dawn for the darkest night, there was—in the heart of the bush homesteader—a dogged persistence that simply would not, could not, give up.

Parker spoke brief words of thanks to Vivian, explained that he would no longer need her services, and sent her on her way. If he noted Herkimer Pinkard's keen glance, he didn't pursue it.

Herkimer was a puzzle—to all appearances a careless, laughing man full of waggery and tomfoolery, but with occasional flashes of wit and wisdom that astonished the hearer. In spite of his buffoonery, Herkimer was considered thoughtful enough to be on the church board and had, at times, served on the school board as well, though he was a bachelor without wife or children.

If Vivian felt his eyes on her back as she drove out of the Finnery yard, it served only to lift her chin and put an angry flash in her eyes.

Mounted, ready to leave, Parker Jones looked down into the face of Jake Finnery, seeing kindness, respect, and perhaps love there, and said heavily, "I'm sorry, Jake. I'd give the world to have the afternoon to do over again . . ."

"Ma woulda been the first one to say it's all right, you couldn't have known. It was awful sudden. I just took out and tried to find you, not even thinkin' you might be busy somewheres else. But the buryin', preacher? You'll take care of all that."

It wasn't a question. Jake, and all the congregation, had full confidence in their pastor. Only Parker knew the hollowness.

He was thankful for the quiet time alone as he made his way homeward on a horse that was reliable—an old plow horse and not given to friskiness—with time to think. To try to pray.

"O God," he cried silently, "what now?"

A t the sound of the child's ululation of anguish, everyone froze momentarily. The silence itself seemed to scream portent; it was the prelude to a great hubbub: The pan of scones in Tierney's hand, about to go into the oven, poised in midair for a second then crashed to the open oven door; the big wooden paddle in the grip of Quinn Archer, lifted for a moment, splashed into the boiling piccalilli; Alice, her mouth agape and the empty tongs in her hand fluttering ineffectually above the kettle of near-boiling water on the table before her, dropped them among the remaining sterilized jars, setting off a sharp clatter. Even the chicken in Barney's arms was shocked into a silent huddle before it lunged, with a flapping of wings and a high screeching cackle, making a bid for escape.

Leaving the oven door hanging open and the doughy scones scattered far and wide, Tierney turned in the next instant toward Billy.

Still on his knees at the side of the table, his mouth stretched and shrieks continuing to issue from it, Billy held his burned arm stiffly, like a poker out before him. One side of his face was an ugly scarlet, his eyes were shut, and one was red and already appeared to be swollen. It had been just seconds since Alice, half dreaming as she lifted the hot jars from the water, had let one fall, to break, to splash, to scald.

Tierney was the first to reach the side of the boy; Quinn was beside her in a moment. Alice faltered back, wide-eyed and breathing shallowly, her hand going to her face in a gesture of helplessness.

Young and inexperienced with tragedies of this magnitude, Tierney looked helplessly at Quinn. It was almost impossible to make herself heard above the hullaballoo, but her lips formed the words *What shall we do!*

Quinn Archer was no callow, inexperienced youth. Whatever life had held for him (Tierney recalled that he had been a teacher of children; one among them, perhaps, had burned himself), he rose to the need of the moment with clear thinking and sensible solution.

"Ointment!" he said strongly. "We need something to keep the air off these burns. Alice!—"

Quinn turned to the stricken Alice, took her by the elbow, and spoke forcefully into her ear, not only to make an impression but to be heard over the din of the boy's continuing howl, "Ointment—do you have any?"

At Alice's shake of the head, Quinn spoke again, "Well, then, lard . . . grease of some kind. Where do you keep it?"

Alice turned to the cupboards, Quinn on her heels. At her pointed finger he located a can of grease, left over from bacon and roasts and other fatty foods.

"Scissors!" Quinn barked, and Alice shuffled through a drawer and came up with them. Quickly Quinn cut the boy's shirt from top to bottom and side to side, and peeled it from him. Taking the grease and disregarding the increased shrieks and the boy's flinching, he began systematically slathering it on the burned arm and face.

"Bandages," he commanded, and Alice, like a puppet on a string, obeyed. As Tierney steadied the stiffened child, Quinn wrapped the torn sheeting around the arm and, with more difficulty, around the head and over one side of the face. Still the gaping mouth screamed and one eye, peering from under the side of the bandages, streamed tears. The stiffened body, now, was shaking like an aspen leaf.

"Take him; hold him," Quinn said, turning to Alice.

But Alice was digging feverishly into a cupboard. Cans and bottles flew and dropped as she shoved them aside, tearing past them to a back corner. Here she grasped a couple of dark bottles and, breast heaving and eyes glittering, began working with the cork in one of them.

Quinn and Tierney watched, momentarily startled into motionlessness.

But when—the cork removed and tossed aside—Alice raised the bottle to her lips, Quinn leaped into action.

"Here!" he said roughly. "Give me that!"

With a sob Alice released the bottled potion and sank into a chair.

His brows knit in a sort of scowl, Quinn lifted the bottles and read the scrolled labels—first of one, then the other: Brandy Cordial, Laudanum.

Quinn studied the print, studied the weeping face of the woman, and shook his head—compassionately but firmly.

"Alice," he said, "Alice!" And Alice ceased her gasping and weeping and focused on the man before her.

"You need to be a help right now, Alice. And *this* won't help." Quinn shook the bottles in his hands. "This is a time for clarity, for sanity. You'll need to be strong. Do you understand what I'm saying?"

Alice reached a beseeching hand, her face anguished. "I *need* it!" she said huskily.

"No, you don't. What you do need is a clear head. Your child needs you—no!" he said, to her raised head, pleading eyes, reaching hand. Alice capitulated, sinking back like a drooping flower.

"I'll tell you what I *am* going to do with it," Quinn continued. "I'm going to give some of the laudanum to Billy. He'll be more comfortable soon. Sit over here—"

Quinn helped Alice to a rocking chair.

"And I'll put him in your arms . . . like so."

Suiting action to words, Quinn put the terrorized Billy in his mother's arms and then, with Tierney's help to hold the tossing head still, measured a spoonful of the medication into the gaping mouth. Billy, taken by surprise, gulped automatically, his mouth closing and his caterwauling hushed, though he spluttered for a while. Quinn and Tierney looked at each other with relief, relaxing, with long sighs, muscles that were more tense than they had known.

"These burns will need more attention than this. We'll have to get him to the doctor," Quinn said, and Tierney nodded agreement.

"I'm worrit aboot that eye," she said. "Seems the hot water splashed into it."

Billy quieted in his mother's arms under the effect of the laudanum, but even in a doze his small body shook from time to time with dry sobs. Alice, her head back and her eyes closed, could have been praying.

Eventually Tierney remembered Barney and turned to find that small boy crouched in a corner of an overstuffed chair, tears streaking his white face, the chicken still clutched in his arms.

Gently lifting the chicken from him, Tierney took it to the door and released it. With renewed vigor it streaked off toward its companions, squawking its unbelievable story at the top of its voice all the way.

"Everything's going to be a' reet," she said, sitting beside the trembling child and putting her arm around him. "It's jist a . . ."— with a few words she relieved him of the lifelong burden of believing he had been the cause of bringing terrible pain to his brother—"a wee burnie. Mama will take him to the doctor. Would you stay here with me, an' help me?"

Barney, with a quivering sigh, slumped against Tierney's side and nodded.

Now Tierney's eyes, which had been dry throughout the ordeal, filled with tears. Hugging the little boy to her, she muttered "Silly!" to herself.

Quinn was doing a hasty job of scraping the scone dough from the floor, pulling the boiling picallili to the back of the stove, and, in general, bringing order out of the chaos of the previous few minutes.

"I've been thinking about how to handle this," he said, turning to Tierney. "I'll have to take them to Prince Albert, I suppose. It'll be some trip, but with this," and he pointed to the dark bottle, "we should make it just fine. At least the boy will. I don't know about the mother."

Having deprived Alice of her support, he wondered and watched her but firmly kept the cordial and the laudanum beyond her reach.

"I'll need to take the Bloom buggy," Quinn said to Tierney. "I'm sure Lydia and Herbert would give their blessing if they knew what had happened. I didn't see the Hoy horses in the barn or in the corral; perhaps Robbie is using them today. What will you do? Stay here until I return? Walk home? Remember, you'll have the boy with you."

"I'll stay here the rest of the day, I think," Tierney said thoughtfully. "Lydia will no' be expectin' me till later. Then, when Robbie cooms to do the evenin' chores, I'll have him take the news to the Blooms an' I'll stay on here wi' Barney until you coom back. Then we'll go back home together. How's that sound?"

Quinn nodded his approval and went to hitch the horse to the rig.

The sun was high overhead when Quinn put Alice into the buggy and handed a drowsy Billy to her waiting arms. Alice had roused herself to fix her hair and put on her hat, and though she was pale and tense, was much more in control than at any time that day. Tierney wondered just what the real Alice was like—out from under the influence of whatever it was she imbibed, whether cheering cordial or numbing laudanum.

Tierney stood with her arm around Barney watching the buggy pull out of the yard, then turned back to the house and the tasks awaiting her there. With the fire stoked and blazing and the piccalilli bubbling once again, she proceeded with the canning, trusting that, in the deprivation of winter, the tomato pickles would be acceptable, though overcooked.

Later, with the sun sinking toward the west, there came a light tap on the door. It opened to reveal the bronzed face of Robbie Dunbar, quickly turning darker still with the flush that mounted to his cheeks when it was Tierney who turned from the stove rather than Alice.

Tierney was stirring a mix of potatoes and onions in a frying pan, and at her elbow, ready to come from pan to table, were delectable scones such as Robbie hadn't seen or tasted since leaving Binkiebrae.

If Robbie's first reaction was "This is what it would be like to coom home of an evenin' if—" he checked it before it reached his lips or even conscious thought. Robbie Dunbar was a man of character, and though that character had been flayed bitterly recently, it had found no way to honorably speak of his deep love to one woman while promised to another.

Consequently he stumbled a little. "Wha . . ." he began, his confusion and surprise showing in more than the color that flooded his face.

"Coom in, Robbie. Sit ye doon a bit, if ye will, and I'll tell ye wha's been happenin'."

Barney crept near, to be gathered into the circle of Robbie's arm and to eventually climb up on his lap while the story unfolded.

"So Quinn and Alice and Billy are probably in Prince Albert by now," she finished, "and should be startin' home anytime. I dinna ken what more a doctor can do than Quinn did, but he'll have ointment, I suppose. I tell ye, Robbie, we had reason to be grateful for those bottles o' Alice's—withoot 'em that puir bairn couldna put up wi' the pain."

"You say Quinn wouldna let Alice hae any o' the medicine hersel'?" Robbie asked. "How'd she seem, goin' off like that withoot it?"

"Once she got used to the idea, she seemed to pull hersel' together. Does she take that . . . that stuff all the time, Robbie?"

"Aye, all the time. An' she's a different person when she does—the laudanum makes her drowsy and slow, the cordial—well, she acts happy, cheerful, sort of. It takes a little gettin' used to, the change in personality from one time to another. I sometimes wonder if I've met the real Alice."

"Aye. I was thinkin' the same. Well, sit up and eat, Robbie. Come, Barney, climb into your own chair now and eat your supper."

For Robbie, sitting across the table from Tierney was both misery and ecstasy. Never had fried potatoes and onions tasted so like angels' fare, never had tea so much resembled nectar. As for the scones, a reminder of home, family, and Binkiebrae, they were lighter than clouds on a summer day.

More than once, almost overcome, Robbie dropped his eyes to his plate, swallowing convulsively and commanding his exhilarated pulse to be still as he made an effort to bring his heart's feelings into subjection to his head's wisdom. The one cried out for satisfaction, the other commanded duty.

Once, raising his head, he looked straight into the amber eyes of Tierney Caulder and was lost. Starting to his feet to—he knew not what—rush to her side, perhaps, he was halted by the swift averting of her eyes, and her quick "An' would ye like some more tatties, Robbie?"

Shaken at how nearly he had betrayed his word, Robbie sank back. Tierney fell silent, as though caught in the same torment of the moment.

Barney sat between them, slurping his milk and probably keeping restraint in the midst when desire threatened to put reason to rout.

Finally Tierney breathed deeply a few times and resumed eating, though it seemed her food, as his, had turned to sawdust in her mouth; even the scones failed to wheedle either of them to continue with their meal.

Was there ever a more unnatural, miserable situation! Sitting across the table from each other yet miles apart; lips locked while words threatened to tumble out. It was torture, Robbie concluded broodingly, and he savagely crumpled a scone in his fingers.

"Excuse me," he said eventually, preparing to rise from the table and flee the house. "I'll get on wi' the chores. Allan is takin' care o' ours, as he often does these days. Between us we manage to keep all three places goin'—his, mine, this one. You coomin' wi' me, Barney lad?"

"When y're done here, Robbie, will ye no' stop by the Blooms' on yer way home and tell 'em why Quinn and I aren't back yet?"

Robbie promised to do so.

When the buggy pulled into the yard and Quinn, Alice, and a sleeping Billy unloaded, quiet reigned in the Hoy house. It was clean and shining, a dozen jars of piccalilli gleamed in the lamp-light, Tierney sat reading by the same light, and Barney, in his much-washed and faded nightgown, slept on the nearby sofa.

But the kettle was simmering, and hastily Tierney poured water into the waiting teapot. Almost before the travelers had crossed the threshold, she was pulling scones from the warming oven, preparing to feed the weary adults when Billy should be carried up to his bed and Barney hugged and kissed and taken to bed also.

Over tea, Quinn and Alice told how the trip had gone—for them, and for Billy, who, with occasional drops of laudanum, had dozed his way to town and back.

"Lucky for us," Quinn said, "the doc was in, and sober. There was some squalling and battling from Billy, but Doc got the burns cleaned and fresh ointment put on, professional bandages. Gave us medication to bring home."

"It seems the burns aren't as bad as we thought. The water wasn't actually boiling," Alice explained in a strained voice, "though it was hot enough, goodness knows." She shuddered at the memory. "His eye, though, may have permanent damage. Oh, I pray not! I feel so responsible, so guilty—"

"Now, Alice," Quinn said gently, as though they had gone over this ground before, "nobody is blaming you; try not to blame yourself, all right? It was the chicken's squawk as much as anything that started the whole thing. Put it behind you, and get on with the healing." Whether hers or Billy's, Quinn didn't specify.

Alice, weary and somewhat disheveled, managed to look queenly as her small head lifted, her narrow shoulders squared, and a glint of determination lit her delicate face.

"It doesn't matter what you say, though you are very kind. I know I was responsible. And maybe it isn't such a bad thing to know, after all. I've . . . I've not been myself ever since Barnabas died. Maybe it's time to . . . to take hold again. As much, that is, as I'm able."

Remembering that Alice was far from being well and that she had put in a day that would have taxed a strong woman, Tierney was stricken at her own pettiness where the fatally ill woman was concerned. Getting to her feet, she hastily cleaned up the table and all signs of the midnight repast.

"Get to bed, Alice," she suggested. "Sleep while Billy sleeps, if you can."

If Quinn saw Alice's eyes stray to the cupboard and its empty corner, he didn't mention it. It was only after Alice had taken a lamp and gone upstairs that Quinn, ushering Tierney before him, blew out the table lamp and turned to the door and the tired horse waiting there.

Whether he was awakened by the passing rig or had been on the edge of a restless sleep, Robbie didn't know. But he tossed on his bed and knew without doubt it was Tierney and the manly, clean-cut, educated, capable, respectable, excellent—Robbie's galling evaluation went on and on—Quinn Archer, passing in the night. Together.

21

"S he hath done what she could,'" Pastor Parker Jones quoted. "Mark fourteen, verse eight.

"Our Sister Finnery," he said, "reminds me of the woman with the alabaster box of ointment, who broke it and poured its contents on the head of the Master. The Bible hints that it was all she was able to do—she did *what she could*. We know she did it freely, in spite of criticism."

The mourners—the good people of Bliss—nodded. A few wiped eyes damp with ready tears, a few murmured amen.

"Sister Finnery did what she could," Parker Jones continued, his own voice thick with the depth of his feeling. "It may not have been what other followers of Jesus did for Him, but she offered the Lord her best. Who among us will ever forget her vibrant witness? I, as her pastor, was often uplifted and encouraged by her simple words of cheer when we met. We all benefited from her Wednesday night testimonies. Even the hard places that she faced, life's difficult times, were touched and changed by her courage and her tenacious grip on God's promises."

In the little white schoolhouse, Jake, bereaved son, with no family member to comfort and sustain him, drooped sadly on a straight-backed chair in the front row, set out just ahead of the desks, sighing deeply from time to time. At his sides, two of the ladies of the congregation offered support, and other friends sat close by and all around, ready to do what they could but feeling sadly inadequate at this time of parting. Almost without exception they had been through the experience—and still they had no words to lighten the sorrow of others when it came to saying good-bye to a loved one.

"Jesus said that wherever the gospel would be preached, this woman's act—anointing Him for His burial—would be remembered. And we remember it today, even as He said. And it helps us. It helps us think on the life and deeds of another good woman—Sister Grace Finnery. And we know that God, even now, is welcoming her to her heavenly home. Just think of it, folks! Think of the heavenly home that Jesus has been preparing—"

Heads lifted, quivering lips were stilled; eyes saw beyond the battered desks, the handmade coffin, the work-worn congregation, and they envisioned, with the pastor, the "land that is fairer than day" and rejoiced, "and by faith we can see it afar."

They rose to their feet and sang it together . . .

> In the sweet by and by,
> We shall meet on that beautiful shore . . .

It was their promise and pledge.

Middle of the week though it was (bodies did not keep well in the heat of summer, and burials were speedy), the people of Bliss had laid aside the pressing need to gather and store before winter's icy blast would send them, like beavers, to shelter for the long, cold season. Pity the family with a death in winter! Often the corpse was shrouded and laid in state in a shed or granary, there to await the kinder, gentler season of spring, when spades went into the ground at last. And for reasons more than sowing; the Bliss cemetery population burgeoned, come spring.

His brief funeral talk concluded and the final prayer uttered, Parker Jones stepped to the side of Jake Finnery, there to speak words of comfort and consolation.

Arms straining and muscles bulging in the tight sleeves of their "Sunday" suits, four neighbors hefted the coffin of Sister Finnery to their shoulders and carried it through the schoolhouse and the hushed crowd, outside, and to a waiting wagon.

Parker Jones rode with Jake Finnery. What their conversation was on the trip to the cemetery, no one ever knew. But when they arrived, Jake's shoulders were back and his head up, and his puffed eyes, waiting one more spate of tears at the interment, were filled with peace. Parker himself was pale, worn, as though he had poured his strength into all that had been done this day and yet remained to be done.

"Ashes to ashes . . ." he said, and Jake and others dropped a handful of good Saskatchewan soil into the gaping hole wherein the coffin rested, reminding one and all of their mortality. So little time, so much to do! They turned as one person back to the heavy burden of living. . . .

Molly, along with her parents, stood silently at the side of the grave, sharing the moment of final parting with their neighbor and friend, Jake Finnery. Because the Finnery house was now so bereft, so vacant, the meal that followed such an occasion would be transferred to the Morrison home. Molly would need to hurry away from the cemetery to reach home before the crowd, to help Mam, her grandmother who had remained at home, put the finishing touches on the repast.

Before she moved to the family wagon, Molly turned toward Parker and found herself hesitating. Ordinarily she would have moved, confident and sure, to Parker's side, to squeeze his hand or pat his arm. *I'm here,* the touch would say, *and I care.*

But something, somehow, someway, had changed. Her very hesitation spoke of it. Grief, that was not for the day's bereavement, touched her eyes.

Silly! she said sternly and silently, reproaching herself for her own foolish imaginings, and she took a step toward Parker Jones.

Stepped, and stopped. Stepped toward Parker and the face he raised toward her, lit with welcome. Stopped when Vivian Condon moved, lightly and quickly in between, her attention fixed on the minister.

It was, after all, Vivian's hand that rested lightly, confidently, on the arm of Parker Jones. It was Vivian's face that turned up to his; it was her voice that stopped his move toward Jake and the Finnery rig.

To be honest, Parker turned startled eyes, perhaps guarded eyes, on the young woman who stood looking up at him, coquettish in spite of the occasion. This much Molly saw before she turned away.

"Do you remember—" Vivian began, almost intimately.

Parker's attention turned reluctantly from Molly to Vivian.

"Remember," she continued confidingly, "I mentioned that I had something to talk to you about? Well, now that this . . ."—and her hand waved to include people and cemetery and grave—"is over and done with, I would like so much to continue with the topic . . . which is—*very* important. Truly," she said persuasively, noting Parker's hesitation, "you'll find it so. I know you will."

"Today," Parker said, polite but firm, "is not a good day for it." The girl's persistence in the face of his duty toward Jake and his parishioners was surprising! Obviously she had little or no understanding of ecclesiastical concerns—

"Of course," she said smoothly, quickly, "I know you have grave responsibilities—*grave* responsibilities . . . oh!" and Vivian put a gloved hand to her mouth to stifle the indiscretion that, she seemed to confess, was most naughty of her.

Parker Jones watched the slim back of Molly Morrison out of sight and felt a fury toward this stranger to the community who, by her very presence, had rather successfully exacerbated the restlessness he was already feeling in regard to his call to the ministry.

Under the gaze of nearby Herkimer Pinkard, watching with keen eyes from the farther side of his horse, Parker managed, gently enough, to remove the clinging hand from his arm, and say, "Another time, Miss Condon—Vivian. Now I really must go; Jake Finnery needs me, I believe."

"But we *will* talk, won't we?" she persisted. "Perhaps when we all get to the Morrisons'. Would that be a good time to talk . . . later on?"

"Yes, of course. Now, if you'll excuse me. I believe your uncle and aunt are waiting for you."

Parker turned toward Jake, who was receiving the last hugs and damp sympathies of the dispersing group, and together they mounted his buggy and wended their way toward the Morrison homestead. The day was flitting away, and soon every male there, and most females, would be called to the urgency of the chores awaiting them. Life would go on for these who remained in the bush, though one of their number had exchanged her cross for her crown. "Remember Sister Finnery . . ." they would say, and say it less and less as the days came and went and as the immediate burdens of life dimmed their vision of things other-worldly.

"Allow me," a masculine voice said in Vivian's ear.

Startled, about to clamber into her uncle's wagon where Bly and Beatrice waited, Vivian's head jerked around to see at her side the large form of Herkimer Pinkard.

Reaching a callused, hairy hand, Herkimer took hold of Vivian's elbow, firmly gripping it and lifting, helping her to the hub of the wagon wheel and on up over the wheel into the wagon box. Her assent was so fast it could almost be compared to dandelion fluff being tossed into the air.

Vivian's hat, set awry by the motion, was tipped over one eye, an eye that was quickly changing from startled to angry.

"I'll thank you—" she spluttered, then stopped in the face of Herkimer's innocent expression.

"You're welcome, I'm sure," he said politely, doffing his hat and stepping back. "I expect I'll be seeing you over at the Morrison place."

"Nice fellow, Pinkard," her uncle said reflectively as Vivian breathed deeply a few times and settled herself on the wagon seat.

"He's nothing but a bumpkin, a country bumpkin!" Vivian fumed. Then, noting a strange expression on Uncle Bly's face, added quickly, "Not that the country has anything to do with it. He'd be a bumpkin no matter where he was . . ."

"Maybe," Bly said briefly, "maybe not."

At any rate, Herkimer's buggy followed the Condon wagon in the small cortege making its way from the cemetery to the Morrison home and the abundance spread there. Glancing back once, Vivian was chagrined to have Herkimer lift his head, smile largely, and wave, almost coyly.

"Yokel . . ." she muttered, her face flushing.

Beatrice, at Vivian's side, looked uncomfortable, and Vivian subsided. Why had she come to the funeral anyway! She didn't know the bereaved man and had only seen the deceased woman from across the room at church. Vivian sighed. What a bore—when attending a funeral offered entertainment in the dullness of one's existence! And yet it had given her the opportunity to speak to the good-looking man of the cloth—Parker Jones, a challenge if she had ever met one.

Parker Jones's integrity and moral ethics were part of that challenge. Here was a man who professed virtue, honor, scruples—but underneath, would he be like the men of the world who were part of her circle back home?

Vivian, not accustomed to challenges, was becoming a little weary of this one and the slowness of the progress she had made. If the handsome minister could not be wooed and won by feminine wiles, what would it take? Money? Prestige?

"Hmmmm . . ." Vivian half-crooned, wondering, thinking, planning.

The wagon made its rattling journey along a Bliss road hemmed in places by pressing bush, open in other areas to fields becoming burnished with golden grain, and the girl was oblivious to it all. She fretted over the dust that rose and settled on her clothes and was blind to the goldenrod nodding by the side of the road; she waved away the flies that accompanied the horses and the wagon and was deaf to the plaintive, penetrating cry of the killdeer; she wrinkled her elegant nose over the smell of warm horse flesh while the potpourri of the bush escaped her.

How could Herkimer, who had been behind them, get his horse tied up at the Morrison fence and be at the side of the Condon wagon when Vivian was ready to descend? Yet he was. His big face beaming, his red-gold beard glinting in the sunshine, his shoulders covered with dust, his hat on the back of his head, he reached a hand upward to the girl preparing to climb down, a move as treacherous as the climb up had been. Pausing, she saw, this time, how the sun glistened on the thick mat of hair on the back of his hand and shuddered visibly.

Heavens! What a bull moose he was!

If there was a glint in Herkimer's eyes, Vivian, in her agitation, failed to notice it.

Holding to the wagon she ignored the hand and reached a leg over the side, furious that he should stand there and watch her in this undignified pose. Why couldn't these rubes have carriages like civilized folk!

She should have taken his hand. Her foot, searching for the hub, missed it, and with a small shriek she plummeted toward the ground. Plummeted and would have fallen except for the strong arms of Herkimer Pinkard.

"Whoops!" he said, catching her, holding her . . .

"Let me down!" she ordered, her hat atilt once again, her skirts in disarray, her face flushed and damp.

If Herkimer's bushy beard touched the scarlet cheek for an instant before he set her on her feet, who was to say? No word of hers gave it away, and no one at all noticed the reappearing glint in the narrowed eyes of the man.

"Careful!" her aunt instructed. "You could take a nasty tumble if you don't watch!"

174

"There you are, Missy," Herkimer said smoothly, setting the irate woman on her feet, standing back, his head cocked, his lips smiling, his eyes admiring.

Vivian, without waiting for her aunt and uncle, flounced her way into the house. Here people were already filling plates, some to return to the yard and seats set up there, some to stand around the walls, a few to find chairs.

Molly was busy at the table, helping fill plates, pouring drinks, engaged in conversation with the friends passing through the line. Nevertheless, she noted Vivian's entrance and, in spite of herself, her heart sank. Clearly Vivian was looking for someone—Parker Jones, of course. For as soon as she spotted him she began weaving her way through the crowd toward the corner where he stood, leaning against the wall, watching Molly.

Watching Molly Morrison! Vivian's lips tightened. As slender as she was, it was no chore to slip between people. It was a wonder, then, that Herkimer Pinkard, as large as he was, had, once again, managed to precede her. Vivian, within a few steps of her goal, found her nose pressed against a broad chest, a chest that smelled disgustingly of horse and man. Wrinkling that delicate feature she raised her gaze impatiently to find herself looking into the placid face of Herkimer. Again!

She stepped to the right; Herkimer was there. She moved left; Herkimer was there.

Though he spoke quietly into the hubbub of the chattering group, she heard him clearly: "'All the thoughts of a turtle are turtles; and of a rabbit, rabbits.'"

"Whatever is that supposed to mean?" she asked furiously.

"Just recalling something I read once. I think a man named Emerson said it. I thought you might find it amusing."

She looked at him blankly. "Amusing—you? Laughable, maybe, but amusing? Think again! Now, will you let me pass?"

"You've passed the table, that's what you've passed. Now come, Miss Condon. Let me help you into the line . . . here, take a plate."

With his big hand once again under her elbow, lifting, propelling her forward, Vivian had no choice but to dance on tiptoe to the table. Helplessly she took the plate put into her hands, helplessly she was herded along the display of food . . .

"I was wondering," Herkimer behind her was saying, bending low, speaking intimately into her ear, "if you would do me the honor of allowing me to drive you home?"

I hate oatmeal!" Barney said crossly, mixing the thick serving his mother had set before him, stirring in a generous helping of brown sugar and good, rich milk until his breakfast was more a soup than a porridge.

"Why, Barney," Alice said reproachfully, "you've never said that before, and we have oatmeal every morning."

"That's why I hate it. I'm tired of it. Sick and tired of it."

Barney's rising tones and the use of the unaccustomed, unchildish phrase, startled his mother. Uneasily she wondered if she used it, more, perhaps, than she should. It wasn't the only matter she had been pondering recently.

"Yes," the small boy repeated, relishing the words, "sick and tired of it. Sick and tired. Sick—"

"All right, I hear you. You're sick and tired of oatmeal. Eat it anyway."

It wasn't as if there was any choice. Breakfast, on the home-steads of the vast area that was becoming known as the prairie provinces and settled largely by immigrants counting themselves fortunate to have anything at all to eat, was usually oatmeal. Yes, and it was oatmeal for too many dinners and suppers for many a frustrated bachelor. Coming in from a long day's work, with no wife to do the womanly things, and with no meal ready and perhaps only a few coals alive in the range, oatmeal was a quick and simple solution after the fire had been roused to life again.

Oatmeal for breakfast, however, was a staple. Oatmeal "stuck to your ribs." At five years of age, Barney had had a lifetime of breakfast oatmeal.

Bacon and eggs would have been a fine alternative, and eggs were in vast supply. But bacon? In summer? No one butchered in summer—there was no way to keep the meat from spoiling. One could hang only so much in a pail down the well, and that space was needed for milk and butter. A few fortunate families had an icehouse; dug into a hillside, it was filled, in winter, with ice from the lake and smothered in sawdust and usually lasted throughout the summer months, offering a way to keep food—meat particularly—fresh, even frozen.

Alice studied the rebellious face before her, tousled her son's unruly mop of hair, and suggested eggs. "I'll be happy to cook them for you," she said. "A poached egg, maybe?"

Barney made a face. Billy, in his high chair across the table, gravely spooned up his porridge with his good hand, the left arm still bandaged. His face, however, was free of the bandages that had annoyed him endlessly and at which he had picked and pulled until Alice had removed them. Air was good for the burn, it was supposed, and it *was* healing, leaving scarlet patches over the left side of his face. No one knew how well or how poorly he saw from that eye; he was impatient with testing, jerking his head away and refusing to say what he saw and what he didn't see.

Barney, it seemed, was as sick of eggs as of oatmeal.

Alice pressed a hand to her middle, drew a few deep breaths, and cast a desperate eye toward the corner cupboard. Only she—and Quinn Archer—knew how barren it was. Still, turning toward it, she scrabbled blindly in its depths, coming up, half sobbing, empty-handed. After a moment's thought, she ran for an ancient bag hanging on a nail with coats and sweaters by the door. Feeling it, her eyes lit, and she reached a greedy hand inside. Unsteady now in her excitement, she withdrew a dark bottle, held it up to the light, observed its half-contents and, flushed and victorious, withdrew the cork, taking a long and satisfactory swallow of the contents. Recorking it, she leaned momentarily against the wall, eyes closed, the paleness receding from her face, her breathing steadying.

Barney banged his spoon loudly on the tabletop, drumlike.

"That's enough, Barney," Alice said, straightening herself, turning toward the boys.

Barney was making strange noises, loud noises, silly noises.

"Eat your porridge," Alice said unsteadily.

"Shan't."

Barney stopped playing with his breakfast, sat on his hands, and set his small face in determined lines. What was wrong with the child! He had been more or less unmanageable for . . . well, since Barnabas died.

Where, oh where, was Robbie! Often, when the boys' antics were too much for their mother, she turned them over to the handling of Robbie Dunbar. She, Alice, had been incapacitated (a good word, she thought guiltily) ever since the loss of her husband, surely an understandable and excusable reason. The boys, and Barney in particular, had caught on to her spells of . . . of weakness and took advantage of them.

"I guess, then, you won't be able to help Robbie today," Alice offered as a desperate ploy. "He'll be disappointed."

Barney looked up uncertainly.

"A weak, hungry boy doesn't have any strength. I thought you were going to ride the rake with him this morning. Too bad—"

One hand came free, hovered over the spoon, grasped it, and slowly stirred the despised porridge.

But he didn't give in easily. "Why can't we buy that Cerealine stuff?" he asked sulkily.

"Cerealine Flakes? They cost a lot of money. Fifteen cents a box in fact."

Barney's face was mulish.

"I'll tell you what—why don't you try and find old Biddy's nest hidden out there somewhere in the bush and gather the eggs and take them to the store and sell them. Maybe you'll have enough money to buy a box of Cerealine Flakes. I think there may be other secret nests . . . I hear cackling out there in the bush every day, don't you? You could be," she inserted cleverly, "a big game hunter in search of prey."

Barney, pondering the suggestion, was intrigued, in spite of himself. While he gave his mind to the idea of stealthy searches, moneymaking, and cereal buying, his spoon rose automatically to his mouth.

"How about that Granula?" he asked, not giving up entirely, gulping a mouthful of porridge and allowing a little excitement and hope to filter into his voice. "The stuff in the catalog—the stuff you read about."

True, at one of their catalog-studying sessions—a favorite pastime—they had lingered over the "Farinaceous Goods." Listed along with flour, popcorn, beans, barley, corn meal, farina, hominy, and the ubiquitous oatmeal—fine ground, medium steel cut, coarse steel cut, Scotch ground, rolled—was the mystifying Granula. "One of the best known foods for infants and children. It is thrice cooked and will keep for years," was the promise. Why would it last for years if it was tasty, Alice wondered privately.

"I remember the Granula," Alice answered now. "Sell enough eggs, Barney, and you can try that, too, if you wish. We'll have to check the catalog and see how much it costs."

Barney began a scramble from his chair in the direction of the catalog, never far away.

"Hold on, young man! The porridge? Finish it first."

It didn't take long now. Barney shoveled oatmeal into his mouth, cleaning his bowl in seconds, wiping his mouth on the back of his hand, and returning to his pursuit of the catalog.

He paused, abashed, "But I can't read!"

"Just look through it until you find the proper page," Alice said, reaching for his bowl and spoon, preparing to wipe up his spills and make a clean place to lay the cherished book. "It's near the front with the other foods—tea, coffee, spices, canned and bottled goods, things like that." With almost 800 pages, that should keep the child quiet for a while!

"And I can pick out the Granula by its picture. It has heads of wheat on it."

"That's right. And you know your numbers, so you can figure out how much it costs." (Twelve cents a package, if her memory served her properly.)

Barney was engrossed in his search; it didn't matter how long it took, the search itself was satisfying.

But as so often happened, he lingered over men's watches, pages and pages of pictured watches—14 karat, gold plate, silverine case, solid coil silver, hunting case, glass on both sides, 18-size, screw back and bezel, dust proof, engraved, thin model, and the awesome timers and chronographs. Barney knew them all, knew them by sight, by description, knew them by name: Trenton, Appleton, Crescent Street, New Railway, Special Railway, Vanguard, Boss, Giant Elgin, and more.

He had a preference, a strong hankering, for the "Glass on both sides," model.

"'You can see the movement in your watch at any time without opening the case,'" he had memorized.

"It's a man's watch, Barney," his mother had said dampingly at one of his dream and scheme times.

"But you said," Barney reminded her quickly, "that it is 'spesh'lly strong!"

Alice had sighed but had to agree. "'Don't be afraid that they are not strong enough,'" the catalog had assured, and she had been foolish enough to read aloud, "'for we believe that if they were placed on the floor, they would support the weight of an ordinary man without breaking.'"

"Do you s'pose it would hold Herkimer?" Barney had asked, marveling at the catalog's claim and longing to test it.

"It says *ordinary* man, Barney," Alice had explained, and Barney had subsided, for the moment.

"Well, Robbie then."

Ordinary Robbie. It was true. Robbie—in Alice's estimation—was ordinary. Perhaps that was why she had had the courage to approach him with her momentous proposal—to marry in order to leave the homestead and the boys in good hands. Thinking about it now, Alice took a deep breath and assured herself that it didn't matter whether he was ordinary or out-of-the-ordinary—love was not involved. And wouldn't she, after all, be joining Barnabas soon in the great beyond, forever free of anxiety and responsibility and heartbreak?

Shaking herself, Alice put doubts away from her concerning her agreement with Robbie Dunbar. She had made her decision.

Barney was still poring over the catalog, detoured from his search for Granula. This fetish of his for watches was unsettling; Barney had a way of putting his mind to something and clinging to it grimly, willing it to come true by his very persistence. In a contest of wills, Barney had the edge these days.

"It wouldn't *have* to be the one with glass on both sides," he said wistfully and quoted, "though 'nothing is more fas . . . fascin-a . . . ting than seeing its different parts, such as train wheels, the pallet, the hair spring—'"

"Oh, Barney, must you go over all that again?"

"'An' the balance wheel,'" Barney quoted without pause, "'which makes eighteen thousand beats per hour, four hundred and thirty-two thousand per day or'—read this for me, Mum. About the millions of times it beats per year, I mean."

"Forget the watches, Barney—"

"One million . . . read it, Mum!"

"No, Barney, I'm not going to read it again. Who do you suppose counts that many ticktocks, anyway? It's a lot of foolishness—"

Barney looked stricken.

"It wouldn't have to be this one, Mum. But it's almost the cheapest one in the book. See, it's only $4.25 for seven jewels with Seth Thom . . ."

"Seth Thomas," Alice provided reluctantly, proud of her son's memory and sorry for her foolishness in aiding and abetting his fantasies.

"Seth Thomas movement. What's a movement, Mum? Does that mean works?"

"I think you're giving *me* the works," Alice said, with a firmness she hadn't shown for a long time. "Now give your attention to something else."

Barney, recognizing the authority, cocked his head on one side, listened as to some distant drumbeat, and slowly turned from the fascinating watches.

"The Granula, son?" his mother prodded.

With a sigh Barney moved on.

Before he had located the proper page the door opened and Robbie leaned in.

"Good mornin'! Is there a laddie in here thass goin' to work wi' me today?"

With a joyous squeal Barney climbed from his chair and flung himself at Robbie.

"Me! It's me, remember? You said I could ride the rake with you!"

"So I did. An' are ye ready then?"

Robbie closed the door behind him and moved into the room, going first to the side of Billy, to caress his head lightly and pat his good arm. Billy ate on placidly, reduced now to the stage where his small finger swiped the inside of the bowl, scooping out the last of the porridge.

Alice retrieved the bowl and substituted a piece of toast.

"And how are ye this mornin'?" Robbie asked, turning at last to Alice.

And it was with reluctance. The hesitation he was feeling regarding marriage to Alice—to *anyone* other than Tierney Caulder—was turning, in his troubled heart, to grim certainty that this was wrong. All wrong! And yet he was bound by his word. *God help me!* he cried and not for the first time.

But God—if He heard and if He cared—was silent. Was it, Robbie wondered uneasily, because he, Robbie, really wasn't on speaking terms with the Lord of the universe?

Robbie had no trouble believing that God was indeed Lord of the universe. But anything more personal—that was harder to grasp.

And was he, Robbie, in any position to claim a personal relationship with God? Didn't one need an *introduction* to Him or something like that? Robbie, at his prayer times, brief and desperate as they were, felt like a voice crying in the wilderness, a wilderness of ignorance and blindness.

But for the first time in his life Robbie Dunbar was attending church with some regularity. True, his purpose was to get a glimpse of Tierney, but the Word, sown faithfully by the pastor, was being planted and, as promised, some of it fell on good ground—the ground of his empty heart—and took root. New at farming, still Robbie could grasp the concept of rooting and sprouting.

Robbie felt the stirrings of the new growth and, at times, pondered the seed. Now, thinking of his miserable fix where Alice Hoy and her property were concerned and his need for peace about it all, he recalled Pastor Parker Jones's recent sowing— "Come unto me, all ye that labor and are heavy laden, and I will give you rest" (Matt. 11:28).

Needing the rest—badly needing the rest—he hadn't done the coming. "Come unto me," Jesus had said. This must be the invitation to the introduction.

But this was a workday morning and no time to ponder Scripture; it was no time to question his arrangement with Alice.

With a sigh Robbie turned to the work that awaited him, and him alone.

"Come along, laddie," he said. And to Alice, "Maybe there could be a bite of sum'mat at noon . . . if ye feel up to it? That way I can keep on wi' the rakin', hopefully gettin' done today."

But it was not to be. Having barely begun, Barney perching happily on Robbie's lap, it became obvious that something was wrong.

Robbie and Barney climbed down and examined the dumping mechanism.

"This lock lever is as perfect as they come," Herkimer had said. "And the teeth should raise easily with a slight movement of the foot."

The teeth—twenty shining steel teeth—seemed to grin wickedly at Robbie, stubbornly refusing to dump.

"Practically a self-dumper, is it?" Robbie fumed, quoting Herkimer. "Well, Barney, lad, it looks like I've got to try and free up this lock system. Or somethin'."

Already wise in some ways and cautious about injury so far from a doctor, Robbie unhitched the team from the mower, not about to have twenty shining steel teeth take an unexpected bite out of his anatomy.

Barney watched for a while. Robbie, grim-faced, was fiddling with the dumping mechanism.

"What about me, Robbie?" the boy asked, restless and whining.

"Ah, laddie . . . why'nt ye run an' get me a drink o' cold water. That'd taste good aboot now. There's a fine mannie . . ."

Barney turned away, a mutinous expression on his face.

Noontime came, and Robbie was no nearer an answer to the mower's problem than when it happened. Wiping the perspiration from his brow, he turned toward the house, and dinner.

"Is there a problem?" Alice asked brightly as he stepped into the house, and Robbie, who was beginning to know her well, recognized the effect of her "medicine." Moreover, on the table, laid out ready for him to take to the post office, was an envelope addressed to the catalog's headquarters.

Though Barney had rattled on about chicken eggs and catalog orders, Robbie was quite sure the order was not for Granula.

"Where is the spalpeen?" he asked, missing Barney's welcome.

"Isn't he with you?"

"Na na. The mower broke down, and I've been workin' on it for a coupla hours."

Alice sat down heavily onto a kitchen chair. "Then where is he? What do you suppose he's up to?"

C ome, Molly," Grandma Kezzie wheedled. "Lay aside your work for a few moments and sing for me."

"Mam" Kezzie Skye had lived a long life without knowing the saving grace of the Lord Jesus Christ. She was a newcomer to His blessings, and all His springs flowed joyously through her ancient body and lifted her old heart to realms never known before, and only imagined. Not able to do much physically herself, she was now coaxing her granddaughter to pause in the day's activities and take a moment to worship. And what better way than by song?

Being Molly's confidante to some extent, and observant as well, Mam knew something was bothering her "bairn." It didn't take much insight to suppose it had to do with Parker Jones. If Molly could be brought to a decision to cast her worry on the Lord, she could once again go smiling about the house, a joy to all who knew her.

"Good suggestion," Molly said, brushing a wisp of her vibrant black hair out of her eyes and laying aside the butter mold—such labors would keep; Mam would not always be with her. But oh, praise God!—they were united in praise as in purpose now, and a few minutes to remind themselves of this would do them both good.

Sitting at the little pump organ, pedaling steadily and running her fingers over the keys, Molly's hymn choice began satisfactorily:

> Awake, my soul, to joyful lays,
> And sing thy great redeemer's praise,
> He justly claims a song from me—
> His loving-kindness, O how free!

Molly sang, lifting her voice and her eyes heavenward; Mam hummed along, her spirit soaring.

But there came a verse that, in spite of good intentions, rang with dire truth and hollow praise:

> When trouble, like a gloomy cloud,
> Has gathered thick and thundered loud,
> He near my soul has always stood—

Trouble, like a gloomy cloud. Molly's hands fell from the keyboard to her lap. Her head bowed, her slender shoulders shook, and even from her chair Mam could see the tears sparkling on her lashes, breaking free, and running down her face.

"Come, love," Mam said gently, and Molly slipped from the stool to her grandmother's side, falling onto the rug at her feet and laying her dark head on her Mam's knees.

With a gesture as old as motherhood, Kezzie stroked Molly's forehead, brushing back the lively hair lovingly. With the other hand she tendered a handkerchief, and Molly mopped her tears.

"I'm just being silly, I know," Molly sniffled at last, her voice muffled in her grandmother's skirt. "But, Mam, I was so sure—

so certain that God wanted me to be a preacher's wife. I felt as called, in my way, as . . . as—"

The tears threatened again. Eventually Molly drew a deep breath and straightened herself to continue with her thought.

"You know, Mam, that Parker, like other ministers I've heard about, referred to his 'call.' It brought him here, to Bliss, with definite purpose. He seemed, at first, so sure of himself. Then there came this little nibble of uncertainly—it happened when Henley Baldwin died, you remember, and Parker learned of the miserable life he had led with Della and hadn't even known about. He blamed himself for not being involved enough in his parishioners' lives. That's where it all started—this questioning, wondering, this dissatisfaction."

"Aye," Kezzie, Scottish through and through, said in her thick brogue, "I ken."

"And now another death and more questions. This time, he was off . . . off somewhere with that . . . girl."

And fresh tears threatened.

"Aye." There was no use Kezzie denying what she already knew to be true. "Aye," she said again, "an' he's struggling with his conscience, feels he failed Sister Finnery and God."

"We all make mistakes . . . if it was a mistake."

"Aye. I think it was a mistake, a' reet. And I think that's what has his heart so twisted and his opinion o' himsel' so low."

"His whole ministry is in question, Mam. His ministry . . . and my future. He'll be here soon, and I don't know how to help him. I can't give him any advice when my heart is . . . is so torn up over it all.

"You see, Mam," she continued earnestly, "regardless of what he does, I've got to know what's right for *me*. That's the only way I'll have any peace. Pray with me, Mam!"

Two curly heads, so much alike except that one was black and the other white, bent in earnest petition to the One whose Word advised, "Give diligence to make your calling and election sure."

And, as always happens when hearts are sincere and willing to trust, rest came, with the assurance *This is the way, walk ye in it!*

"I know what's right for me," Molly said eventually, getting to her feet, her voice calm and her eyes peaceful. "And that's enough."

This assurance held her steady when she and Parker, late in the afternoon, walked down the lane side by side.

"It's so peaceful," Parker said, breathing deeply. "At moments like this I wonder why I wrestle so with my call. This seems God's perfect plan for me, and Bliss seems like the ideal place. And then . . ."

"Then," Molly supplied, "the tempter comes with his suggestions and his lies."

"Do you really think it's that? Can it be that simple? Is that why I have these terrible moments of doubt—about myself, about Bliss, about—"

"About me, Parker?" Molly asked quietly.

"Never! Never about you, Molly," Parker said, and said it with such passion that the small misery that Molly had been carrying around in her heart was stilled.

"About the future. The future that I want to be yours as well as mine . . . our future, Molly."

"And what is that future, Parker? *Where* is that future?"

"That's what I'm struggling with, of course."

"You'll find the answer, I know you will. You have so much ability, Parker, so much to offer, and a long life ahead of you in which to serve God's people. No wonder Satan tries to sidetrack you! Can you just hold steady until the answer comes, clear and simple?"

"I have no choice," Parker said simply. "I'm miserable this way. I've got to come to some conclusions. Will you wait with me, Molly, and pray with me?"

"Yes—to both."

Parker reached out, almost as a drowning man, and took the slim hand that was waiting for him.

"Show me, Lord!" he said, and it was half groan, half prayer.

Molly's squeeze was reassuring. The walk back to the house was peaceful, their hearts lighter than they had been for a long while.

"Now," Parker said reluctantly, "I've got to go to the Condons'. It's been hanging over my head like a dark cloud for days. I don't know what that girl—Vivian—has in mind, but she won't let up until I go by there and listen to her. Maybe," he said, without much hope, "she is interested in salvation."

"Maybe," Molly repeated and hoped her skepticism didn't show.

———

Through the kitchen window Molly saw Parker's return as he rode back up the lane. Horse and rider moved briskly; if looks spoke at all, it had been a satisfying meeting. Perhaps some serious spiritual business had indeed been attended to. Somehow she doubted that, but thinking it, her heart reproached her.

Molly went outside to greet him. Parker swung from the back of the horse, tossed the reins over a post provided for the purpose, and turned toward Molly. "Let's sit down somewhere," he said.

Beyond the garden was a large poplar, and it was on the grass under this tree that Molly and Parker settled themselves. Angus, at the barn, waved and went about his duties. Somewhere a calf bawled, and then silence reigned.

Molly eyed Parker cautiously. What could possibly have happened to perk him up so? She felt quite certain that Parker was not drawn physically to Vivian Condon. What then did the girl use, almost like some magic spell, to disrupt his life?

She waited for him to speak. Parker, on the verge of doing so, seemed restless, shrugging himself into place, drawing up his knees, putting them down again, leaning back on his elbows, straightening up, plucking grass, and tossing it loose without thought.

"I had supposed," he began, "when I left here, that things were getting more settled in my mind, that I was close to a decision. Now . . . I don't know . . ."

Still she waited. Her own peace of mind, so recently sought and won, should not be disturbed, nor her conclusions changed.

Challenged, perhaps, but not changed. Molly felt she knew the Lord's will—for her.

"She—Vivian, that is—didn't have a personal need or problem that she wanted to talk about," Parker said finally, opening the subject that was on both their minds.

"No?"

"What she had was . . . this." Parker pulled an envelope from his pocket, held it in his hand uncertainly.

Molly made no move to take it. Rather, she looked at Parker steadily, waiting for him to make what explanations he would.

"It's a letter from Mount Moriah. Have you heard of Mount Moriah, Molly?"

"In the Bible—"

"Not that Mount Moriah. This one is located on Prince Edward Island, near the city of Summerside. It's not a mount, of course, but a . . . place named for the biblical Mount Moriah. Actually," Parker cleared his throat, "actually, it's a Bible school. That's why I thought you may have heard of it."

"No, I never have."

"No reason why you should have. There are a few Bible schools dotted over the country now; this one is the most easterly. It offers two-year courses to young people wanting to prepare for Christian work. Anyway," Parker turned the full gaze of his dark eyes on Molly, "this letter is an offer to join the faculty."

"I don't understand," Molly said slowly. "Why would they offer you a place? How did they hear about you? What's the . . . the connection?" Asking, Molly thought she knew, and she returned his gaze steadily.

"It's Vivian, of course. She has an uncle who is on the board of regents there, or some such place of responsibility. She recommended me—"

Vivian had been two months or so in Bliss, and she recommended him?

So thought Molly. What she said was, "And what is your reaction?"

"Molly, it may be the answer to my cry! Think of it—just when I'm so full of uncertainties, here comes this—"

"This 'out'?" Molly wanted to say but didn't. Being so sure, so very sure of her own place in God's plan, she could afford to be quiet. Parker Jones would have to find his answer for himself.

"Just think of it, Molly—a teacher! A teacher of the Bible! Helping young people get ready to serve the Lord. And, Molly—"

"What else?"

"A salary. Not large but regular. Large enough to get married on! What do you think of that, Molly?" Parker's voice bordered on exultant; certainly it was urgent, hopeful. His eyes, turned on Molly, were bright and questioning.

"It sounds . . ." Not knowing how to answer, Molly's feeble response faded away to nothing.

"It could be our answer, Molly!"

"*Our* answer, Parker? Do you mean . . . what I mean is . . ."

Parker had spoken words of devotion before this. He had broached the subject of marriage, he had walked all around it—the pros and cons, the inadequacy of the small house, the uncertain salary—but this was the first time he had put it into anything definite.

"I mean, Parker . . . is this a proposal?"

"It is! Molly—will you marry me? I love you, Molly girl! Will you go with me to Mount Moriah? What do you say, darlin' Molly?"

It's Rob Dunbar," Lydia said, laying aside her book and pulling back the lace curtain at her side.

Incapacitated much of the time with her aching joints, Lydia would have much preferred to be crocheting, or knitting, or engaged in tasks she felt were constructive and helpful. Reading! It was for idle hours—and who, in their right mind, could expect any of those?

Still, she was reduced to sitting, rocking, flexing her twisted fingers gently, hoping and praying for better health, trying to do a little mending, and reading. In the meantime, she thanked God daily for Tierney Caulder. Not only was she a willing worker but a cheerful, pleasant person, made more so, no doubt, by the One who indwelt her.

But how long, Lydia thought with a sigh, could they keep her with them? Lydia sometimes watched the faces of Tierney and Quinn Archer, looking for signs of a secret attraction, for some clue that there was some magic at work between them. Quinn was a gem of a man, capable and reliable. Quinn would make a wonderful husband and father. He was mature, seasoned, thoughtful, a man of humor and wisdom. And fine looking!

At times Lydia was sure she intercepted a glance that was more than casual between her two hired people. Being an inveterate romantic at the core of her staid English being, Lydia found opportunities, *made* opportunities, for Quinn and Tierney to be together—sending Tierney to the barn or field with messages, arranging for Tierney and Quinn to make trips to Bliss together, occasionally seeing them off to church alone when her health forbade her going and she persuaded Herbert to stay with her.

Now, having announced the rider who was approaching the house at a gallop, Lydia turned to study Tierney: slender, taller than many women of the day, with curves in all the right places (Lydia knew where they should be, though she couldn't boast of them herself), a mass of auburn hair that continually strayed from its pins to riot in abandon around a face that was piquant, Tierney was filled with the love of life and smiled often. Yes, Quinn Archer would be blind and dumb not to see what was set deliciously before his very eyes every day.

Just now, her hands in a dishpan of hot, soapy water, washing up the noon dishes, Tierney's lips were moving, as though she were praying, perhaps. And that was best of all—Tierney Caulder, not too long ago, had given her life to the Lord Jesus Christ and knew Him on a personal basis. Her witness was bright and clear, her mind and heart fervent in their devotion.

With a start Tierney lifted her head. "Who . . . who is it?"

"Robbie Dunbar. I wonder what he's doing here this time of day. And in a hurry, too," Lydia said.

Even as she spoke, Robbie was springing from the horse's back, striding across the porch, knocking at the door.

In a wink Tierney had it opened.

"Robbie . . ."

"It's Barney," Robbie said, stepping quickly into the house. "I've come for help. Barney is lost—"

"The little boy?" Lydia inserted rather blankly, being caught so completely by surprise.

"Aye, Alice's son, Barney. He's jist five years old, and he's lost."

"Lost?—"

"Somewhere in the bush, we suppose."

"O Lord . . ." Lydia breathed, and it was a prayer. How often she had worried and prayed over her own small grandson on the prairie, that God would keep him from wandering away in that unending sea of grass. It happened. Many were the stories of people—adults and children—lost on the prairie, lost in blizzards, lost, yes, lost in the bush. That it should happen here!

"There isna time to tell you all aboot it," Robbie said desperately. "We looked the best we could, and when it seemed he wasna in the farmyard, we knew we needed help. I stopped at Allan's, and he's headed over to help look. Can someone from here—Quinn maybe—give us a hand?"

Robbie's usually bronzed face was white and taut with anxiety.

"Of course! Tierney, run and get Quinn. Tell him to hitch up the buggy, and you better go with him."

For once Lydia had no secret motive in sending Quinn and Tierney off together; her concern for the lost child was uppermost in her mind.

Robbie was already turning toward his horse, mounting, heading out. "I'll stop by Herkimer's, too. Thank you—" And he was gone in a cloud of dust, pounding down the road.

Tierney and Quinn pulled into the Hoy yard to find Alice, half collapsed, leaning against the post on the porch, Billy beside her, sucking a thumb, looking solemn.

"Any luck?" Quinn asked after alighting from the buggy. Tierney hurried after him to Alice's side. Putting her arm around the trembling woman, Tierney persuaded her to sit on the step.

"No, there's no sign of him. Allan is out in the woods somewhere. I've looked everywhere . . . everywhere except—" Alice's eyes turned fearfully toward the well.

What a thought! In spite of reluctance to consider such a possibility, all three adults turned apprehensive eyes on the well. Quinn cleared his throat.

"I'll check it," he said.

"Come inside," Tierney urged, feeling Alice could withstand no more. Alice complied, moving, under the pressure of Tierney's guiding hands, into the house, sagging into an overstuffed chair.

When Quinn reported that the well was clear, thrusting his head in the door to do so, Alice whispered, "Thank God. Well, then, it's got to be the bush. We've looked everywhere else."

Almost immediately Robbie and Herkimer were galloping into the yard, to be met by the news that there was no news.

"Which way did Allan go?" Robbie asked, but Alice seemed not to know. "He tied up his horse and just headed out . . . somewhere."

"We three will start—one this way, one that way, one over there," Robbie said, "but I think maybe you better stay wi' Alice, Tierney. A' reet?"

Tierney nodded and headed for the stove to build the fire, boil the kettle, and apply the calming properties of a soothing cup of tea.

The three men started out blindly, doing the only thing they knew to do. Clattering off the porch, they scattered out toward the bush that pressed the farmyard on three sides, the road making the fourth.

"Hey, fellas! Alice! Tierney!" It was a shout from Herkimer Pinkard.

Robbie and Quinn, about to slip into the circling bush, paused and turned. Alice heard and opened her eyes and made an effort to struggle to her feet; Tierney left the teapot and hurried to the door.

In the fading light of the sun, standing in the open barn door—a small figure.

Barney stood, alone and forlorn, while the searchers gathered round him. Robbie and Quinn strode toward the barn from the edge of the bush; Tierney and Alice—suddenly invigorated and flying toward her son on light feet—came from the house. Herkimer, the first to reach the child, stood looking down on him.

About to snatch the small boy up into her arms, the others standing in a semicircle, watching, Alice paused.

With a curious dignity, she spoke. "Barney, where have you been?"

Barney's head drooped. "In . . . there," he said, indicating the barn.

"We looked in there. Where, in there?"

"Up there . . . in the hay," Barney admitted in a low voice. It didn't take a close inspection to see the telltale signs of his hiding place—hay stuck to his clothing, hay clung to his hair. Burrowed into the hay, he had been invisible.

"I looked there," Alice said. "I called, again and again. Didn't you hear Mother?"

Slowly, slowly, Barney nodded.

"Were you hiding?"

Barney looked at his feet. Barney squirmed. Barney—finally, reluctantly—nodded.

The semicircle stirred. Tierney, Quinn, Herkimer, Robbie—looked at each other and blinked their shock and surprise.

Alice, it seemed, was moving ahead with purpose and with surprising calm.

"I see. I think, son, that we need to talk. All right?"

Now a tear appeared in Barney's eye, to trickle down his cheek. Alice reached into her apron pocket, pulled out a handkerchief, and handed it to him.

Stepping to his side, she put her hand on his shoulder and drew him to her momentarily.

"Go on into the house, Barney," she said firmly then, "and I'll come in a moment."

Barney shuffled, sniffling, past the ring of searchers, his small brother in his wake. The little group watched in silence; the slam of the screen door brought them from their silent study, to look at Alice.

"You see how it is," Alice said, turning to them.

"Not really—" someone said doubtfully.

"It's my fault," Alice said, her face white but her eyes set with purpose. "It's my fault. I haven't been . . . myself since Barnabas died. I've been excusing myself. Selfish is what I've been, lost in my own grief. Barney is smart enough to see it. What he needs—now that he doesn't have a father—is a mother."

No one argued with her.

"I'll go on in to him now," Alice continued. "But I want you to know how much I appreciate you. Thank you . . . thank you for coming. I believe I can do what needs to be done—"

Quinn stepped toward her. Alice looked up, met his gaze, gave him a small smile. Robbie cleared his throat; Alice turned to him, nodded. She squeezed Tierney's outstretched hand and touched Herkimer on the sleeve.

Slowly the group dispersed.

Alice stood on the porch until Quinn and Tierney had pulled out in their buggy, until Allan and Herkimer and Robbie had mounted their horses. Watching them go, she lifted her hand in a small salute and turned toward the house.

Barney stood uncertainly beside the oak table in the middle of the room, his eyes, large and round, fixed on his mother. Billy was curled up on the sofa, thumb in mouth and clutching a scrap of a blanket, a serious onlooker.

Crossing the linoleum to her son's side, Alice's eyes fell on the envelope, addressed to the catalog, ready to mail. With no hesitation at all she swept it up, walked to the stove, removed a lid, and thrust the envelope inside. Watching it catch fire and curl into ash, a curious expression touched her face. One would almost say it relaxed; perhaps it was the ruddy reflection of the fire, but Alice's face seemed brighter, free, at rest.

While the boys watched—Billy's bright eyes peering over the edge of his "bankie," and Barney staring openly—Alice turned and marched to the corner cupboard. There the usual blind scrabble brought forth the familiar dark bottle. Holding it by the neck Alice walked to the wood box, gave the bottle a smart rap on the edge, another and another, until the bottle broke, scattering its contents into the box and down the sides of the box onto the linoleum, to puddle harmlessly there.

For a five-year-old, Barney's eyes looked wise indeed. Wise and comprehending. With a rush he was in his mother's arms, his tears, checked until that moment, flowed freely, his voice choked with sobs, his body racked with sobs.

"I'm sorry, Mama! I'm sorry!"

"And I'm sorry, too, Barney. So sorry."

Alice, with the dusty, sticker-covered boy in her arms, sank onto the sofa, there to gather her sons to her. Rocking, crooning, she held them until Barney's weeping subsided.

It was as Alice suspected. Though Barney wasn't able to put his grief, frustration, and anger into words, they were there. Alice did little but listen and hug and whisper, "Things will be different now, Barney. We'll work on it together. I know I can count on you to be the man of the family. Little Barnabas."

Eventually a supper of sorts was set out (not porridge!) and the family of three ate together. Alice brought in the galvanized tub, filled it with warm water from the reservoir, bathed both boys tenderly, and took them upstairs. Billy, sleepy-eyed, was tucked into his small cot and almost immediately went to sleep.

"Come, son," Alice said, taking the nightgown-clad Barney by the hand and leading him into the adjoining bedroom, the room that had been hers and his father's.

Alice went to the bureau and opened the top drawer. From it she removed a small wooden box, and together she and Barney sat on the edge of the bed, the box between them.

Alice lifted the lid, moved an item or two aside, and located what she was looking for. Holding it up in the day's waning light, she said, "Do you know what this is, Barney?"

Barney's eyes were big and dark. "Dad's watch."

"Your father's Royal Waltham. The one he carried every day of his life."

Barney seemed mesmerized. "But . . . but . . ." he stammered.

"But what, son?"

"But I thought . . ."

"What did you think, Barney? You can tell me . . . please tell me."

"I thought," Barney stuttered, "I thought it . . . went into the hole in the ground."

Having seen his father in the coffin, dressed in his suit, Barney had assumed that the watch, as always, was in the fob pocket. In the pocket and in the grave.

Alice barely refrained from snatching the boy into her arms, falling into a spasm of grief once again for the husband and father who was gone from them. Only her newfound determination allowed her to put it aside, to smile, somewhat shakily, and put the watch in Barney's hand.

"This is a man's watch, Barney. Only a man can carry it. I think you are on your way to being such a man."

Barney looked at the watch with awe. With his thumb he rubbed the scrollwork. With a little effort he pressed the magic spot, and it opened. Not yet able to tell time, still he studied the numbers critically.

"I think a boy like you can look forward to the day when he can wear his father's watch—"

"Yea-a-a-ah," Barney breathed, caught up in the wonder of the moment and not finding words to express himself.

"In the meantime, we'll keep it safe here in this box. What would you say if—every Sunday afternoon—we get it out, wind it, check it over, and let you wear it around the house?"

"Yea-a-a-ah," Barney breathed again.

With Barney tucked into bed, falling asleep almost at once, Alice sat in the gloom beside the two small creatures who had, in God's wisdom, been left in her care.

One step. She had taken one small step in the right direction. With His grace, the next one would be forthcoming, and soon.

P arker Jones, heading for the schoolhouse and the Sunday service, walked through the early morning dew, his troubled soul feasting on the freshness and quiet of the new day.

It was the harvest season. Summer had slipped away, gone on the warm wings of bird and butterfly, never to return again. Reaping time, and his harvest had been discontent and uncertainty. Rather than offer the Lord of the harvest a bounty of joyous service rendered, he came with empty hands, barren heart, faded hopes. What had begun as vision had turned to empty shadows. His high-flying dreams of the pastorate had wavered and reshaped—under his doubts—to the routine of a job, a job not that well done. Or so it seemed.

The offer of a teaching position at Mount Moriah—it had all the earmarks of a plain old "job" also. But if it were not possible to work under the high command of a "calling," any job would do. And this one would offer a certain balm to his conscience, because he would be teaching the Bible. This one promised a salary sufficient to live on. To marry on.

Parker's footsteps dragged, his ear lost its ability to hear the muted sounds of the bush all around him; his nose failed to catch the autumn scents of grain and straw, drying grass, shriveled berries; his eyes were dimmed to the changes of color in bush and field. Beautiful Bliss. Blessed Bliss. Could Prince Edward Island and Mount Moriah offer the feast for body and soul that he had found in the bush country of northern Saskatchewan? Parker trudged on, caught up in another round of introspection, trying to solve the problem that plagued him.

On this morning, of all mornings, Parker needed to avail himself of the healing peace of the bush, for his heart was sorely torn since his last talk with Molly; his mind had performed whirligigs of thought and emotion—round and round and round—and still no answer.

One thing was clear: If he left Bliss, it would be alone. Molly had refused to go with him.

❦

Having declared his love and having finally, even passionately, asked her to become his wife, Molly had sat in silence for . . . for far too long. Her gaze was lowered, her fingers plucked at the grass on which they sat, while she hesitated.

"Well, Molly?" he had urged.

Parker Jones felt that, if he knew anything at all, Molly Morrison loved him. At a time when everything else seemed uncertain, he knew Molly loved him. Knew it, depended on it, cherished it, and—now—claimed it.

"Molly," he said again, reaching for her hand and speaking gently, "Molly girl, have I made it plain? I love you. I love you and want you to be my wife. Well, Molly?"

Parker gazed earnestly at the flushed face, so dear, usually so full of life and now so still. He gave her hand a little shake.

"Am I so hard to love, Molly?" he asked, a little puzzled now, a little uneasy.

"Not hard to love, Parker. Not hard to love. Lord," she murmured, and it startled Parker, "help me say it right."

"Say what, Molly?" Parker asked, his heart beginning to beat heavily.

"I've been aware of some of the doubts and questionings you have been going through . . . we've talked a little about them from time to time. We've talked, and I've prayed. I had to have some answers, Parker—"

Molly's eyes lifted, full of pain and unshed tears. But her voice, though unsteady, carried on.

"I had to know God's will for *me*, Parker—"

"Well, of course. I'd want you to. I've hoped it would be the same as His will for me."

"Anyway," Molly said, continuing on, plowing ahead, "Mam prayed with me—it was a few moments well spent."

"Are you telling me you heard from God?"

"For me, Parker, just for me. I can't tell you what God's will is for you. Don't you see—we each need to know for ourselves. I was miserable, uncomfortable, trying to . . . to hitch my wagon to your star. It wasn't working."

No mention of the fact that Parker, at the moment, had no star, that he seemed, to Molly, a soul adrift. A soul not one bit sure of his place, his future, or God's plan. Or whether indeed God had a plan.

"All I know, Parker, is—" Molly's voice quavered. She was, after all, responding to the marriage offer about which she had dreamed and hoped and prayed. To be the wife of Parker Jones had seemed heaven on earth to Molly Morrison for some time now.

"My place is here, in Bliss, for now," she continued, rather desperately but firmly. "I know it. The realization gives me peace of mind, and I can't jeopardize that, Parker. It's been too long in coming. It's like . . . like a very narrow path, and I can't argue with it or stray from it, or I'm truly all at sea again. I have this little bit of knowing in my spirit, and it came after prayer. I can't ignore it. So you see, Parker, I can't go to Mount Moriah."

"I . . . see," Parker said slowly, hungry for the same knowing in his spirit about what was right for *him*.

What more was there to say? When eventually Parker rose to his feet, offered a hand to Molly, and helped her up, both faces were stiff, perhaps to keep from weeping, certainly to keep from looking into each other's eyes and falling into each other's arms. But Molly had found her answer, and Parker, who had preached faith and trust, would not attempt to budge her from her place of peace and confidence. He understood the biblical principle of Isaiah 30:21: "This is the way, walk ye in it," and he could wish her nothing better than to know and do God's will.

———

His mind full of his conversation with Molly, his senses blind and deaf to his surroundings, heavy of heart, Parker made his way, Sunday morning, to his pulpit, there to preach—as best he could in this state of mind—the Word of God.

Arriving before anyone else, the only tasks he had to perform—except in winter when the fire had to be lit a good hour before church started—were to bring in the bench that served as an altar, place it at the front of the room, just below the blackboard, and dig the battered songbooks out of a cupboard that was designated for church supplies.

"Good morning, Pastor!" It was the Dinwoody family, come early so that Sister Dinwoody could practice the hymn selections on the pump organ. The Dinwoody children distributed the hymnbooks, Brother Dinwoody laid out the offering basket, and all was in readiness.

The Condon family group came in—Bly, Beatrice, a cowed Vivian. For close on her heels, grinning from ear to ear, pressing close, hat in hand—Herkimer Pinkard.

Almost desperately Vivian crowded in between her aunt and uncle, but to no avail. Herkimer would not be denied. "Move over, Missy," he urged, and though Vivian rebelled and kept her place without budging, Aunt Beatrice, with an uncertain smile, moved, and Herkimer sat down beside Vivian.

"What kind of man do you suppose Boaz was before he married?" he asked chattily, leaning close to Vivian's pearly ear to speak intimately.

Vivian jerked away, put a hand up to adjust her hair and her hat.

"Ruthless," Herkimer said happily, supplying the answer to his riddle, and Vivian looked as though she would commit murder, if such a thing were allowable.

When the singing began, Herkimer cheerfully shared his hymnbook with her, his off-key bass rising above her obvious distaste for all things associated with the large man at her side. It didn't help any to note the curious glances of those seated around them: A few people nudged each other or shrugged; a few smiled; and one or two—knowing Herkimer well and wondering what he was up to now—tittered. Once, fishing around in his pocket until his elbows dug into her sides, Herkimer produced a mint, much the worse for wear, and offered it to her.

Vivian's fury was hard to contain. "Put that away, you lout!" she hissed, and Herkimer good-naturedly popped the rejected sweet into his own mouth.

Parker looked out over the assembled group and found the attendance good. Already winter's chilling breath threatened, and they all knew there would be Sundays soon when it would be difficult, perhaps impossible, to get to church. "Make hay while the sun shines," had a great deal of meaning to the people of the north. And yet they were willing to lay work aside for the Lord's day and felt the blessing of the service was reward enough.

At the proper moment, Parker Jones opened his Bible, prepared to announce his text. All week he had labored over Jeremiah 8:20: "The harvest is past, the summer is ended, and we are not saved."

With the Jurgenson boys in mind, Parker meant to expound on the swift passing of time, the certainty of the harvest, the seriousness of the reaping. And as he had hoped, the three Jurgenson boys sat—shining of face, clean of shirt, slick of hair—before him, having laid aside their usual worldly Sunday pursuits in favor of church attendance. Surely God had a message for them.

Instead, he found his attention given to another portion of Scripture, one that had plagued his mind all week, but which he had ignored and turned aside as being his own thoughts, certainly not God's message for the church.

Now he found himself reading the worrisome verse. Perhaps his ponderings on it during the week would not be silenced and were struggling for attention. Whatever the reason, it seemed the Scripture rang in his own heart; perhaps it would be meaningful to his listeners.

"For the gifts and calling of God," he read from Romans 11:29, "are without repentance.

"More clearly stated," he explained, "is to say that God doesn't take back His gifts, doesn't take back His callings. They are irrevocable; that is, they are unalterable, incapable of being revoked. That's good news. If you've been the recipient of any of God's gifts, you may claim them with your whole heart—the world can't have them; Satan can't take them from you; God won't take them back—they are yours.

"The same may be said for God's calling—"

Parker could hear himself speaking, could hear the very answer he was seeking as it came from his tongue. Part of him spoke God's truth; another part of him listened. Listened, accepted, and marveled. How simple it was, after all. What was it the Bible said? "The word is nigh thee, even in thy mouth, and in thy heart" (Rom. 10:8).

The answer! He had known it all along—God's plan hadn't changed; God's call hadn't changed. The problem was his questioning heart, his doubting spirit. In this moment when the Scripture came close and searching, the light dawned.

Somehow Parker finished his message, his own heart lifted; he could only pray that his people found what he said as helpful as he did himself. But if no one else listened, on this day, Parker had a congregation of one—himself, and felt the time not wasted.

Now came the serious moment, the time for honesty, for soul-searching. Having faced himself and his recent bout with unbelief, his toying with disobedience, Parker gave what he termed an "altar call," urging the sinner, the backslider, to make peace with God, and found that, once again, he was speaking to himself. And when the congregation stood and sang the old favorite, *Just As I Am,* with lusty voices, Parker, forgetting the Jurgenson boys and their need, sang to himself and for himself.

And then they came to a verse that needed, in Parker's case, to be prayed:

> Just as I am, Thou wilt receive,
> Wilt welcome, pardon, cleanse, relieve;
> Because Thy promise I believe,
> O Lamb of God, I come! I come!

And the Bliss congregation saw a sight never seen before.

The singing faltered, faded, dwindled away as Parker Jones laid aside his hymnbook and stepped toward the rude bench, called the "mourner's bench" by some. There, alone, he knelt—to pray, to repent, perhaps to weep.

Startled, amazed, even humbled, his people watched. Time passed, and still Parker prayed. People began gathering up their Bibles and, slowly, as though undecided, moved toward the door. Silently they dispersed, casting glances back, creeping away to the family wagon, clambering aboard and wending their way home, discussing around the dinner table the moving sight of the seeker-pastor who had knelt at his own altar.

Only a few lingered with him, sitting quietly in their seats or kneeling, waiting and watching with Parker Jones in his time of repentance and his hour of victory.

Finally, looking up, Parker was surprised to see the dear ones who had watched and waited with him. Rising to his feet, it was to turn toward them a countenance of peace.

"Woe is unto me," he quoted, "if I preach not the gospel!" But it was said with such joy and complete lack of woefulness that his people smiled with him; a few laughed aloud, sharing his joy, and a few said "Amen—so be it!"

Herkimer, during all of this, had refused to budge. Silently he had waited with his friend and pastor, and the Condon three, wedged in against the wall, had no choice but to stay, without creating a scene.

"Now," he said, rising, his face almost as peaceful as Parker's, "we will go home."

"And home I shall go!" the irate, flushed Vivian gritted. "I mean back home—out of here—and as soon as I can pack! And," she said in a fierce undertone to Herkimer, who, with an innocent expression on his face, was listening politely, "I'll thank you to keep your distance from me and never to speak to me again!"

Humbly, hat held against his chest, his whiskers quivering suspiciously, Herkimer took the tongue lashing, though a close observer might have seen a twinkle in his eye. Still on Vivian's heels—in spite of her tirade—he followed the small group from the building. Treading closely, he kept in step right up to the Condon wagon, Vivian glaring over her shoulder, her hurrying steps availing nothing—Herkimer clung like poplar sap all the way.

As for Parker Jones, he received the hugs of numerous members of his group, the hearty handshakes of others, then gathered up his Bible and turned toward the outside. Molly was climbing into her buggy.

"May I?" a well-loved voice asked at her elbow. "May I drive? And Molly girl—"

Parker couldn't wait for a more convenient season, a more romantic setting. "Will you," he asked softly, earnestly, his voice thick with a depth of feeling that would not wait for a more propitious moment, "throw your lot in with mine, Molly girl? Will you become a poor, foolish, pastor's wife?"

"No, I will not," Molly answered with spirit. "But I'll become *your* wife, Parker Jones!"

And without hesitation Molly turned the reins over to her future husband.

The small group watched, smiling, content, as their pastor drove away, Molly Morrison at his side, as was right and proper. If the buggy wasn't out of sight when Parker turned her toward him, drew her to him, and kissed her with all the vigor and passion that any woman could have dreamed of, only a few people saw, and no one, no one, was surprised.

Their departure coincided with a deep breath, a mighty sigh, heaved by Herkimer Pinkard. Now at last he stepped back, watching as Vivian Condon flounced her way up and into her uncle's wagon, not an easy thing to do.

Nostrils flaring, face scarlet, breath short, she turned one last furious glance on her would-be suitor, and said—and all her superficial graces fled in a second—"Good-bye, Mr. Herkimer *Lumpkin!*"

Herkimer lifted his hat in a salute of sorts and said politely, "As Mr. Abraham Lincoln said, ma'am, 'When you have got an elephant by the hind leg and he is trying to run away, it's best to let him run.'"

Tierney had lived through her first threshing, though there were moments when she wondered if she would fall asleep on her feet or keel over from sheer exhaustion.

The work on the Bloom farm had started before dawn. It seemed to Tierney that she had just blown out the lamp for the night when the whistle of the arriving engine rent the darkness, calling the household awake. Soon lights were twinkling all over the house, everyone was astir, and with the kindling of the fire in the range, work was underway for breakfast. Men were gathering in from surrounding homesteads, moving from farm to farm until the district's harvest was complete, each man helping his neighbor. It not only strengthened the bonds between them, and was the wisest thing financially—the only wages paid out were to the owner of the threshing machine—but was scriptural: "They helped every one his neighbor; and every one said to his brother, Be of good courage" (Isa. 41:6). Almost without exception, the people of the bush recognized their dependence on each other, and on God.

And, on threshing day, it was not only the men who gathered in to help. Women came, too, knowing how very much they, in turn, would depend upon their neighbor in the mammoth job of feeding workers three meals a day plus lunches taken to the fields morning and afternoon.

Lydia and Tierney had been busy for days. With threshing time in mind, barrels of sauerkraut (chopped by a new spade), had been put down when cabbages were ready in the garden. Cucumbers and tomatoes, in turn, had been pickled and were waiting in stone crocks; butter churned and hung down the well to keep sweet. Thick cream was on hand for applying to nearly every dessert served; pails of eggs were ready and waiting for breakfast. Finally, the baking was done—cakes, pies, cinnamon rolls, doughnuts.

On the last evening, Lydia and Tierney had prepared for the morning rush. The table had been opened full length, spread with oilcloth, dotted with butter dishes, sugar bowls, cream pitchers, and, in the table's center, the cranberry-glass cruet with its salt and pepper shakers, its mustard, vinegar, and oil bottles. Bacon had been sliced, potatoes peeled and waiting in huge pots of cold water. Frying pans were assembled for pancakes, for scrambled eggs, for onions. Coffeepots—their own and those borrowed—were filled and ready to be pulled to the front of the stove as soon as it was hot.

Already Tierney had caught the importance of the kitchen and its output; the reputation of the lady of the house was at stake! Pity the woman who bumbled and failed, who was unprepared for the awesome responsibility of threshing day, allowing the menfolk of the district to be wretchedly fed. She was as much an object of scorn as the expectant mother who had no flannel in the house when the baby came.

In Bliss and surrounding districts, first thing upon arising on threshing day, the sky was checked for signs of rain; clear skies called forth fervent thanks lifted to the Lord above. Many prayers

211

had gone up from earnest hearts for days, even weeks; every pulpit in the land had voiced the concern of one and all that the Almighty look with favor upon their need of good weather for harvesting. Knees unused to kneeling, mouths unaccustomed to praying, now bent, now spoke, in heartfelt petition for enough rainless time to get in the crop.

On this morning, though under pressure to get breakfast started, the cooks could not resist stepping outside to watch the threshing machine's arrival. The powerful engine, replacing the three teams of horses needed in years past, hauled the thresher, followed by the water tank; the earth was deeply patterned by the huge wheels as the outfit came down the lane, past the house and farm buildings, heading for the nearest field.

The ladies turned from the exciting sight back to their tasks, but the hustle and bustle in the kitchen could not completely shut out the distant chuffing of the machine, a constant reminder of the appetites raging in the hardworking crew.

When everything was set up in the field—the men in place, a hayrack of sheaves waiting—the "pitcher" climbed into position to begin throwing the sheaves to the platform below where the "band-cutters" waited with their knives. The great belt turned, the white canvas of the carriers began to revolve, the "feeder" tossed the sheaves into the machine. What a sight—golden straw arcing into the air, golden grain cascading into a wagon!

All this Tierney was able to observe firsthand when, in the middle of the morning, she loaded a cart with big jars of ice-cold lemonade, piles of sandwiches, dozens of doughnuts, and went to the field. The men, having shed their shirts early on, labored over the mighty monster, feeding its voracious appetite, appeasing its hunger. Scattered across the field among the stooks, other men and boys loaded the racks, pitching sheaves high into the air where another worker layered the load precisely. One by one the loaded hayracks were trundled to the threshing machine, pulling into position at the proper moment and followed closely by another, so that there was no break in the process.

It was a marvelous example of teamwork. Looking around at the men, like ants busy everywhere, Tierney was awed. At the same time, back at the house, equally hard at work and equally coordinated, half a dozen women perspired in the blazing-hot kitchen, cleaning up the remnants of the last meal while preparing the next. Dishes, washed and dried, were carried right back to the table and put into place again. Frying pans were emptied only to be filled again, the only difference being that they held chicken rather than bacon. A huge pan of rice pudding bubbled in the oven; pies cooled in the pantry, vast loaves of bread awaited slicing, fresh grounds were added to the big enamel coffeepots clustered on the range top. Someone was kept busy trotting to the well for water, carrying out the potato peelings and other slops, feeding wood into the cookstove, shaking down the grate, filling the wood box. It was no place for shirkers.

Just outside the door, benches were set up with numerous basins, bars of soap, and stacks of towels. Pails of warm water must be ready and waiting when the crew came in covered with sweat and layered stickily with chaff. When they made their way, shining of face and damp of hair, to the long tables, even the sturdiest house shook with the vibrations of their boots—oil grain two-buckle plow, seam-riveted western, best Kip with bellows tongue and dirt excluder, fully warranted spring heel plow. Their tread was businesslike as they approached the spread boards. Very little was said as they passed the bowls and platters, filled their plates, and shoveled in the food that had taken so long to prepare and which disappeared in a matter of minutes.

About to go around the table with the coffeepot, Tierney paused, her heart coming up into her throat, her eyes smarting with something more than heat from the kitchen. Seated among the men of Bliss—Robbie Dunbar, her one love and her great sorrow.

Tierney had tried, over the months, to expunge the passion of feeling for Robbie Dunbar that had affixed itself, years ago, to her heart. She had loved Robbie Dunbar for so long it was as if he were part and parcel of her very being. No words had been spoken over them, making them one; no kiss had been exchanged. But if love were a flower to be seeded and grown, Robbie Dunbar was planted, entwined, *established*, in Tierney's heart, and try as she would, pray as she did, work at it as she might, Robbie Dunbar would not be rooted out.

I am Robbie Dunbar's, she had finally admitted to herself. Admitted it helplessly and hopelessly. He might never be hers, but she was his and his alone, and for all time.

I'm doomed. Blessed—and doomed! she had thought. *I'll never be heart-free in all o' me life. Oh, Robbie!*

"More coffee?" she asked him now, seemingly as cool as the bowl of sliced cucumbers in sour cream on the table. But the coffeepot, as she poured, was unsteady, and with his thick head of hair so close and his bronzed cheek only a few inches away, Tierney was captured by thoughts other than of coffee, and the cup overflowed.

"Oh, I'm sorry!" she gasped and leaned to mop at the stain spreading on the oilcloth.

Robbie's face, as she bent past him to the task, was as tight as an Indian drum. His nostrils flared, his dusky skin deepened in color, his breath shortened. One would almost think his head reeled.

Fortunately the other eaters were absorbed with their plates and, after a glance at the accident being repaired at one end of the table, gave it no heed. But the little drama continued.

Robbie, perhaps unable to stop himself, turned his head slightly and looked at Tierney. Pulling back from the spill, Tierney's face was only a few inches away from his—kissing distance. For a second that seemed an eternity, their eyes met.

Tierney and Robbie, for as long as they could remember, had communicated by glance. Very little—back in Binkiebrae—had been said, very little needed to be said, their feelings were as plain to be seen as to be stated. A glance said it all, said it poignantly, said it graphically. There was sweet certainty in waiting. And there was time—or so they had thought—time for the fulfillment of the love between them. Were they not destined for each other? Would they not spend their lives together? Would they not grow old together?

Now, again, at an oilcloth-covered table in the middle of the bush country in a remote northern district called Bliss, the language of the heart was blazoned between them, by glance. One short glance—a volume of meaning.

Knowing it was wrong, that he was promised to someone else, still it happened. In spite of tight reins and good intentions—it happened. Like a spark from a struck anvil, it happened.

The moment passed; someone called for coffee, and the moment passed.

Trembling like a Saskatchewan aspen in the spring breeze, Tierney moved on, Robbie turned blind eyes on his plate, and life went on.

Both were grateful for the workload that called them, catching them up in exhausting physical labor. But to turn off the thoughts—that was another matter.

Tierney, doing tasks with which she was well familiar and no challenge mentally, went over and over the explosive moment when her eyes had met Robbie's. Unexpectedly her heart lurched, and her eyes filled with tears, threatening to expose her turmoil. She swiped at her face furtively with the corner of her apron but found no relief for the pain that twisted her heart.

Robbie pitched sheaves like a madman—with no letup of the misery—all the livelong day.

B ack home in his own "wee hoosie," with threshing completed at the Blooms' for the day, Robbie was bathed and ready for bed but too torn of heart to sleep, and the tumult of his heart brought him to the point of decision. With no one else listening, Robbie found himself talking—at last, at long last—to God.

Lying back on his cot, staring up into blackness, it seemed darkness was no thicker anywhere than in his soul.

"God," he said, and it was a cry in the night, "listen to me, please. If anyone ever needed You, I'm the one.

"I'm confessin' to You that I love Tierney Caulder. I'm admittin' to You that I made a mistake in agreein' to marry Alice. It was wrong, wrong for me, wrong for Alice, a wrong toward Tierney. Please forgive me for that.

"An' while we're on the subject, forgive me—oh, please forgive me!—for my lifetime of selfishness and sinfulness. Forgive me for ignorin' Your Son, Jesus. Forgive me . . . forgive me . . ."

All that and much more he said . . . prayed, for Robbie slipped from bed to floor, to kneel there and find that his conversation with the unseen Listener had turned to prayer, a prayer between a mortal man and his Maker—a prayer of contrition. It was a time of drawing nigh, of touching grace, of knowing cleansing.

Robbie rose to his feet a man born again—"If any man be in Christ, he is a new creature: old things are passed away; behold all things are become new" (2 Cor. 5:17).

Oh, blessed newness! Robbie's poor, battered heart was light as dandelion fluff as all the old things passed away and the new touched him with glory. The log walls echoed, for a time, with spontaneous expressions of praise.

Lying back once again on his cot, Robbie looked up now into darkness that no longer seemed impenetrable. Perhaps his inner eye saw beyond to a throne room and perhaps his inner ear heard distant rejoicing, the "joy [that] shall be in heaven over one sinner that repenteth" (Luke 15:7).

And gleaming through the window—a star; the blackness of the Canadian night had been pierced by a single light. Robbie's darkness, now, had been lit with hope. It was a small glow but enough to point the way.

"Now help me, Father, to do what needs to be done."

<hr/>

Robbie waited until the chores at the Hoy place were finished for the day, until supper was over, until Billy and Barney had been put to bed. If Alice wondered why he lingered, she said nothing.

When the day's activities were over for her, Alice returned to the room where Robbie sat waiting, seated on a straight-backed chair pulled up to the round oak table, hands clasped before him, face serious.

Seating herself across from him, some inner sensing prompted Alice's "Yes, Robbie?"

Robbie tried to speak, failed, cleared his throat, began again. "Alice, I've sum'mat to say to ye . . ."

"Yes, Robbie?"

"It's aboot us—you an' me."

"Yes, Robbie." Alice's glance sharpened, but her tone was gentle.

"It's aboot . . . aboot our agreement to marry."

"Yes," she said, somewhat breathlessly. "Go ahead, Robbie. We haven't talked for a long time."

Robbie, breathing a prayer, felt encouraged to proceed. At least Alice was open to talk about this most important aspect of their future.

"Our arrangement," he began, "wasn't fair to you. You made it at a time when you were vulnerable, full of grief over the loss of your husband. I feel now that I took advantage of you—"

"But, Robbie," Alice said softly, "I was the one who brought it up. You merely agreed to my . . . my proposal. You were very kind—"

"Maybe not kind, Alice," Robbie said slowly, flushing a little, shifting in his chair. "Greedy, maybe. Oh, I was willin' to take on the care o' the laddies. But—you see—I wassna free to pledge myself to anyone."

"Not free, Robbie?" Alice was puzzled.

"Nae. Not free. My heart was promised elsewhere. I shouldna hae—"

"Oh, Robbie—don't! You see, I've . . . fallen in love! I haven't been able to find a way to tell you, but I'm in love!"

Robbie's heart plummeted. This—Alice's love—he hadn't counted on. What, oh, what had he done, that she should fall in love with him!

"In . . . love!" Robbie stammered.

Of all the ways this conversation might have gone, to learn that Alice had fallen in love with him was not one of them. To break off a business deal was one thing; to boldly break free from someone who had just proclaimed love for you—Robbie didn't know how to do it, what to say, how to proceed. He barely stopped himself from groaning aloud.

"Yes, in love!" Alice was saying, her face pinker and healthier than he had ever seen it and her eyes brighter than any bottle could have made them. "And I didn't know how to tell you. I was afraid . . . I didn't know how to go about confessing something so . . . so special and so wonderful."

"Confessin'," Robbie repeated, dazed.

"Oh, Robbie!" Alice laughed. "Don't look so astonished! Surely you guessed—"

"Why should I? There was nothin', nothin' . . ."

Once again words failed Robbie Dunbar. How, oh, how would he handle the situation now? Wanting, needing, praying to be free, it seemed he was more enmeshed than ever. What was the honorable thing to do?

"There will be someone else," he explained, desperately. "God will send along someone . . . someone better than I could ever be—"

"Robbie—don't you understand what I'm saying?"

Apparently Robbie's face spoke of his confusion, for Alice continued, "I don't believe I'm making a bit of sense to you, Robbie. Weren't you about to tell me you wanted to be free of our arrangement?"

"Aye, oh, aye," he said humbly, still not wanting to inflict hurt on this one who had offered him so much.

"And I'm telling you it's all right. In fact, it's just perfect!"

"It is?"

Relieved to hear her say so, still Robbie was taken aback. Alice, happy to be free of him?

"But," Robbie stumbled on, "you said . . . you said you're in love—"

"With Quinn, Robbie! With Quinn Archer!"

Quinn Archer! Comprehending at last, Robbie fell back weakly in his chair, overcome.

"You . . . an' Quinn Archer?"

"Yes, Robbie—a love match. It's been developing right under your nose, and you haven't caught on. At first I couldn't believe it—that God would send along someone to love me. Not just to care for me and the boys—no," she cried, believing Robbie was about to interrupt, "it's all right; don't apologize, Robbie.

"You and I, we never pretended it was anything but necessity," Alice continued. "But even so, I was so hesitant to bring it up, to tell you the way things were going. I knew you had your heart set—if not on me—then on the farm."

Robbie squirmed. But the farm had been laid on the altar, and Robbie was happy to leave it there.

"Na na," he disclaimed. "Nae more, nae more. I'm happy as a lark at daybreak, wi' me own sma' holdings."

"Oh, I'm so glad! And Robbie," Alice pinked again, "I'll be in good hands. Quinn is a fine man."

"The best!" Robbie agreed wholeheartedly.

"And, Robbie—there's been no more of the . . . the medicine. That's over and done with. I think, Robbie," Alice said hesitantly but bravely and honestly, "I wasn't sick after all, except maybe in my mind and in my heart. I was just so weak; I didn't want to face life without Barnabas. I was just . . . just taking the coward's way out.

"But when my carelessness caused Billy's burn—oh yes, it did, Robbie. I feel terribly responsible for that. And when I saw what my withdrawing from Barney was doing to him—well, I just had to come back to them and to life, even if it were hard. And thank God," Alice said softly, "Quinn was there for me."

Robbie, dumbfounded, could only shake his head.

"Are you sure you don't mind, Robbie?" Alice asked anxiously, and they were the very words he had been struggling with, wondering how to say them to her. Surely God was good. Good to both of them.

"Na na! I'm happy for you!"

And with those words, Robbie Dunbar was once again a free man.

<hr/>

It was that very evening—why wait?—that Robbie wended his way to the Bloom homestead. He had no right to Tierney's love, but he had to have her forgiveness. But yesterday, at the Bloom table, he had seen something . . . something in her eyes akin to the flame that had blazed between them in earlier days in Binkiebrae, and it gave him hope. At any rate, he decided doggedly, he had to know.

The evening shadows were lengthening when he rode into the Bloom yard, slid from the horse's back, and knocked on the door of the house.

"Why, hello, Robbie. Come on in." It was Lydia, friendly, inviting.

"I've coom to talk wi' Tierney," he said without preamble, looking over Lydia's shoulder, into the room beyond.

"She's not here, Robbie. She may be in the pasture with a pail of milk, teaching a calf to drink, or she may be taking a walk, which she does often of an evening. If it's important . . . will you come in and wait?"

Lydia was cautious in her invitation, remembering the moment Tierney had shared with her about Robbie's agreement to marry Alice Hoy. In fact, she had often prayed with Tierney, when her heart was about to break and she needed comfort and strength to face the future. A future without Robbie Dunbar, it seemed, was almost more than Tierney could contemplate. The thought of it, or prayers about it, may have been what drove her to these times she got away from the house, to walk the wilderness roads, to sit beside the lake, to be alone with her pain.

"Or," Lydia offered, "you might rather come back another time—"

"Na na," Robbie said, studying the farmyard, looking for a glimpse of Tierney. "I canna wait."

"I hope, Robbie," Lydia said gently, "it's good news. That is, it isn't anything that'll upset our Tierney."

"It's good news, ma'am. The best!" And Robbie's eyes, turned on his questioner, blazed with something Lydia had never seen in them before.

"Why, Robbie," she said, "you look—"

"Look how, ma'am?"

"I don't know how to put it . . . you look—you look *different,* somehow."

"I *am* different!" Robbie, it seemed, could keep it a secret no longer. "I'm as different as night an' day! An' thass what I need to tell Tierney . . . it's part of what I need to tell her."

Lydia's eyes, studying Robbie's face, were slowly filling with comprehension.

"Robbie!" she said wonderingly. "Robbie Dunbar—is it possible you've given yourself to the Lord, that He's become your Savior?"

The answer was clear to be seen. Robbie's face—in spite of a deep tan and a day's growth of beard—radiated the transaction that had changed him. Lydia caught her breath, with wonder and with awe.

Robbie looked happy enough to caper; Scotch dignity kept him flat-footed but couldn't disguise the happiness that glowed from his eyes.

"Yes, ma'am. Thass what happened, a' reet! An' thass the first thing I want to tell her.

"I know I have no reet . . . no right," he continued, humbly now, "to Tierney, *or* her love. But I jist have to try, don't I? I've niver told her how much . . . how much I care. Though I think she knows."

Lydia, a romantic at heart, was nodding.

"She needs to hear it, Robbie; she needs to hear you say it."

"But first—*after* I tell her about accepting the Lord, and *before* I tell her I love her—I have to tell her how sorry I am—"

Robbie's voice faltered. He scuffed his shoe on the porch as he took a moment to get his feelings under control. It was a time of highs and lows for Robbie Dunbar.

"I think, ma'am," he said, taking a deep breath, "I'll jist wander off toward the pasture an' see if she's there."

Lydia watched him go with a prayer on her lips—for him and the urgency upon him, and for Tierney, who needed, more than anything, to hear what he had to say.

Turning to the house, the motherly woman wandered aimlessly around the kitchen, checked the reservoir for bathwater, flexed her aching fingers . . .

The screen door slammed.

"Oh, it's you, Tierney," Lydia said, asking immediately, "Did you see Robbie?"

Tierney stopped short. "See Robbie? Na na—"

"He's looking for you. I didn't know for sure where you were . . . he's out there, somewhere, looking for you. He wants to talk to you."

Lydia could barely keep from blurting out the secret.

Her expression turning heavy, Tierney headed for the stairs and her room. "I dinna care to see him. I canna see him . . ."

"But maybe you should—"

"Na na. I made up my mind to that when . . . when—well, you know," Tierney said firmly yet with a sigh, and she took another step toward the stairs and escape.

"Wait!" Lydia was desperate. "I think . . . I think you should talk to him, Tierney."

Surprised, Tierney paused. "Whativer can ye mean?" she asked slowly.

"There've been some changes . . . changes in the way things were."

Tierney's glance sharpened, and she asked again, "Whativer do ye mean? Tell me . . . oh, do tell me!"

Lydia could keep it a secret no longer.

"Tierney, darling Tierney," the older woman's voice trembled, and her eyes misted with happy tears, "he's come . . . Robbie's come to tell you that he's accepted Jesus Christ as his Savior. And to ask, now, your forgiveness, too—"

With a choked cry, Tierney was across the expanse of the kitchen; the screen door slammed behind her, the porch resounded to the clatter of her shoes, the steps never felt the touch of her feet as she flew to find Robbie.

Flew to find Robbie Dunbar and saw a vision she was to remember the rest of her life: Striding toward her across the pasture, Robbie's beloved figure was etched against the last rays of the sun, ringed about with an aura of light. Coming toward her. Robbie, coming to her at last.

Robbie, seeing her, breaking into a run, his leaping and bounding feet—feet that had once taken him away and were now bringing him back to her, his raised arm, his shout—expressing what words had not said all these years.

Stepping out of the loose shoes that so hindered her, her bare feet flying over the grassy expanse that divided them, Tierney sped, straight and true, into the arms of Robbie Dunbar.